IT'S F...
EVERYTHING'S
FINE.

the bestselling author of *One Percent of You*

michelle gross

It's fine. Everything's fine.

ISBN-13: 979-8-9896212-1-7

Cover Design: © 2023 L.J. Anderson of Mayhem Cover Creations
Editor: Shantella Benson of S.T.A.R. Editing

My gran used to say, "If I didn't have bad luck, I wouldn't have any luck at all."

The words have followed me all my life. They couldn't be any truer than the situation I find myself in.

Within twenty-four hours, I lost both my apartment and job. With no one else to turn to, I reached out to my brother, who lives on the opposite side of the state. Due to a situation in his home, he sends me to Hudson Henderson, a complete stranger, until his giant dog jumps on me in his driveway.

I intend to crash under his roof for a week, just until my brother's houseguest leaves. Plans can be tricky, though, and often never go as arranged, especially for me. Hudson is cranky and handsome, and I'm positive he loathes that I'm in his home.

Yet, despite the exasperated sighs that frequently escape his lips, he chooses to help me when I'm in need. His brows pinch together and his forehead crinkles when I trip over my own feet, but... He's always there to extend a hand and lift me up.

One week stretches into two months.

I never leave, and I believe the jerk is my best friend, but he gets that look in his eyes sometimes. I feel it all over me, and when it happens, nothing we do seems like friendship.

CONTENT WARNINGS

Please do not read if you don't want spoilers. This is for my readers who need to know what they're going into just for peace of mind. Last chance to stop reading if you don't want any spoilers. There is an assault (not sexual) on heroine near the end of the book. Don't worry, it's not her love interest. Hero goes ballistic when it happens. I'll also mention the heroine had a rough upbringing. Mainly, she grew up poor, and she has a hangup about it. Hero is slightly judgmental of her at first encounter, but if you've read One Percent of You, then you know it's not going to last. If you feel like I've missed something that might be triggering for my reader, please reach out to me via any of my social media. I might not see it right away, but I always want to make sure you guys know what you're getting into!

This one is for all those who don't know how to ask for help.

You're not a burden.

This one is for all those who are their own worst enemy. For those who would rather suffer in silence than ask for someone's shoulder to lean on. For the ones who have the best intentions for themselves and somehow still make mistakes.

<u>You're not a burden</u>

Someone might have convinced you otherwise, or maybe you've witnessed a thing or two that's altered your perspective on living. Even so, that doesn't mean you're annoying.

Life is hard.

Let's not make it harder on ourselves.

1

EUGENE

I was born for bad luck. The day the hospital allowed my mom to name me Eugene, my fate was sealed. Who would name their daughter Eugene? My name sounded like I might be some old creepy dude who followed you around in the grocery store. After giving me a boy's name, the woman didn't keep me either. She tossed me to my gran the second she got out of the hospital with me, just like she had my brother.

My misfortune started before I had any control over it.

So, silly me for thinking it was going to be a good day when I didn't misplace my keys that morning or trip over my own feet. I found myself on the side of the road instead. I had a flat tire. It wasn't the end of the world, but my thought process made the situation worse. The pothole I hit a few miles back was likely the culprit. My bad luck would say otherwise. It was me. I was the problem.

"I'm going to freeze a tit off." I rubbed my arms as I squatted in front of the tire.

A Kentucky winter could be below freezing one day and seventy degrees the next. Unfortunately, it was below freezing outside that early December day.

"That kind of language is off-putting for a woman. No man is going to find you attractive if you talk like your brother," my gran's voice drifted through my thoughts.

Gran was wrong. That was *my* voice and my personality. It might have come from hanging out with my brother and his friends all my life, but it was still me.

The woman died a couple of years ago from cancer. Besides my brother, Edwin, no one gave a damn what happened to me. She tried her best to raise me to be proper, but proper never wanted shit to do with me.

"What's wrong with titty, anyway? Sounds so much more colorful than booby," I said to myself. I mostly talked to myself *inside* my head, but sometimes, when irritated, it felt good to let the words leave my lips. It felt good to let my thoughts out. And those no-good words women shouldn't say.

I snickered.

"Do you need help, miss?"

Startled, my lug wrench went flying from my hand. A hoarse laugh erupted as the tool clattered somewhere in the distance. I turned to find an elderly man sitting in a very nice truck with his head hanging out of the window, looking down at me. A red baseball cap covered most of his gray hair. How long had he been there?

Grabbing my chest, I stood. "I didn't hear you pull up," I said as I tried to calm myself.

"I noticed."

"You scared me."

He smiled. "I know."

I looked left and right, bending every which way, until he laughed again. Where did that stupid wrench go?

He pointed toward the truck's tailgate. "Your wrench is in the back of my truck."

"Really?" I scratched my head. "How did it get there?"

He threw his head back and laughed. "You don't remember throwing it?"

"I mean, I do, but I'm a little impressed at my ability to throw it so far," I said as I moved toward his truck. "May I?" When he nodded, I climbed up on the back wheel and hopped into his truck bed. Sure enough, the dang wrench was there.

I jumped out quickly and said, "Whew, you could have totally kidnapped me there."

He quirked a brow. "You would have jumped out."

"You're right," I agreed.

"Besides, my old lady has kept me on my toes the last thirty-five years. I don't have time to kidnap a child. Wife is at home cooking me up a mean meal, and I've got a few hours before I make it home."

"Damn," I muttered. "I can't cook. She's got me beat."

"At all?"

"Who knows?"

"Well, it looks like you can change a tire. Are you sure you don't need help?"

"I got it." I held up my skinny arm.

He smiled. "I have two sons, though. Both are single, but my oldest one... I believe you'd like him."

"Does he know you pimp him out to women beside the road?"

"He needs all the help he can get."

"That bad?"

He nodded.

I dropped to my knees beside the flat tire. "I believe I'll pass, good sir, but thanks for stopping."

"Shame. He could use someone like you," he said. "And tit is a more colorful word than boob."

That time, I was the one laughing as the old man drove away.

My boss texted me before I got in my car.

No power at the office. Don't bother
coming in.

Danny Hopkins was my boss and a big-time lawyer around those
woods. Not that Huntingsburg was a big or well-known place.

I wasn't going to complain about not having to work, but
missing a day's worth of pay would cut back on my savings. Just like
the tires I bought last month. It was a dang mystery how quickly and
often I managed to get a flat tire a few weeks after *buying* new ones.
It was so hard to save when everything, *everything,* no matter how
big or small, went wrong.

Gran used to say, "If I didn't have bad luck, I wouldn't have any
luck at all."

I was fond of the hardheaded woman. Her words lived in my
head. I missed her so much.

How was I supposed to save money when I had to live?

I sulked and allowed my pity party to go on another thirty
seconds before I shrugged and called up my best friend. Holly
answered after two rings. "Aren't you supposed to be working for the
creepy, old fart?"

"I'm off today. How soon is your next appointment?" Holly was a
hair stylist and the only person I let touch my head.

"I had a cancellation, so not until noon."

"Good. I'm heading over to redo my red."

"Fine. I guess I'll make you pretty again."

"You're the best."

2

HUDSON

THE LUNCH SPECIAL WAS PEPPER STEAK OVER RICE. I MARINATED THE MEAT overnight. Customers were on a seafood and chicken binge that month, which wasn't unusual. The meat I used differed each week. It just so happened that week, steak wasn't the preferred choice. All the fresh beef inside the fridge would expire on Friday, so hence, the special.

"Looks good," Randall said as he fried a burger beside me.

"Stick around." I smiled. "I might teach you something yet."

A loud clattering noise came from behind me. I whipped my head around. My grandma Sue was hunched over, trying to pick up the broken plates with her hand. I swore the old woman helped in the kitchen to scare the hell out of me. She knew I'd rather her visit instead of work.

I sighed. "Or you might end up like this. Older than the town and still trying to work."

My grandma ignored me, so I grasped her hands. "Come on. I'll clean it. Your arthritis is bothering you today, isn't it?"

"Leave me be. I got it handled." She tried shooing me away.

"How about you go take a break?"

"How about ya mind your business? The day has barely started, and you're telling me to take a break."

"I worry about my business," I fibbed, going along with her. "You're the only one that can cook my recipes as well as I can." I'd rather Grandma not help at all, but it was impossible to win an argument against her. She wouldn't listen, so I had to choose my battles with her carefully.

Randall hollered, "Hey!"

"I taught ya those recipes," Grandma Sue muttered as she stood. "Listen at ya, trying to take credit."

I grinned as the old woman grabbed the broom.

"The day I stop doing anything, is the day I die. A body ain't good for nothing if ya ain't moving, remember that Hudson, or I'll outlive ya like I have two husbands."

"Yes, yes," I agreed and took the broom from her. "You taught me everything I know. Now go stir your potato soup before you burn it."

The beginnings of a smile crept up over her wrinkled face, so I continued to beam at her until she swatted my shoulder. "I better. Leave everything to Randall, and your shop will go downhill before it's even been open for two years."

"You two," Randall began with a huff. "I can hear, ya know."

"Hmm. He can hear better than he can cook." Grandma Sue shrugged before trotting over to the stove.

"Hellooo," Georgiana dinged the bell three times as she spoke. "What's going on? Where are the orders?" As she said it, she clipped another order to the board. "We're getting busy." When she finally noticed me scowling, she did a double-take, her eyes widening. "Oh, boss. I didn't know you were back there."

"Don't hit the bell more than once," I said. "How many times do I have to tell you that?"

She smiled sheepishly. "Sorry. Don't be mad. I thought Randall was slacking with you gone."

I narrowed my eyes. "When was I supposed to be gone?"

She cringed. "I don't know." She slipped away from the window.

"Such a pretty little thing, and ya talk to her like that." Grandma clucked her tongue. "How am I ever going to get any grandbabies from ya if you talk down to everyone?"

I shook my head. "You already have ten grandchildren. How could you want more?"

"That doesn't matter. Ya haven't given me any. A nana can *never* have too many."

I snorted. "Yeah. Not going to happen."

She threw a towel at me from across the kitchen.

For an eighty-year-old, she could be quick when she wanted to be.

3

EUGENE

"WHAT DO YOU THINK?" HOLLY LIFTED MY RED CURLS AS I STARED INTO THE mirror.

"How do you make me look so awesome?" I asked, turning my head side to side.

"It's the red," she said. "It's your color."

"I agree. I don't know why I was born a brunette when I was clearly meant to be a fiery redhead."

"Get up." She ripped off the cape covering my body.

"Wow. I bet the world is lining up for you to do their hair with this kind of service."

"You bet your sweet ass they are. But no, my clients are early." Holly stared out the window of our salon as I fished my debit card out of my back pocket. "I can't believe it's almost Christmas. This year has flown by."

I stared at the adorable pink tree she had decorated by the front desk, and a sharp pain snagged my chest. There would be no Christmas for me. I hadn't put up a tree or celebrated the holiday since Gran passed. A tree in my ratty ass apartment would look absurd anyway.

My phone rang as I paid. I frowned as I looked at the screen.

"Who is it?" Holly asked.

"My landlord."

"Have you paid rent?"

"Of course, I've paid rent. I always pay my bills, thank you!"

"Then why would she be calling?"

That bubbling of unease dipped into my stomach. "I don't know." I answered the call. "Hello?"

"Eugene, this is Yolanda, your landlord."

"Hi, Yolanda." I pressed my hand against Holly's lips when she kept mouthing, *what is she saying?*

"I'm afraid I have terrible news. It seems the tenants above your apartment have had a bathroom leak for a few months now."

"Yes. Remember, I mentioned the state of the ceiling in my bathroom because of their leak?"

"Right. Well, their tub fell through."

"Can you repeat that?"

I closed my eyes and took a deep breath. *It's fine. Everything's fine.* My ass knew the ceiling was in rough shape. The wetness was growing, and black mold was setting in. I kept the door closed and only went into the bathroom to take a quick shower and use the toilet. Some mold was in the rest of the apartment, but not as bad. I'd lived in worse.

But I fucking knew better. I didn't allow myself the luxury of acting surprised when I tiptoed over the mess in my bathroom. When I looked up at the gaping hole in my ceiling and saw the little boy snickering, I waved, and he waved back.

I saw myself in that smiling child with an optimism not many could have in our situation. He laughed, peeking his head over the hole, then hiding himself from my view as he continued to whisper hi to me. He was so innocent; he probably didn't realize we were all about to be kicked out. The police were questioning Yolanda when I arrived. I caught bits and pieces of the conversation, but the woman in the tub had gotten hurt and likely filed a complaint.

It was negligence on Yolanda's part. Most likely, I wasn't the only one complaining about the condition of those apartments. I should have moved months ago, but I wanted to save. There were so many things I needed money for.

I told myself that once I paid off my car, I'd find a better place to live. Maybe even buy a home. Once I had a home, I would finally take the plunge and open a shop. A book café was my absolute dream. The bad thing was, I wanted the book café more than I wanted a place to live, which was a fucking problem.

"We can't let anyone stay here," the policeman said as he rubbed his chin. "It's a wonder how none of you aren't sick with the condition of these walls. I'd recommend a trip to the doctor."

There it was. I didn't have a place to live.

I sat in my blue Kia Soul, parked at Dairy Queen. I had gone through the drive-thru and grabbed a burger. Food was good while I pondered my living situation. My churning stomach might disagree, though.

I didn't own much. I bought a cheap futon at Walmart when I moved into the apartment to keep from overspending. My washer and dryer came from my brother's brother-in-law, who happened to be someone I kicked in the balls when he kept pushing himself on me one night. I bought my fridge from Facebook Marketplace, which could be a shady place to buy from, but it worked out for me. It didn't always. Once, a woman tried to sell me a twenty-four-inch TV for a hundred bucks but claimed it was a fifty-five inch. I didn't buy it once I met up with her and saw the TV. When I thought back, I realized the deal had been too good to be true to begin with. I didn't know which of us were sillier. Me falling for the post or her thinking I wouldn't realize it wasn't a fifty-five inch the second I saw it.

You live, and you learn.

My brother moved to the southern part of Kentucky a year before Gran passed. Which was bad since I lived in the eastern part. My nerves were all jumbled and lodged in my throat as I forced down my burger. I could call Holly, but her relationship with her boyfriend was still new. I hated feeling awkward in someone's home. I was going to feel uncomfortable no matter where I went if it meant having to stay with someone.

I thought of the little boy, wondering if he and his family had the luxury of having someone to call like I did. I'd be welcome, whether I called my brother or Holly. But if there was anything I hated more, it was asking someone for help. It made my insides go all wonky, and my heart felt like it might rip out of my chest.

I thought of Gran's screen door and shook my head quickly, as if to make the image fade from my mind.

The biggest problem was that I had to get my stuff out of the apartment ASAP. I grabbed what I could before I left, but there was a risk someone might steal what little I had if I held off too long. I still had my key, but with the hole in the roof of my kitchen, my neighbors had free access to my stuff. They could lock the door as they left, and I'd never know if they were snooping.

The thought made my skin crawl. I grimaced and took another bite of my burger.

It's fine. Everything's fine.

I decided I'd hold off calling my brother until the next day. Instead, I'd rent a room at the Holiday Inn. My boss had a lot of connections. Maybe he knew of someone who had a place to rent.

Yes. I'd find out tomorrow, I thought as I sat in my vehicle and munched on my food with renewed vigor.

4

HUDSON

"Max," I warned my giant white Pyrenees as he stepped on my flannel slippers. He had a bad habit of getting right in front of me when I walked. He wagged his tail and must have decided to behave since he stuck to strolling alongside me instead. All I did was leave the kitchen and move toward the window, but Max still treated it like an adventure.

I made some hot cocoa and chocolate chip cookies. The forecast indicated snow during the week. Besides some flurries, we hadn't yet had a bad storm that winter and Christmas was a few weeks away. I peeked out the blinds. Nothing moved. Everything was dark and still. The trees were bare. Honestly, snow would make those mountains beautiful.

Max whined at my feet, and I walked away from the window. "No cookies for you. Go to your food bowl."

I stoked the fire before getting in my recliner. Putting my plate on my lap, I patted Max on the head before sitting back.

I groaned as I stretched out and turned on the TV. Max plopped beside me on the floor. *This is nice.* Really fucking nice. I worked seven days a week, but I saw change in the future. More plans. More time to relax. My restaurant, Homestyle, might not have been what my father wanted for me, but it was what I wanted. And I was doing really damn well with it. The restaurant had only been open for a year, but I could branch out if I wanted and see if the place had the potential to do well elsewhere. Like my grandma said, my recipes were passed down through her family, but with my own added touch.

My food was my pride. In a kitchen, I was the fucking king. That was why I didn't want to rush the process of opening another place. I had to find the right people. Those who could do right with the food we served. Randall and Daisy were getting there, but they'd been working with me since the restaurant opened.

It didn't help that Grandma Sue pestered me about finding love and starting a family. Yada, yada, yada. She didn't realize I'd never give her grandchildren. I preferred animals. In my younger days, I chased after women for fun—not marriage. I had a lot of good memories doing shit I shouldn't have. I'd had one relationship that lasted a year. Hilary and I drifted apart because I couldn't give her my time. I'd finally left my dad's construction business and thrown most of my savings into my restaurant. Because of that, I was busy, but it wasn't like I wasn't busier working with my dad. We had been out of town most of the time on jobs, but Hilary hadn't complained then. I was probably giving the woman too much credit. It was clear she hadn't had faith in my restaurant. I made great money working for my dad and would have made more if I had taken over his business, but that was more my brother's thing. Not mine. But I wasn't a prick when it came to people's wants. I knew I wanted to put all my time into Homestyle when it opened, and I couldn't give Hilary the time she wanted.

For a moment, I let myself wonder: Was I too harsh on our relationship? Should I have gone slower with the restaurant to make things work with Hilary? The answer to my doubt ended when I saw how quickly she chased after my younger brother the second we split. He would inherit the company one day, since I didn't want it.

I questioned everything after that. Whether she liked me at all during our time together. Whether I liked her. Why were we together? Was it money or status for her? Ending things with her had been more of a relief, which made me wonder if I had the capacity to give love to someone romantically. Wouldn't I have been angry, at least, about Hilary chasing after my brother so quickly if I cared? None of it hurt. I was excited to have all my time to myself again. Which proved I wasn't the man my grandma wanted me to be. I couldn't— I *wouldn't* change my lifestyle to make anyone happy.

A sharp pain snagged my chest, and I grunted, rubbing the spot. I didn't need the company of others to be happy. Not having to worry about anyone else seemed better than feeling alone while with someone. I supposed Grandma's words did get to me every so often. Maybe something was wrong with me.

Why didn't I want to share my life with someone?

I took a sip of my hot cocoa. "Ain't nothing better than this, Max. Ain't no woman better than my own company."

I believed those words. Spending a year with someone taught me one thing. I didn't know how to care, and part of me did feel sick at the thought.

5

EUGENE

I was sweating bullets as I waited for the sheriff in his office. I shouldn't have answered my phone that morning. In fact, I should have stayed in that uncomfortable bed with my blanket pulled over my face. I was so nervous my stomach rumbled. If the dude wasn't quick, I was about to wreck their poor toilet.

It didn't matter that I was innocent. My skin itched at the situation I'd gotten myself into. All because I worked for Danny Hopkins. Apparently, the lawyer was more of a sleazeball than I thought. After the call from the sheriff, I guessed the electricity wasn't out at the office the day before.

"Sorry to make you wait," the sheriff said, his black shoes squeaking on the tile as he stepped into the room.

I sat straighter in my chair. "It's no problem."

The questions began, "Did you notice anything strange? Did you know Danny was planning to take off with everyone's settlement money?"

Surely, that was a misunderstanding. I had known Danny was

working for a lot of men with their black lung settlements from an old mine they had worked for. I thought of all those old grumps, coughing, back hunched over with so many health problems from a lifetime spent working under a mountain, and my heart ached. Danny wouldn't steal those people's money. They had nothing. Most of them lived off SSDI, *Social Security Disability Insurance*. Their bodies couldn't withstand another two decades in the mines to receive their retirement. With the cost-of-living skyrocketing, I didn't see how some of those people were surviving off those checks either.

"I'm sorry." I shook my head. "Danny wasn't the nicest person, but he wouldn't take off with these people's money. They're barely getting by with what they have each month."

The sheriff gave me such a pitiful look. "I can assure you, he most certainly did. He was being questioned about his wife's disappearance last year."

"He had a wife?" I didn't know that. Danny never wore a ring, and by the lewd suggestions he made toward me all the time, I would have never assumed he had one.

My head spun. I gripped my stomach as the pain got worse.

"So, he never mentioned he had a wife?"

"No!"

"Did you have relations with your boss?"

"Eew, no."

"I'm sorry. I had to ask."

"I understand, but this is all really shocking." And terrifying. I might have been working for a murderer. Scratch that. Since I was sitting in the police station, I most likely was. If they were questioning me, did that mean... "Why bring me in? Why not question him?"

"Danny's gone." The sheriff took a deep breath. "You said he told you not to come in yesterday, correct?" When I nodded, he continued. "My guess is he planned this for months, maybe longer."

"Can I use the bathroom before we continue?" I said as the rumbling worsened.

The way he nodded, along with the understanding in his eyes, kind of sucked.

When I returned from the bathroom, I answered a bunch more questions. I told the sheriff I knew Danny liked going to Tennessee in the summer. Plus, he owned a beach house in Florida. I knew which bank he processed all orders from. I even knew one of his account numbers since I had overseen signing people in and charging them when the case was finished. I doubted it would help, but I gave the information over anyway. I tried to recall anything that seemed important, but I was stunned.

I felt like I was walking in a dream. I'd lost my apartment and job in one swoop. To make it worse, I felt dirty because of Danny's wrongdoings. My arms were itchy and broke out from the stress. My legs felt like lead as I walked out of the station. The sheriff told me I'd likely have to return for more questions, but he assured me I wasn't in trouble. It was procedure to interrogate all those who knew Danny.

All the assurances in the world, however, wouldn't make the gross sensation go away. When I got inside my vehicle, I finally allowed myself to cry. If I didn't, the funk would cling to me.

I thought of my gran and how someone had sold her a shitty vehicle. She'd handed over her money in blind faith before realizing the problem. Those old miners had put their trust in Danny to win the settlement for them. He won it and then took off with the money. How was that possible?

It was like life was trying to prove to me how unfair living could be.

I wiped my eyes, then squeezed my butt cheeks as the rumbling returned. I was going to have to walk right back into the station and use the bathroom before I drove away.

It's fine. Everything's fine.

I ate at Wendy's, then went back to my car and called my brother. He answered on the third ring, "Genie!"

"Eddie."

"What's wrong?" he asked.

I perked up because I didn't want to worry him. "About that... How mad would you be if I had to come stay with you for a few weeks?"

6

HUDSON

My phone vibrated nonstop for the last hour inside my back pocket. After getting the bulk of my lunch meals out the window, I removed my iPhone. I frowned as Edwin's name flashed on the screen. I met him through his wife, my cousin, a couple years ago. He was a good guy, but I found it strange that he kept calling. We weren't exactly close, but we hung out with the same people.

"Ed?" I asked.

"Good. You answered." He sounded a little winded.

"Is everything okay?"

"My wife and I are good, but that's not what I called for."

"Oh?" I didn't like where the conversation was headed. With my last name plastered all over Dad's company, people expected the family to have nice things and money. We did. Edwin didn't seem the type to be calling for money, but I'd heard too many lines like his not to expect something.

"I need a favor."

"I'm not sure what I can do for you—"

"It's not for me exactly, but my sister."

"You have a sister?" I asked, not that it mattered. "I don't know what I could do for—"

"She needs a place to stay this week. It's only for a week. Her apartment flooded, and she lost her job, which was kind of a good thing. I'd been trying to get her to move anyway."

Was losing her job a polite way to hide that she was fired? Was he trying to hand off his problematic sister to an innocent bystander?

I rubbed my temple. "I don't understand. You have a home."

"Michael's staying at my place for the week, and you know him. He's a prick, and I don't want him near my sister."

Michael was Francis's brother and my cousin. A fucking joke of a man. Still, that didn't mean a stranger should be pushed off on me because of him.

"Ed…"

"I know this sounds like an odd request, but I don't want her wasting money on a motel. She has a lot to figure out, and she needs to leave that godforsaken town. She'd do well here."

"I don't think I can, Ed. I don't know her—"

"I can pay you. She won't accept any help, but if she doesn't know about it, it won't bother her."

"I don't need your money."

"You're the first person that came to mind. It's just a week, Hudson. I know we're not close, but I'd be in your debt."

"This is ridiculous," I said as my shoulders sagged. "You know that, right? I don't know her. Wouldn't she be uncomfortable staying with a stranger?"

"Yes, but Genie is also obsessed with saving money, so she'd do it."

What kind of name was Genie?

I sighed long and loud.

"You're going to let her stay?" he asked.

"Why me? Why not call Jack? Or Freddy?" Even as I asked, I knew the answer. I stopped hanging out with those men years ago. They lacked decency.

"Jack is an ass toward women, and Freddy is no different. She needs a few days to relax and figure out what she's going to do. Not be around men trying to make her situation worse."

"I could very well be worse than them. How do you know I won't seduce her?"

Edwin laughed. "No offense to you or my sister, but I've seen your type. Genie's not anything like that one chick you dated who always wore heels and never had a hair out of place. You know all put together and shit like you."

Something about his words irked me, like I was being judged. Hilary might have been a well-loved person in the community, but she had been cutthroat and often cruel, especially when it came to other women. Something else that confused me to no end was the competition women had with each other. Edwin probably thought Hilary was as sweet as she made herself look, which could be a problem. If he thought that, then he was clearly suggesting his sister was a hellion. I didn't want anything to do with someone who disturbed my peace.

"If you're suggesting that your sister is trouble..."

"She's clumsy, awkward—a complete nerd, actually. She spends her free time reading on her tablet. That's what I meant. She's a mess, but I promise she's not trouble."

A mess? Trouble? What was the difference when a person was describing their sister as a mess? It wasn't reassuring. I should have told him to fuck off already. I normally would have, but something was stopping me. I couldn't put a finger on the feeling. I couldn't be curious. No way. Concerned? Maybe? *Why would a guy I wasn't exactly close with want his sister to stay at my place?*

"And if I say no?" I asked.

"She'll stay at a motel until Michael leaves."

"I know Michael's a prick, but is he so bad you want to keep your sister away from him?"

"Trust me. Genie doesn't like him. She won't stay while he's here, and I don't blame her."

Fuck. Why wasn't I saying no. "Just a week?"

"Michael's apartment will be finished next week, so yeah, just until then."

"She can stay until he's gone."

Why did I agree to that madness? I wasn't what I'd call nice or helpful. I'd get nothing but the inconvenience of having a stranger in my home.

Edwin let out a breath before saying, "Thanks, man. I owe you."

I ran my fingers through my hair. "I'm not home much, so your sister better not be a problem."

"She's not. She's not."

Why did I get the feeling he was lying? I should have said no.

7

EUGENE

I was going to kill my brother. Stay with a friend of his? One I didn't know, which would be the way of things, since he made all new ones when he moved to the opposite side of the state. Men, in general, sucked most of the time—plain and simple. I loved my brother, but I couldn't stand most of his friends growing up. There were no innocent crushes, either. I'd been sneaking into my gran's Harlequin romance books since I was eleven. When I read about those sexy and heroic men, then saw how teenage boys acted? *Bleh*.

But I was still a hormonal, curious teen who read things she shouldn't, so I got sexual way too early because of it. If I could go back, I would have changed some horrible experiences, but *you live and you learn*.

I thought of my ex, Jared, and my insides knotted. He was one lesson I wished I never had to experience.

I deserved more in life than I allowed myself when it came to the opposite sex. Since I was almost thirty and still doing absolutely nothing I wanted in life, fear had set in. I'd been obsessed with love when I was a teen because of all the romance books I read. I wasted a lot of time trying to make my partners happy. One guy wanted me to stay home while he worked. I did, and my soul was chipped away in the process. I spent a year with him before I had to leave. I'd been cheated on and lied to, enough that I was over it.

Before any man, family taught me how little I could depend on anyone. Anytime my parents popped in at Gran's growing up, it was to ask for money or her vehicle. If Gran didn't comply, my sperm donor would threaten to take Edwin and me from her. Anytime they mentioned us was the only moment I remembered my gran looking fearful. Our so-called family took advantage of her so much, and she allowed it. My two aunts were the same way about using Gran. The door was in constant use during my childhood. People were in and out of the trailer, asking something from Gran. For such a proud woman, she let her kids get away with everything. Aunt Cheryl had been a good soul, but she always chose men who abused and used her. In the end, she became no different than the men who hurt her.

Being in love must be a trick. I should have learned my lesson during my childhood. Regardless, I knew those days. *Depend on yourself, Eugene.* Don't become like those who aggravated Gran. *And for goodness's sake, don't trust a man again.*

Love was better in books. I could turn on my Kindle and read whatever type of man I wanted at the time. It was convenient and satisfying, no matter what anyone said. Once I stopped dating two years ago and focused on me and my needs, I became happier.

The problem was that I'd made good money working for a lawyer. Between the pay and my cheap apartment, I had saved so much within two years, and that income was gone along with Danny.

I tried not to panic about the future, but my thoughts were swirling. I had no money coming in. If I didn't find work soon, I would have to dip into my savings and find a permanent place to live.

I refused to stay at my brother's house while Michael was there.

My brother, being my brother, found me somewhere to stay, so I didn't have to spend money on a hotel. Still, it would be awkward to stay with someone I didn't know. But screw my awkwardness and pride when it came to saving money. Edwin said the man's name was Hudson and gave me his address, which I put into my car's GPS.

I hoped he wasn't a pervert or something. Obnoxious behavior wasn't worth it to save a dime. I'd give the first night a try, but if I didn't feel safe, I'd give my brother the biggest smackdown of his life for putting me in that situation. I'd never allow myself to feel afraid of living with someone again. Jared was enough of a mistake.

"What's this on the floor?" Jared's voice drifted through my thoughts, and I shuddered. He would come home from work and yell over a speck of dirt on the floor I couldn't even see.

Stop. I didn't want to dwell on a mean ex, so I refocused my attention on driving.

I should have asked for a picture of Hudson or his place, at least. My odds with a GPS weren't the best. To make matters worse, I'd wasted the day spending time with Holly while she worked. It had been nice to confide in her, but I regretted overstaying. I hated driving in the dark.

The interstate was a breeze. I'd only taken one wrong exit along the way, but it became more stressful when I reached Jefferson County—an area made up of small roads and dirt turnoffs. I gave myself another mental fist bump when I didn't miss the tiny sign for Boogey Lane.

"Woot, woot. I found it first try," I said, pulling onto the bridge and heading up the small, graveled road. The navigation's voice said I had another half a mile to go before reaching my destination.

I did it. *Go me!*

It was a little after nine, and my stomach bubbled with nervousness. Edwin said Hudson lived in a huge cabin—all fancy and shit. My brother's words, not mine. When I arrived and saw the place, I muttered, "Holy shit."

It *was* all fancy and shit.

Cabins were always beautiful. No matter how big or small. But that two-story was beyond anything I'd be able to afford in my lifetime. Not that I was sad about being unable to live in a home like that. What would make me miserable was being unable to achieve the things I wanted in life. A nice, comfy home to go along with my dream would be nice, but I didn't need it to be so big.

The cabin was perfect, though. I opened the door and whistled. From the looks of it, the porch wrapped around the entire house. There seemed to be another rooftop, but the wooden fence was obscuring my view of what it was. The light on the power pole behind the house illuminated the place enough for me to see the looming trees and hills in the distance.

The clinking of what sounded like windchimes had me looking at the porch again. The porchlight was on, and the chimes slapped together, dinging more as the wind picked up. Thank God the bottom floor was lit up. Hudson was still awake. Edwin said he told him I was coming.

I inhaled deeply, then exhaled. "You got this."

I hopped out of my car. As I was shutting the door, I heard the crunch of what sounded like someone stepping on gravel and went completely still. I squinted my eyes as if that would help me pinpoint where the sound came from. When I saw the animal, I screamed. Clearly, I knew it was a dog, the lights made it easy to spot him, but my brain said, "Polar bear."

The dog was a massive ball of white fur, and reality hadn't mattered for a moment. My brain tried to convince me a bear was coming for me. The dog's head came up to my hips. Clearly, it was overgrown!

"Ah," I said as I pressed myself against my car as the beast stalked closer. "I hope you're nice. Please don't eat me." I held out my hand. A wet nose pressed against my palm, followed by a bunch of slobbery licks. His tail wagged, and I sagged against the vehicle. "So nice of you not to eat me, Bear."

"Max!"

I screamed again and clutched my chest at the thundering voice. The dog stopped licking me and took off running. Glancing toward the porch, I saw a man descending the steps. Oh, shit. Hudson was a big dude. He had to be well over six feet. The man wore black pj's and house slippers. He walked holding a coffee mug. His strides, posture, and the way he stared at me screamed unfriendly. I was intimidated. I gulped and peeled myself off my car to greet him.

"I just let him out to use the bathroom before you arrived. Max isn't used to guests, but he's harmless. You don't have to be afraid of him," Hudson said in a husky voice. At least, I hope that was Hudson, and I didn't pull into the wrong place.

"I thought he was a polar bear." When I realized how ridiculous I sounded, I blurted, "I mean, of course I know he's not a polar bear. This is Kentucky. But he's so big, and it's dark out..."

The place was lit up by the giant light on the power pole, so I knew my blabbering about it being dark out wasn't helping my case. I couldn't help it, though. He made me more nervous than the sheriff ever did.

"Are you Edwin's sister, Genie?" Hudson asked as he stopped at the front of my vehicle.

I couldn't be sure, but his hair looked blond or light brown. It hung over his forehead slightly. I tried not to stare too much because his jaw was hardened and... *Oh shit,* I was really going to kill my brother. Hudson didn't want me there. I gathered that much from his severe scowl.

"Uh, yeah. Hudson, right?"

He nodded. "I didn't think you were going to show since it was getting so late."

I fought the urge to touch my hair or face. He was staring awfully hard at me. "It was a four-hour drive, which became five hours for me since I suck at directions." I laughed, but it only made it more awkward when he didn't smile or anything. "Are you sure it's okay for me to stay here this week?"

"I told your brother you could." The words dripped out of his mouth like they were acid. "I can help with your bag. Is it in the back?"

"Yes. Thank you."

I popped the trunk and waited while he grabbed a bag for me. I retrieved the one with my toiletry items and followed him to the porch. "Your place is beautiful," I said to ease into a conversation with him.

"Yeah," he said.

I frowned at his back.

Handsome men were always boring. He wasn't dark-haired with dreamy eyes, making him a failure as a book boyfriend. Still, in terms of height and stature, he passed with flying colors. I snickered and didn't notice he'd stopped at the top of the stairs. A gasp escaped my lips as I collided with him. I looked up at his scowling face and smiled.

"Oops. Sorry."

One of his brows was arched. "Why are you laughing?"

My face and neck heated. "I don't know."

I live inside my head and was thinking about how you fail in book terms since you are blond...?

In the porchlight, I saw his blond hair more clearly and his eyes. He didn't have baby blues, like I would have guessed, but very light browns instead. Maybe even a green or hazel.

"Mm-hmm," he said way too snootily and turned back around.

That made me want to laugh again because I was nervous. He likely thought I was a weirdo, which wouldn't be wrong. I completely owned who I was, so it didn't bother me most of the time.

Once inside, I ogled him some more. The man was gorgeous. I might have sworn off dating for the last two years, but I could still appreciate a man who looked good in pajamas. When he turned, I glanced up and away from his rear. He didn't seem to notice since he was pointing toward the stairs. "You can stay in any of the rooms upstairs. Mine is down here."

"Awesome. Is there any specific place you don't want me to go?" I asked.

It must have been a weird question because he cocked his head slightly, his lips flattening. "Is there anywhere you should be other than the guest room or bathroom?" He pointed toward a doorway. "Of course, you're welcome in my kitchen, too. All I ask is that you clean up after yourself while you're staying here."

"Right. Of course," I agreed, then looked down at my muddy boots. "Um..."

"You can put them by the door."

I put my boots away and looked up to find him staring at my socks. He sighed and shook his head, then headed up the stairs. I peeked down at my feet. What was the problem? Sure, they didn't match, but if I tried keeping all my socks the same, I'd never be able to keep any because the dryer ate them all.

Maybe it wasn't about my socks, even though he was looking at them when he did. I'd give the man the benefit of the doubt. I ran up the stairs behind him. He dropped my bag at the top. "Pick a room."

And with that, he walked back down and left me to myself.

My stomach grumbled as I slipped into one of the rooms. I should have grabbed something to eat on the way, because I refused to go downstairs. I'd inconvenienced him enough for one night. Maybe there was a shower upstairs I could use, though. I'd never be able to sleep unless I cleaned up.

There was a scratch at the door, then a whimper. I smiled and opened it. "Hey, Bear," I cooed as I rubbed his head.

"Max!" Hudson yelled. The dog and I flinched. "Get down here."

Max wagged his tail and went downstairs.

"*Okayyy.*"

The good news was that Hudson didn't seem to be a creep. He might be an asshole, though.

8

HUDSON

Edwin was right in his assumption. His sister was nothing I desired in a woman. Even when she didn't say anything, she was still loud. From her bright-red hair to her black nails, I felt ensnared, like I couldn't look away. I didn't like that. It was bad enough she was in my home, and she was so *noticeable*.

Her hair had been so vibrant beneath my light outside that it appeared to glow. Her voice was soft, yet I felt like a siren had been speaking, about to drag me to the sea. And her eyes were brown, but so fucking bright.

And she had way too much personality for one woman. What reason did she have for laughing out of nowhere as we walked inside the night before? She called Max a bear since she thought he was a polar bear. As odd as she was, she had stolen my focus since she pulled into my driveway. My heart felt tight and weird when she smiled. I felt exhausted just at the idea of her smiling and snickering more in my home. After only a few minutes in her presence, and I was positive I was correct in my judgement of Genie.

I heard her showering the night before when I went to bed. It was disconcerting and a bother to my schedule to have someone in my home. Thankfully, it would only be a week, and I could chalk it up as being charitable. Proof that I could be a good guy when I wanted. I still didn't understand how I ended up in that situation. Yet, I had been curious about Genie the entire time I worked. It had to be because a stranger was in my home while I was at the restaurant. *Had to be.*

My guest must have gone out while I was at work because she parked in the middle of my driveway when she returned. I couldn't get into my garage or park beside her. I had to leave my truck *behind* her Kia, despite there being plenty of room for two vehicles to park side by side. *Women drivers.* I snorted.

I was walking by her car when the door opened. I barely saw the movement and wasn't quick enough to step away. But I fucking felt the door as it smacked into my knees. I stumbled back a step.

"Oh, shit," Genie mumbled as she jumped out of the tiny vehicle. She had a hoody over her head. Her nose and cheeks were pink, like she'd been outside in the cold for a while. That red hair of hers was even brighter in the daylight as she pushed the hood off her head. My heart did the weird thing again.

Fuck. She was so easy to look at. It pissed me off.

"I saw you pulling in the driveway," she said.

"You couldn't wait until I walked by?" I scowled but refused to rub my knee in front of her.

"I didn't realize you'd move so quickly," she blurted as she glanced behind me. "I'm sorry. Did you want to park in your garage?"

"For a vehicle so tiny, it amazes me that you've managed to take up my entire driveway with it."

"Sorry about that. I can move it right now. I didn't know how long you'd be gone, so I was thinking about heading out until you got back. It's why I parked like that."

"You're a guest. I offered you a place to stay this week. You don't have to wait on me."

"Yeah, but I locked the door when I left this morning and didn't think about how I'd get back inside."

I stopped and turned. She held her hands to her mouth, blowing them. It dawned on me. She was red in the face because she was freezing. "How long have you been out here?"

"Not that long." She waved her hand quickly and averted her gaze, which told me one thing. Genie wasn't a good liar.

Fuck. I should have given her my spare keys. Why would she willingly freeze? Making me feel like a total shithead for allowing it to happen, as if I had control over my guest.

"Does your car not have heat?" The vehicle looked brand new.

"Yes, but carbon monoxide poison is a real thing."

"So, you were out here for a while," I said, and pulled my keys out of my pocket, singling out the house one before handing them to her. "Unlock the door and give me your keys. I'll move your car."

It should have been a simple exchange, but Max barked. Genie looked toward the door as she passed me her keys. Her hand was nowhere near mine when she let go, and the keys fell to the ground between us.

"Shit," she muttered.

I bent to retrieve them as she did, and our heads bumped.

"Fuck," I hissed.

"That's what I say." She groaned.

We were rubbing our heads when our eyes met. I was closer than I should have been. Her breath fanned my cheek, and she smelled good, like strawberries, and clean. She wore a bit of eye makeup. Her brown eyes were...

Fuck again. I fixated on her. The longer I looked, the more I felt like I was getting pulled into her orbit. Was it the red hair or the eyes? What sucked me in? She still stared at me with those brown eyes, lips parted, as if she were studying me too. The odd chick was making me odd with her. I didn't know how else to explain it.

I made a sound in my throat and took her keys, then dropped mine in her palm before creating distance.

She's not my type, I told myself. She seemed all bright and shit, and I was more like gray.

"Go on in," I told her.

When I made it to the driver's side, I heard her screech. Turning around, I spotted Genie on the ground with Max licking her face. "Max!" I yelled, and the dog sauntered off like he hadn't bulldozed into our guest. "What is with you, man?"

Maybe I wasn't doing my dog any good by not having any visitors. He didn't know how to behave around women.

"It's okay." Genie stood and started patting her ass off.

Just as I was turning away, something about her actions made me do a double-take. Even a woman would have looked for a second. My eyes widened, and I palmed the back of my neck, knowing I should have turned my damned head. She had a hole in her black leggings, right at her ass crack, and she noticed it when her finger snagged the spot. She twisted a bit, trying to see. "Are you kidding me? Did I leave the house with this hole?"

I placed my fist over my mouth and averted my gaze. Was she not wearing underwear? From the amount of pale skin I saw, she fucking wasn't. *How could she not notice the breeze with how cold it was?*

"Maybe it happened when Max jumped you," I said as I opened her vehicle's door. That had to be the explanation. The other possibility didn't make sense.

"I hope," she mumbled, then stiffened and eyed me suddenly. "Did you see?"

I decided it was better not to answer and hopped in the car to straighten out my driveway.

"Did you see Bear?"

"His name is Max!"

"What are you doing?"

Genie jumped at my voice and palmed her chest. Water sloshed over the edge of the bowl in her hand and spilled to the floor. Did the woman jump at everything? I took a deep breath as I stepped into the kitchen and placed her keys on the island between us.

"I'm so sorry. I'll clean it up right now!" she blurted.

She was so frantic, it made me nervous just watching her. Why was she so panicked? I wasn't upset with her for spilling water, but she acted like I was.

"I was just going to make me some ramen." She set the bowl down and walked around like she was searching for something.

"In a bowl?" I asked, then pointed toward the paper towels to the left of the stove.

"Yes. I was going to microwave them."

"Don't bother. I'll make some."

She paused with a few paper towels in hand. "Oh, okay. Are you sure?"

"I'm sure."

Genie stood nearby while I retrieved a carton of eggs and a bunch of green onions from the fridge. She moved out of my way each time I walked toward the stove. I pointed toward one of the stools. "You can sit."

And get out of my way.

"Right." She hurried and nearly fell over Max in the short distance it took her to get around to the other side of the kitchen island. "Do you need me to help with anything?"

I raised a brow. "How often do you use a stove?"

The blush that swept across both of her cheeks was answer enough, but I still listened as she huffed. "Hey now. I might eat out mostly, but I can cook a few things. My gran would have killed me if I didn't learn a thing or two after all those years spent in the kitchen with her."

"Hmm."

"I can make gravy and biscuits, meatloaf, and spaghetti...Wait, are you judging me? Can you cook more than ramen?"

I poured the noodles into the pot and looked over my shoulder at her. Her sneaky laugh and twinkling eyes told me my guest didn't think I could cook. The reality was that I turned down a position in the family business to work in a kitchen.

"Your brother said you lost your job and home all in one swoop," I said, changing the subject as I turned back to the stove.

"Mm-hm."

"That's it?"

"What about you? You have this massive cabin and live all alone with Bear—"

"Max."

"*Max.* What do you do for a living?"

"I cook."

Silence. Such a long, wonderful stretch of quiet that my mouth twitched upward.

"You cook? And afford this place?" she finally asked.

"I cook at *my* restaurant."

"Ooh, fancy. I knew that the moment you stepped out the house."

"Me? Fancy?"

She pointed downward. "Your slippers. I bet you have more than one set of pj's. too. Am I right?"

I looked at my house shoes and frowned. Who liked getting stuff on their feet? The floor could be cold. I thought everyone wore them, and I *did* have more pajamas. Several.

"You don't wear house shoes? And everyone has pj's."

"Not me."

I turned around again because I had to look the woman in the eyes. Those chocolate orbs were expressive, narrowing as she smirked.

"Then what do you wear to sleep?"

"T-shirts that are way too old." She held up her hands, and then covered her mouth. Her cheeks reddened the longer I watched her, and she started fidgeting with her long sleeves. It was like watching someone try to hide themselves right in front of me.

Was she embarrassed? Was she lying? Was she trying to be nonchalant and failing? I didn't know, and that bothered me.

Genie was a frustrating mess. I suddenly wanted to crack her open like an egg to see what lay inside.

One thing was certain. Genie wasn't my type.

9

EUGENE

Gʀᴀɴ ᴡᴏᴜʟᴅ ʙᴇ ꜰᴜʀɪᴏᴜs ɪꜰ sʜᴇ ᴋɴᴇᴡ I ꜰɪɴᴀʟʟʏ ꜰᴏᴜɴᴅ sᴏᴍᴇᴏɴᴇ ᴡʜᴏ might be a better cook than her. That was saying something because all I'd had was Hudson's *fancy* ramen with its egg and vegetables. I didn't need to know what the veggies were since the meal was delicious. I even told him so, but he didn't respond.

I had to make sure I never cooked in that man's home while I was there. Although he never said anything, I was sure he saw the crack of my ass where my leggings ripped. Jesus, I really hoped I didn't go into town like that. Cooking around him would just embarrass me more.

Hudson left the kitchen after he cleaned up, so I washed my dish when I finished. As I headed upstairs, I spotted him by the fireplace, resting on a recliner. That fire sure looked cozy. I wondered if he'd mind if I joined him and read while he watched TV? Max was at Hudson's feet and jumped up when he spotted me.

"Max," Hudson warned, and I couldn't help but notice that

Hudson styled his hair with product. His blond mane was slicked back perfectly. *Fucking fancy-ass rich man.*

"It's fine." I dropped to one knee and beckoned the bear dog forward. "He's not bothering me."

I got a grunt in reply.

I petted Max for a bit before I finally worked up the nerve to ask, "Do you mind if I sit by the fire to read?"

Without making eye contact, he beckoned me toward the fireplace as he browsed Netflix on his TV. I took that as a yes. With a grin, I ran toward the stairs to grab my Kindle. Big mistake! Max chased after me and stepped right in front of me at the top step. I nearly tripped over him. I caught myself on the banister with a loud 'oof', then looked over the edge to see if Hudson heard the mishap. If he did, he never moved from his recliner, but he sighed long and loud. I was more careful going back down with Max since he liked to trot under a person's leg. It was cute. I had a giant animal chauffeur.

I plopped down right beside the fire with Max and began to read.

Rubbing my feet together, I leaned forward and swiped on my Kindle. I didn't know if I was getting warm from the fire or the absolute smut in my current book. The first time the word *cock* popped up, I touched my cheeks and looked up. *Mistake!*

I made eye contact with Hudson. He stared at me with his arms folded over his chest as he reclined. I looked away and the magic of the book faded as awareness crept in. Normally, I didn't care where I read my romance. I'd gotten used to reading sex scenes in public with a straight face. I had wandered into my little Eugene bubble where nothing else existed, including the man sitting next to me in a recliner. And, well, he popped my fantasy bubble with his eyeballs. He was supposed to be watching TV instead of looking at me. He ruined my sanctuary with those hazel eyes of his. Why was he staring so intently, anyway?

No matter how hard I tried reading, the words looked too much like words, and I couldn't dive into my imagination. I looked at him again, and sure enough, he was still ogling me. I took a deep breath.

"What are you reading?" he asked in a gruff voice.

How long had we been sitting there for his tone to sound like that?

A question I hated being asked by men. I wasn't ashamed of what I enjoyed, but the look in a man's eyes when I told them annoyed me all the same.

"Nothing you'd enjoy." When he didn't respond, I added, "I read a lot of romance and fantasy."

There was no hint of a smile or a tease on his lips. Instead, his forehead crinkled, and he surprised me by asking, "Is your natural hair color brown?"

What a strange thing to be curious about.

I cocked my head to the side as I brushed my fingers through my hair. "Yeah."

Easy guess, I supposed, since my eyes were brown.

"Your brother said you lost your job and apartment."

"I did."

"You don't seem like someone who just lost their home and income," he stated.

I tried not to let his words get to me. Whether he was being judgmental or curious, he pushed a button I didn't like being pressed.

I hit the power button on my Kindle and stood. "If I cried and fell apart every time things went wrong in life, well, I'd always be crying and falling apart." He made a sound in his throat, and I thought he might say something, so I blurted, "I'm going to bed."

I was optimistic about finding work. Almost every place in town had a *Now Hiring* sign. The problem was that the pay wasn't going to be what I was used to working for the corrupt lawyer.

That asshole. My stomach got all bubbly at the thought of the creep. I made the mistake of looking at a Facebook news post about him and regretted it. Of course, I was mentioned—not by name--but as the secretary who the police questioned for being in contact with him. Some of the slandering comments were about me, saying the assistant would have known what he was doing.

"He or she was likely working with him!"

"These people deserve their money."

"Arrest everyone who worked for him until they talk!"

I had to stop reading because it was fine. *Everything's fine.*

Every second, I tried not to peek at my phone, expecting the police to call me in again. Maybe they would think the same things as those people.

Driving back to Hudson's, I sang along with the radio until my throat was hoarse. Singing helped keep my thoughts quiet. Hudson had been kind enough to leave a spare key out by the front door with a note that said, *"Use it and don't wait outside again."*

The gesture wasn't enough for me to forget his eyes on me the previous night. I spent way too much time thinking about it and decided Hudson was judging me. Was he doing it the entire time he watched me? I could only imagine the facial expressions I made while reading. I also thought about his comment about my hair. He must be one of those people who disliked women dying their hair bright colors. Why else would he ask about my natural color?

Ugh.

Just a few more days. I could do it for my savings account's sake. While I couldn't handle a creep, I could handle a jerk.

When I reached Hudson's cabin, I let Max out to pee. The big guy nearly knocked me over every time he greeted me, but it was okay. I'd always wanted a dog, but I always lived somewhere that didn't allow pets or had a boyfriend who hated animals.

As a teen and then as a young adult, I was such a dumbass when it came to men. Oh well. I forgave myself, but that didn't mean I didn't cringe. I fell prey to pretty men and nice words. Their fake words always turned to venom.

While waiting for Max to finish up, I pulled out my phone to check the weather. It was so cold that day and had been raining the last couple hours. I wondered if it might turn to snow because of how fast the temperature seemed to be dropping. Before I opened the weather app, I spotted Max running for the front door. My heart stopped. The giant dog was solid white, but you wouldn't know since he was buried under a layer of mud. Max looked as if he'd found a puddle, then caked dirt and grit onto his fur. Oh, no. I tried to beat him to the entrance, waving my hands to get his attention.

In my head, all I could see was Jared's furious face and how angry he'd be if an animal tracked mud all over his home. My stomach cramped.

"Oh, my God! Oh, shit! No, Bear," I yelled, but it was pointless. Max darted into the house. I chased after him and screamed every time he tried to jump onto the sofa or anything he could dirty up.

As soon as I got close enough, I tackled him, not caring how dirty I got in the process. I cared more about how furious his owner would be if I let him destroy his furniture with mud. The floor was already a mess at the entrance. "Let's go to the bathroom," I said, leading him by the collar.

Max was super satisfied with himself. His tail was beating the shit out of me as I walked him between my legs. I didn't trust him to bolt. I had to clean up Max and the mud before Hudson returned from work. My stomach bubbled with unease.

"You betrayed me, Bear," I told him as I stepped into Hudson's room. I gawked. His room was beautiful. The bedroom furniture was made of wood similar to that in his cabin but stained a darker color. The bed sheets were solid black. There were two doors in his room. The closed one must be his closet. I went to the bathroom and flipped on the light. I gasped. A huge porcelain tub rested in the center. A shower was at the other end of the room and took up the entire back wall. He had his and her sinks. Like his sheets, every-thing was black, including his sinks, shower, and tub. The lights were dim, and looking at the wall, I believed there was a knob to adjust the brightness. It was breathtaking, and I fucking shouldn't be in there.

"Maybe I should have used the upstairs bathroom," I whispered as my anxiety skyrocketed.

"What the—"

My soul left my body when I heard Hudson's voice in the distance. Of course, he'd get home before I could hide the evidence.

"Oh, God," I whispered, but it was too late. I'd already created the mess and had to see it through, so I led Max toward the shower. I didn't believe I could keep him in the tub by myself. At least I could trap him in the shower, so I slipped inside with him.

"Genie!" Hudson hollered.

"In here," I called back.

When he stepped into the bathroom, his jaw tightened, and his eyes surveyed me and the dog. Hudson had his hair slicked back again. "Might I ask what happened?"

My grip loosened on Max, and he rushed out of the shower. I rose and stood still, trying not to fidget. "I let Max out to pee once I got back, and he must have headed straight for a puddle."

"Yeah, you have to watch him every time it rains, he will go for any kind of water." Hudson yanked off his jacket and pushed up his long sleeves. He ran his fingers through his blond mane, messing up his styled look as his forehead crinkled. When I felt my attention snagging on his muscular arms, I looked away.

"I wish I would have known," I admitted as I grasped the shower door.

"Here. Let me." Hudson leaned into the shower so much that I had to press myself against the wall.

I flinched when he moved his arm toward my face, and he froze, looking me up and down. Hudson wasn't Jared, I told myself. But Hudson could be like him over a mess. I didn't know, and my body was in a state of fight or flight.

"You're pale," Hudson stated as he grabbed a shampoo bottle behind me.

Shit. He was reaching for the dog shampoo. The tension drained from my body, and I sagged forward a little.

"Sorry," I mumbled. "I can bathe Be— Max. I'm the one who let him out."

Then I realized how close we were in the shower together. I could smell Hudson. His cologne was subtle but extremely pleasant. Inhaling sharply, I stepped out, then Hudson did, before he turned on the water. He told the dog to get in, and the animal listened.

"Are you sure you don't want me to help?" I asked again.

"It's fine. Go wash up." Hudson turned and looked at me. Yes, his eyes were definitely hazel, although they never appeared the same color. "It looks like he got you just as dirty."

I didn't know why, but my cheeks reddened. We were still closer than we should be standing outside the shower. Max was stinky, which meant I was too. I walked out to let Hudson clean his dog or tried to. One moment, I was standing, the next, I slipped and pitched forward. With nothing to grab onto, I threw my hands forward to catch myself. Pain sliced up my palms as I hit the floor, and I winced. "Ow, fuck!" I was wiggling my wrists around when Hudson ran by and slammed the door shut before squatting in front of me.

"I'm fine," I said, showing him my reddened palms.

"What did you trip on?" Hudson asked.

"I don't know," I grumbled.

He grabbed my hands, moving and bending them every which way. When he was satisfied, his shoulders dropped as he met my eyes. "I'm beginning to wonder if I can take my eyes off you."

My face was as hot as a furnace. I made a sound in my throat as I stood. My knees popped, and I fought the grimace I wanted to make. I hadn't realized my knees hurt, too. "I'll get out of your way."

Max pawed at the door. It looked like the big dog wanted to escape his shower, but when Hudson hollered, he trotted to the shower again. I slipped out of the bathroom but didn't shower myself yet. I found the mop in Hudson's pantry and spent the next ten minutes cleaning up Max's pawprints before I went upstairs.

10

HUDSON

MAX AND GENIE WERE A TERRIBLE PAIR TO BE LEFT ALONE TOGETHER. HELL, even without my dog, I was beginning to suspect something would go wrong with Genie involved.

Edwin's sister was a mess, but I only had to survive five more days.

I'd been at Homestyle since six that morning and came home to *chaos*. I was exhausted by the time I towel dried Max. *How* did he manage to find mud when it was colder than a witch's tit outside anyway? Everything was frozen. The weatherman forecasted snow. I was positive we'd get some by the end of the night.

She took a pretty hard fall in the bathroom, too. Should I check on her? Fuck. Why was it something I asked myself? If I didn't double check to make sure she was okay, I'd fixate on her more. I'd been doing it since she arrived and was exhausted with myself for it. Did I need a new hobby? I never recalled being so curious about someone who troubled me so much.

Genie was awfully jumpy, too. Did I imagine her flinching in the shower when I neared, or was I losing my mind having her around? Surely, she wasn't afraid of me. I might not be the most pleasant person, but she was safe with me.

Should I try smiling? *No.* I should keep the smiles to a minimum. I wasn't sure I could handle seeing any more of hers. I felt like my heart might jump out of my chest when she did. Maybe she truly was a siren who escaped the sea to bewitch me.

When I stepped into the living room, the pawprints near the entrance were gone. There was no sign of the muddy mess Max left behind. Genie cleaned it herself. I never would have asked a guest to clean anything in my home. I was raised better. Rubbing my chin, my thoughts drifted to the night before, when she'd been reading. I should have let her be. The moment she caught me staring, I could see I ruined her mood because she had been so animated while she read. I didn't think she noticed how much she smiled and moved around, and then I destroyed her happiness by paying attention to her. But as much as I saw her discomfort, I still had to ask, because it didn't make sense. For the chick with firetruck red hair and a soft smile to be sitting beside the fire reading so peacefully as if she hadn't lost everything.

My question must have upset her. She went upstairs.

I crossed my arms over my chest. "Did you completely forget how to behave once she arrived?" I asked my dog. I got nothing but tail wags in return.

"Sorry for the mess." Genie descended the stairs, patting her hair with a towel. Her wrists must be fine from the way she moved her hands.

She was dressed in raggedy clothing—a T-shirt with a hole right at her navel and a black pair of jogging pants that looked just as worn. Even so, the ragged outfit couldn't hide how alluring the woman was. My eyes strayed to her more than I wanted, just like my thoughts did.

"I was giving him the opportunity to pee, so he didn't have to wait for you to return."

"It's fine," I said quickly and looked away, because, God forbid, I offended her by staring again. She told me what she wore to bed. Her appearance shouldn't surprise me, but it did. "There's a leash hanging by the door. Feel free to take him out that way if I'm not home."

Why did I say that? It wasn't like she'd be in my home much longer.

Genie's hair was so damp that water dripped onto her shirt. And her face was bare and oily, like she put something on it before coming down. It took every ounce of control I had not to pluck the towel from her hands and properly get the excess water from her hair. Her skin was pebbled, and despite the heat running, the cabin was chilled. Seeing her be so willy-nilly with herself, I didn't know why, but my chest tightened, and I became uncomfortable.

"You should blow-dry your hair," I couldn't help but say as I stared at all the wet spots on her shirt. I spotted her navel again, and the tightness increased in my chest tenfold.

"I never blow-dry it," she said with a shrug.

"The cabin can get cold..."

"It's fine." She waved her hand.

I frowned.

"Believe me, I've survived worse."

She wasn't trying and had no idea of the mess she was causing my brain. But every time she spoke, she made me more and more curious. I wish she didn't.

"I brought home some leftover soup." I pointed toward the kitchen. "You're welcome to it."

"If it tastes as good as your fancy ramen, count me in."

Fancy ramen?

Was everything ordinary considered fancy by my houseguest?

Her phone rang. She pulled it out of her jogging pants and answered, "Hello?" There was a pause. "This is she. That would be perfect. I can make that work. Of course, yeah. See you Monday!" She jumped in the air as she ended the call. "I have a job interview already."

"That doesn't surprise me. Every place is hiring."

"You're right, but I'm still glad."

"Where at?"

"Subway." She bounced toward my kitchen, her wet hair flying everywhere. "It's not the pay I want, but it'll do until I can find better."

I wanted to know what she did before losing her job, but I realized I was asking all the questions. Genie hadn't inquired about me at all. Why did that bother me? My heart felt weird, tight, and *uncontrollable.*

In my recliner, I browsed Netflix a bit, then looked toward the second-floor balcony. I supposed she wasn't coming down to read by the fire. Rubbing my jaw, I went back to looking for a movie. I hadn't read a book in a while. Maybe I should. Most nights, I spent more time looking for something to watch than actually watching something.

I looked toward the second floor again and spotted Max in the corner of my eye. He sat at the bottom of the stairs, waiting for our guest.

"Max," I hollered.

Great. I was offended for no good reason at all. Me and my dog were doing the same fucking thing.

When Max laid down beside me with a huff, I shook my head and put down the remote. The lights flickered once or twice before going out. About five seconds later, they came back on. It must be snowing. As I stood, I heard the creak of a door opening and shutting, then Genie's loud footfalls as she came running down the stairs.

"Careful," I said right as she nearly slipped.

She grabbed the banister, caught herself, and gasped. "The power blinked."

Her hair was dry and wavy over her shoulders. I tried not to notice how stunning she was and continued to fail.

She's not my type. She's not my type. The woman was a walking safety hazard. She needed someone to look out for her, though. I worried. But why? Those thoughts shouldn't belong to me. She wasn't my problem. Besides, my last relationship was proof I lacked the ability to care... So, why couldn't I stop frustrating myself over her?

She's a siren. I was doomed.

"Yeah." I walked to a window and pulled the curtain back. It hadn't been thirty minutes since I last checked outside. There hadn't been anything but some slight rain. Suddenly, everything was white, and the power lines drooped in the middle from the weight of the snow. The snow seemed wet, heavy, and it came down hard.

Shit. I wanted snow. Not a power outage.

"We're going to lose power. I'm going to go grab the generator and some more wood."

"Do you need my help?" she offered.

I shook my head. "No. But charge anything you have. You might have time."

11

EUGENE

Hudson looked like the abominable snowman by the time he finished setting up the generator outside and carrying in firewood. No matter how much he patted himself down before stepping in, snow fell everywhere as he untied his boots by the door.

I rushed to the pantry, grabbed a mop, and began cleaning up the mess. Although Hudson had shut the front door, it was still so cold. My skin pebbled, and my hands and feet were numb. I was pretty sure my nipples pointed through my bra. Normally, I didn't wear one in the house, but I wasn't at home. Besides, Hudson stared far too much for me to skip a bra.

The light flickered, and I said, "Power might not go out."

"It's going to go out," he said with certainty. He hung up his coat and finally looked at me. "The snow is too heavy and coming down fast." He planted his hands on his hips. "I can clean up after myself, Genie."

"It's not a problem. It's the least I can do for the person trying to keep us warm."

He stopped and just stared.

I stared right back, arching a brow. *What?*

"The generator won't run the heat pump. We'll need to stay by the fire to keep warm."

"Right," I whispered.

Well, that wasn't awkward at all.

"I'll run a kerosene heater, too, but it's still not going to do much for such an open room."

The lights went out again but didn't come back on. The cabin was pitch dark.

I gripped the mop tighter. "Um, Hudson, I can't see anything."

"You don't reckon." The sarcasm dripped from his voice.

Eew. That man's attitude. I knew I stated the obvious, but he didn't have to be a butthead. If I had my phone, I would have had some light. Unfortunately, I left it on charge upstairs.

"Here."

It was like being touched by an icicle when he grabbed my arm. I flinched, and the mop clattered to the floor. "Your hands are freezing."

"Sorry," he murmured.

When his phone's flashlight beamed straight into my eyes, I held up my hand to shield them.

Hudson moved the light in a different direction and said, "You can have the couch. I'll sleep on the recliner."

I walked behind him.

"Uh." He stopped and turned around at my voice, the light hitting my poor eyelids again. "Do you mind?"

At that point, I was positive he was doing it on purpose.

He grunted, and I hesitated before asking, "Do you care if I use your phone to walk up and grab my Kindle, phone, and blanket?"

Hudson handed over his device. As soon as I moved toward the stairs, I was met with resistance on my legs. Max was right in front of me, and I didn't notice. I gasped. My arms shot out in front of me. Hudson grabbed my forearm and pulled me back.

He sighed and said, "How about I walk with you?"

Was he kidding me? My face felt like it might melt right off as I huffed. "Sure, yeah. If you're afraid of the dark, you can tell me."

Another grunt.

He snatched his phone and aimed the light at my face again.

I shielded my eyes with my hand. "Would you stop that?"

"I'm afraid of the dark, right? I need to see your face to know I'm not alone."

I snorted because he said it with such a straight face. "Do you want to hold hands, too?"

"Yeah. That'd be best." The man took my hand in his, and I gawked.

He pointed the flashlight toward the floor.

I grew more and more flustered as my heart rate quadrupled. "I was joking."

"Look. See how nothing is in front of us." He waved the light around, showcasing the floor. "There's nothing for you to trip over."

Oh, *oh!* I understood exactly why he held my hand like a child. When I tried yanking my hand away from his death grip, I couldn't. The embarrassment burned my face. "Your dog almost tripped me."

"Right, but I'd rather not have to drive in this weather tonight."

"What's that got to do with anything?"

"I'm worried you'll find a way to fall off the second-floor banister and break something. No ER trips tonight, okay?"

"Oh, my God. You're being ridiculous. I can walk fine on my own."

I pushed his phone toward his face to see his expression. My eyes widened as I saw the corners of his mouth stretch upward. Was Hudson smiling? I didn't realize my position put us chest-to-chest until I breathed in his cologne. Inhaling sharply, I stepped out of his personal space.

The fancy-ass rich dude smelled so good.

Hudson pointed the phone back toward the floor. "I've seen *your* walk for two days now. I'm not so sure."

I wanted to defend myself, but I was terrible about rushing and being clumsy. Regardless, I was like a persistent little roach that couldn't be harmed no matter how many times I tripped or bumped my hips into things. Holly was the same way—it must be a woman thing. Of course, men wouldn't understand. Their brains would have to be filled with *thoughts* to understand how easy it was to bump into something when there were a billion scenarios running through the brain. When I was stuck in la-la land, it could make a short walk to the toilet seem like a minefield.

"Oh," I said with dramatic flair. "How did I ever manage to walk up the stairs before you?"

He snorted, and I grinned. I let him continue holding my hand as we walked up the stairs. His knuckles and fingers were so much bigger than mine—that made sense considering he was a man, but it was nice. Big arms, tall man, no electricity in his giant house. I yanked my hand out of his grip the second we reached the top as my insides twisted.

Oh, no, no, no. I'd been great with the no-man's-land lifestyle. While it was perfectly okay to admire the perfection that stood beside me, I didn't need to project a fantasy onto the situation. I'd never speak to Hudson again once I left that cabin in five days.

"You make it a habit of holding your guests' hands?" I asked to ease my discomfort.

Hudson opened the bedroom door, gesturing for me to enter. "You'd be my first guest in a while."

Although he couldn't see it, I arched a brow as I slipped inside and grabbed my things. "It makes sense, but I don't think you should grab people's hands, especially if you hardly know them."

"You're right, but I probably shouldn't allow strangers inside my home either."

Oof. He was right, so I called a ceasefire for the rest of the conversation. Thankfully, he didn't try to take my hand again as we walked back down.

"I'm going to turn on the generator for the fridge," Hudson said as I settled myself in front of the fireplace with my Kindle.

I didn't respond as I wrapped myself in a blanket, but he didn't move from his spot. I glanced up and asked,

"Do you need my help?"

With a grunt, he finally strode off, and Max followed him. Okay. I hoped I didn't somehow offend Hudson. Maybe I was getting too comfortable in his home, and he didn't like it, which was crazy. I was far too relaxed to be in a place I wasn't familiar with. I was usually the very definition of awkward.

When I heard him returning, I set down my Kindle. I wasn't about to repeat his watching me read again until I could forget about that last encounter. His hands were full, and I couldn't make out what he had until he was bending before me. He placed a bottle of water and a sandwich on a plate in front of me, then rose and went over to the recliner with his own food.

"Thank you. You didn't have to."

I noticed lettuce, tomato, and pickles were on the plate beside my sandwich.

"I didn't know how you liked your ham sandwich or if you even liked ham, so I added a few things on your plate in case you wanted them."

Nothing about the bread or ham looked cheap as I added lettuce and tomatoes. I recognized two-dollar ham anywhere since I'd lived off it and ramen a lot in life. That wasn't inexpensive ham. It was finely cut and smelled like heaven.

"You really are a cook, aren't you?"

"It's just a sandwich," he murmured. "But yes."

I inhaled the sandwich and would have asked for another if it wasn't too shameful. The man was letting me stay there for free and had given me food *three* times already. I was taking a drink of water when my phone started ringing.

"Hello?"

"Eugene." My brother's voice was stern on the other end.

"Edwin."

"You've been in town for two days and you haven't visited."

"I've been looking for a job. I found one, by the way. Subway. And I don't like your guest, remember?"

"Power out at Hudson's, too?"

"Yeah, but it's fine."

"He's a good guy," Edwin began. "He's treating you okay, right? No funny business?"

I looked at Hudson and saw him staring. "*Yes.* But I'll talk to you tomorrow, okay?"

"As soon as the snow is gone, I'll meet you somewhere. Michael won't be here much longer."

"Yeah, yeah. Love you. Bye!" I hurried and ended the call.

"Your name is Eugene?" Hudson asked the second I put my phone away, not even trying to hide the fact that he must have heard the entire conversation.

"Yeah. And yes, I'm aware it's a boy's name. I'm not a fan of it, so please stick to calling me Genie."

He flickered his gaze over me, then shook his head. Hudson didn't say a word, so I was confused as to why he looked put off again.

"What is it?" I asked.

"I'm going to call you Red."

"Red?"

He pointed at my hair. "*Red.* And Eugene is nice. Even if you're the only woman on the planet named that, which I doubt, that means it's not just a boy's name. It's your name. So, if you don't want me calling you by your name, I'll call you Red."

This man.

He decided what to call me as if he had the right to do so?

"First the handholding, now choosing what you call me? Hudson, that can come off rude. What if I call you..." I looked him up and down, trying to figure out what to pick. "Non-book boyfriend material. How would you feel?"

He froze, and the way his nose crinkled was cuter than it should have been for someone of his stature. "Huh?"

"All of the popular male main characters in books have dark hair. You're a blond, so you'd never be someone's book boyfriend."

I realized I was talking to someone who didn't know a thing about the precious world of romance books. I'd made a mistake. One that left me wide open to being judged.

A slow smile spread over his lips. "I'm going to look up this material. I'll decide if I am or not. You can't dislike a man because of his hair color."

I tried hard not to snicker. "I wouldn't call you non-book boyfriend material, you know. It's a mouth full."

"I know," he replied. "But I am going to call you Red."

"Fine." My smile waned when I got that warm rush of adrenaline in my chest. I didn't mind the nickname. What I did mind was how okay I was with it.

A loud cracking *snap* woke me. Even if it hadn't, Max would have. The dog started barking as soon as he heard the sound too. Hudson was already up and, on his feet, heading for the front door.

"What was that sound?" I asked as my stomach knotted.

"I'm not sure. I'm going to go check it out." He turned on his phone's flashlight before putting on his boots and jacket.

I saw the fire going out. Grabbing a few logs, I put them in, which might not be the best idea since I wouldn't know what to do if I created a problem. But I didn't want to sit around and do nothing. Once I got the fire going, I looked out the window. A huge tree lay a mere foot behind my car. A few branches were on top of the vehicle. Everything was so white. The moon illuminated the yard, and it still snowed. I spotted Hudson and Max walking around my vehicle. He checked the back end for something while dipping his head underneath the branches, and my insides got worse. *Lord, please don't let anything be wrong with my vehicle.* It was all I had at the moment.

When he headed to the door, I opened it. The snow reached the top of his boots as he stepped onto the porch. He began knocking the snow off as Max jumped up the steps. Even as big as Max was, he was hopping around to move through the storm.

"Is my vehicle all right?" I asked and wrapped my hands around my arms. The air was so cold it stung my skin.

"Yeah. You got lucky. All that hit it were some branches." I moved back as they came inside. "Probably because it's so tiny."

My shoulders sagged. "Luck is not something I usually have."

"I'll get the tree moved when the sun comes up, but you aren't going anywhere. At least not today. I haven't seen it this bad in a while."

"Me either."

He stopped and looked at me before saying, "You're cold. Go sit by the fire. I'll turn the kerosene heater on."

I felt like he might be getting the heater because of me. I didn't want him to do more than he would have if I hadn't been there. It made me feel guilty. "You don't have to. The fire is plenty."

The cabin was getting cold, though. Maybe he wanted to warm up himself. I ran to the fireplace and plopped on my ass as he disappeared again. I couldn't stop shivering, but the heat was nice against my skin.

He must have started the kerosene heater outside, since it was already lit when he carried it in. "It won't smell the best, but at least we'll be warm. The cabin is ventilated enough so we won't have to worry."

I immediately thought of my childhood. A painful snag hit my chest. "Edwin and I lived with our gran growing up. When I was about ten, her heat pump tore up one year in her trailer. It was a long winter because she used a kerosene heater to keep us warm. She put us all in the living room every night to sleep. I was so embarrassed going to school knowing I smelled like kerosene."

I cradled my knees to my chest as I reminisced. Those days, I would have given anything to have a hundred more nights near fumes that were bad for my health if it meant getting to speak with Gran again.

"I'm sorry," he said.

I frowned. "Don't be. I'd give anything to go back and sit in that room with her again."

"No. I mean, I'm sorry for your loss."

My eyes met his. Hudson's expression gave nothing away. I never said she had passed, but he knew. Somehow, I'd given it away, but it was okay. It felt good to talk about her to someone other than my brother and Holly.

12

HUDSON

I was awake before my alarm went off. My recliner was fantastic to sit on, but not my favorite place to sleep. A few feet away, on the couch, Eugene lightly snored with her mouth wide open. One leg hung off the edge uncovered, and she had an arm thrown over her forehead.

Maybe not a siren.

I snorted and shook my head. The woman's ability to adapt to a new environment honestly astounded me. I could have been a serial killer, for all she knew. Yet, there she was, sleeping better than I did in my own home.

I grinned, cracked my neck, and stood to stoke the flames. Max stretched and moved about as I did. Even with the curtains closed, the bright sun shone through the cabin windows.

I peeked over at Eugene again. She hadn't moved. That crazy colored hair spilled out all over the couch pillow. A weird static seemed to take over my chest. I sucked in a breath and looked away. The organ was out of control in her presence.

Eugene, Genie—*Red*. She truly wasn't my type. She was nothing I wanted or needed. Yet, my gaze snapped right back to her. Fuck. She looked... sweet sleeping there. It was pleasing to see something cute resting in my home. Did I really just think that? It was bad enough that I ogled her all the damn time, but she couldn't get a reprieve from my stare while sleeping either. I flexed my hand as I recalled her tinier one in mine the night before. She felt good, soft, and warm. I wasn't a lonely man. Being alone was a luxury, if you asked me. Eugene being in my home was confusing me. I should have been tired after the fitful sleep I had, but I wasn't. There was a lot of energy bouncing around inside me.

Knowing I was being a total creep watching her sleep, I pulled out my phone to distract myself. There were a few texts from my employees already, letting me know they couldn't make it or checking to see if we would be open. With the power out, I figured the latter should be obvious.

My phone rang as I responded to the messages. "You keeping warm, old woman?"

"Likely warmer than you," Grandma Sue replied. "I'm guessing ya won't be opening today."

I rubbed the side of my forehead and sighed. "I hope the emergency generators kicked on at the restaurant. I'd hate to lose everything in the freezer."

I'd give it a few hours before heading out to check on my place. One of the perks of being the owner.

"Those generators cost ya a pretty penny. I sure hope they worked."

Yes, they did.

"I'll go out and check the restaurant later."

"I'll—"

"No, you won't do anything. We can't open without power."

Grandma Sue grumbled. "I'm too old to sit in the house all day."

"You know, *normally*, everyone works their entire life to do nothing all day once they get to your age."

"If I don't stick by your side, you'll scare every woman away. I got to do all the sweet talkin' because you're terrible. How ya got that last one to stay with ya, I'll never know."

"Grandma—"

"Even if she was a snake, I'm still shocked she stayed with a *toad.*"

I closed my eyes. "It's too early for this. Call me if Dad isn't keeping you and Mom warm."

I ended the call and smiled, picturing how hard Grandma was huffing at the phone.

The hardwood floor creaked, and I turned around to see Eugene attempting to tiptoe toward the stairs.

"I didn't mean to wake you," I said.

"You didn't," she replied.

Eugene would probably still be snoring if I hadn't started talking.

"I'm going to deal with the tree in the driveway," I said, slipping on my boots.

"Um... I heard you say something about going out later..."

"Yeah."

She tucked a strand of hair behind her ear. "I thought you said we couldn't get out today."

"I said *you* couldn't in that Kia. I, on the other hand, own a four-wheel drive truck and have driven in worse weather."

Eugene blinked and pursed her lips. "Yes...Well, hmm..."

"Red," I interrupted her, fighting a smile. "You're welcome to go into town with me later."

She hesitated, twisting her fingers together. "If it's not too much trouble."

In the truck, I glanced at her. She gripped her hands together on her lap. Something I noticed she did a lot. My houseguest seemed to be a constant ball of anxiety.

Before we left, I asked, "Do you want to stay at the cabin? I can grab whatever you need while I'm out if you're worried."

Her seatbelt clicked as she buckled up. "No, no. I don't need anything. I just wanted to go out."

I quirked a brow as I backed the truck out of the driveway. "You'll risk being afraid to cure your boredom?"

"I'm trying to get familiar with everything." She was quiet for a second until I started driving through the tiny, one-lane road. "Are you sure this is safe? The road's really narrow..."

She had good reason to be nervous. The snow was at least eight inches thick on the graveled path, but I figured the main roads would be a little better.

"I wouldn't say it's safe. Anything can happen. I don't feel the wheels slipping, so I think the traction is good."

She bounced her legs as she gripped her seatbelt.

"Hey, it's okay, all right? If you're that scared, I can turn back around when I find a spot. I'd rather you stay home than be terrified."

From the corner of my eye, I saw her lean toward the console. "I'm fine. I wanted to come. You were going out regardless to check your restaurant."

"Yes, I, *me*." I looked at her then. She was so close; I saw every tiny shade of brown within her eyes. I swallowed hard, and quickly looked back to the road. Damn it, my heart wanted to pop out of my chest. "Honestly, how have you survived in the world this long? I want to know."

"Excuse me? How does wanting to go to town with you have anything to do with survival?"

"Because you're so careless. And when you walk—"

"You're bringing up the way I walk again?" Her tone became accusatory.

I should have kept it to myself when I noticed the crease in her brows and the pain quivering her chin. But I didn't because I felt like *someone* needed to tell her to be more aware. Three days around her, and she turned my insides upside down.

"You're clumsy, Red. You're not mindful of your surroundings."

"God, so I'm clumsy. Big deal. It doesn't make me helpless. And if I let fear control me, I'd never do anything. There's not much in this world that doesn't scare me!"

She twisted her body toward the door and looked out the window.

My stomach sank to my boots. I understood my words came off as rude sometimes, but I didn't mean them to be. I was terrified by her, but I couldn't explain why. The only thing I was certain of was that I could warn her to be cautious.

13

EUGENE

I wasn't sure what to anticipate. Maybe I assumed he would have leased a structure in the Senkins city area, a location that squeezed in between other businesses, all in the same building. Not a restaurant with a unique layout, décor, and setting. After driving up a short hill, we arrived at a parking lot where his was the only business visible. The area was blanketed in snow, but I could still tell that it was large enough to accommodate numerous customers.

Homestyle was in cursive letters hanging on an oval wooden sign over the double doors. The windows were painted over with pictures of landscapes—hills on one, a giant mountain on another, an ocean, and a gushing waterfall all woven through them. The deep red roof matched the building's brick finish. It was beautiful. I would have told him that if I hadn't been pissed off.

I'd been clumsy all of my life. It took me a while, but I'd embraced my awkwardness. There were always jokes growing up from my brother and my gran about how often I got bruises. They were teasing me, though. I didn't know why Hudson looked so upset. I was the clumsy one, not him.

"This is my restaurant." Hudson said, breaking the quiet tension between us as he shut off the engine.

"It's nice," I said, but my tone was icy.

I should have stayed in his cabin. If I had stayed put, I could have avoided the hurtful conversation. *Damn, my curiosity sometimes.* The fireplace and my Kindle sounded far nicer than Hudson's company in that moment.

"Red..." The soft way he spoke the nickname made my stomach heat.

I hopped out of the truck quickly to escape the feeling.

I looked at him. "Don't you need to check on everything?"

With a sigh, Hudson got out on the other side and shut his door. I followed him, letting the quietness swallow us whole. It was still freezing, and inside the restaurant was no different. I rubbed my ears as they began to ache. Earmuffs would have been great. My ears were sensitive and hurt so bad in the cold.

Hudson must have noticed me rubbing them because he said, "I just need to check the generators. Make sure they're working properly."

As soon as he said that the rumbling of a heat pump started, and a few lights came on.

Wow. The place was the real deal. Gorgeous wooden booths lined the perimeter of the room, with breathtaking nature pictures hung at each. Black tables scattered across the large room. In the center of the restaurant was a rectangular liquor bar with stools wrapped around it. Toward the back, I saw another set of metal-looking doors and guessed it was the kitchen since a window was right beside it.

"Well, that makes everything ten times easier," he muttered. "Let me check the food."

"Do you think you have power at your place now?" I couldn't help but ask. The idea of a hot shower sounded amazing.

"I doubt it. The power company will focus on business areas first, and then work their way into the rural spots."

Not what I wanted to hear.

He rubbed his jaw before letting his fingers slide into his hair. "Do you like steak?"

"Yes, I do."

"Come to the kitchen. It will warm faster."

I arched a brow and tagged along behind him. He picked up a stool on his way past the bar and carried it with him. Once inside the kitchen, he set the stool down and patted it. "Sit. I'm going to check on everything, and then I'll cook us something."

"Tell me what to do, and I'll help," I offered because I didn't like the idea of sitting there and doing nothing while he fed me again.

A door chimed.

"Hudson!" yelled a female with a scratchy voice. "How long has the power been on?"

Hudson swore, looked at me, then at the closed kitchen door, palming his forehead. "She's going to misunderstand."

"Huh?" My insides twisted. "Is it your girlfriend?"

I'd totally been ogling a taken man the last few days. The shame! Gran would disown me.

"No. Worse." Hudson opened the door and hollered. "How did you get here?"

"Your dad dropped me off. I told him to leave when I saw you were here."

Hudson rubbed his temple and stepped aside as a small, elderly woman limped in. "I didn't realize Dad was home, but it's too cold for you to be out. You're lucky the main roads aren't that bad. He should have known better than to get you out—"

"Will you hush? So, are we opening—" The old woman stopped, and her bright-green eyes widened when she saw me.

"Grandma Sue, this is Eugene—"

"You can call me Genie," I interrupted. The old woman's wrinkled mouth kept growing wider the longer she looked at me.

"She's a *temporary* guest I have at the moment."

I quirked my brow at Hudson when he emphasized the word temporary.

Sue turned and gawked at him. "Ya mean, she's staying with ya? At *your* place?"

Hudson dropped his head, and then his shoulders sagged, as if he'd given up. "For a few days, then she's leaving."

Sue seemed to be ignoring him because she limped past him and held her arms out *toward* me. "My child, ya have crazy hair."

I laughed. "I wouldn't call red crazy."

"It's very bright," Hudson's grandma stated. "I'd never lose sight of ya, which is good. My vision ain't great these days." She adjusted her glasses on her nose to prove her point. The old woman looked between Hudson and me, one corner of her mouth curling upward. "So, what are we doing?"

"I'm checking on everything, then leav—"

"Hudson's going to cook us steak after he makes sure everything's good," I cut in, and then frowned at Hudson. Why did he say we were leaving? Were steaks no longer on the table?

She gasped dramatically and covered her mouth with one hand. "My grandson is cooking ya steak."

"I cook *everyone* food," Hudson grumbled. "It's what I do."

Then it hit me. I understood his grandma's reaction to me, and his fear that she'd misunderstand. She must believe we were a couple. If not, she seriously wanted us to be. By the gleam in her eyes, I'd guess she was a schemer and had trapped him in those situations before. I liked her already.

"I'm guessing you're the reason he's such a good cook," I said.

Sue side-eyed her grandson when he muttered something I couldn't hear. "Don't ya need to check on those generators and cook us a steak? And bring me a stool like ya did her."

A slight rush of adrenaline shot through my bloodstream at her words. He *carried* the stool for me. As quickly as the sensation came, I shook my head. Most likely, he didn't want me tripping and destroying his kitchen.

"You don't need a stool. Go sit in one of the booths," Hudson told her.

He must have forgotten that he said the kitchen would warm up quicker.

"Come then, Genie. My grandson doesn't think an old woman can sit on a stool, so join me in a booth. With an attitude like that, he can cook in here alone."

My eyes met Hudson's. Although he'd upset me, I didn't want to piss off the man who offered me his home. "Do you need my help?" I offered.

His voice came out softer that time. "No. Go sit with her if you want."

"Let's go," I said as I picked up the stool. "I'll take it back for you."

"I'd make him do it," Sue said over her shoulder, limping as she walked.

Hudson moved closer, keeping his hand right at her back. Although he wasn't touching it, he was close enough to grab her if she fell or something. I found it sweet, especially when she looked up and scowled.

"Stop hovering. If I fall, I fall."

"Not on my watch," he muttered and followed her. "Behave, will you?"

I followed behind them, smiling.

"Shoo." Sue waved him away as she sat in the booth.

He glimpsed my way, hesitated like he wanted to say something, and then decided against it. He left without a word.

Okay.

I joined his grandma.

As soon as I was sure Hudson was gone, I said, "We're not dating, you know."

"Not yet," she countered.

I didn't want to upset the woman, but I felt it should be obvious we weren't compatible. "He offered me a roof over my head for a week because my brother asked."

Her wrinkled face crinkled more. "Hudson did?"

"Yeah, but I'm sure he's regretting it."

"Might I ask why ya needed a place to stay?"

I gathered my hands in my lap and squeezed. There was nothing to be ashamed of, but embarrassment was all I could feel in that moment, especially sitting in such a beautiful restaurant.

"My upstairs neighbor's apartment flooded, destroying mine in the process." I wouldn't dare admit the state I was living in because I knew better and chose to live there anyway. "I'm actually not from around here..."

"Where did ya live?"

"You know Huntingsburg?" When she shook her head, I added, "It's in the western part of Kentucky."

Her mouth curled into an O. "So, what brought ya out this way?"

"My brother."

Her expression was thoughtful as she rubbed her knuckles. "So, ya have one of those online jobs?"

"No. I actually found one in town."

"If ya need a place, why not work here?"

I blinked. "I found one."

"I'm sure Hudson would pay better than whatever ya found."

"I'm thankful enough and won't impose on him anymore after I leave—"

She waved her hand. "Nonsense."

The woman's intentions could be spotted a mile away, so I had to get the conversation over with. "I don't know why, but I see you're trying to push me, someone you don't know, onto your grandson. While I don't really know Hudson, he looks plenty capable of finding a partner."

Sue threw her hands up, and her shoulders slumped. "I'll be dead before I see him happy with anyone." Despite the dramatic way she spoke, the possibility clearly bothered her. "Aging is a wonderous thing, don't let anyone tell ya different, but it also makes one greedy. I am not happy with what I have left—even if it's another ten years. Because ten years doesn't guarantee what I'll be alive for. All my grandkids have babies now besides Hudson."

I didn't dare say her grandson might not want children. Her stubbornness and willingness to speak about Hudson told me she was used to dealing with a determined man.

"You are greedy, aren't you?" I teased. "How many great grand-babies do you have?"

"Ten." She grinned. "All of them are rotten."

"And you want more."

Her smile waned. "I want Hudson to find happiness, too."

I glanced at the chandeliers lighting up the place, and then at the clean booths. The paintings on the walls and the windows held my attention for several seconds. My pulse quickened as the excitement built. *I wanted this*. Well, not a restaurant, but to open my own place like Hudson did. Instead of steaks and potatoes, I wanted books, coffee, and sweets. The more cookies and cakes available for people, the better.

"I don't know," I whispered in awe. "This looks like happiness to me. *His* happiness. I'd be glad for him if I were you."

When she said nothing, I finally looked over at her. She had a peculiar squint in her eyes as she studied me. It wasn't amused, angry, or sad. Just a look that made me blush for some reason. Like I was being dissected like a frog.

"You're right. You're right." She broke eye contact. "I should leave him alone. He has it all figured out."

"It seems to me he does." I scanned the area again.

"I suppose I'll stay out of his business," she added.

I nodded. "I'm sure your grandson would appreciate that."

"So, you're going to work here. You'd make a pretty waitress."

I stiffened and side-eyed the old woman again as she beamed. The smile was too big, too suspicious. I'd already told her I would start a job soon, and she didn't seem the sort to listen if I repeated myself, so I remained quiet.

"So, ya made this huge change in your life all because you lost your apartment?" she asked.

I didn't know why, but her questions were making me nervous. "Yeah. There was nothing left after that."

"Oh. So, ya left no boyfriend behind?" Before I could answer, she was talking again, "Ya said ya found a job in town. What did ya do before coming to Hudson's and what did ya choose now that you're here."

Oh, God. Why did I feel like I made a grave error somehow? Was it too late for me to tell her she could go back to planning her grandson's wedding and future kids? Anything if it meant escaping the conversation, we were having about me. Sue asked whatever she wanted; despite the fact we'd just met. She was like my gran. The thought was like a sucker punch to my gut.

I felt obligated to answer one of her questions. "Let's just say, I worked for a shitty man and was foolish enough to think my job was stable."

Sue's mouth opened, ready for her next question, when Hudson spoke first. "It's none of your business, so don't pester her."

As he placed two drinks down, I couldn't help but wonder how long he had been there. The idea of him hearing anything was unsettling. "Are you okay with Pepsi?" he asked me.

"Yeah. Thanks."

"Give me a few minutes on the food." He crossed his arms and stared at his grandma.

She rolled her eyes. "Would ya leave?"

I fought chuckling. There was something amusing about those two together.

Shaking his head, he went back to the kitchen. My heart nearly jumped into my throat when Sue started sputtering. I would have thought the woman was choking until she shoved her drink aside.

"He gave me orange Crush Soda." She glared at the door. "The nerve of this boy."

I liked Crush, but I'd side with Sue just to help her aggravate her grandson. "You've got your hands full."

She stopped fussing and glimpsed at me. The look in her eyes as she held my gaze and grinned caught me off guard. "Yes, I do."

Why did I get the feeling we weren't talking about her grandson anymore?

14

HUDSON

The steaks weren't my best.

In an effort to save Eugene from my grandma's interrogation, I rushed. The old woman was my favorite person—I'd never tell her that—but she could drive anyone mad. She didn't give a shit what she said or did. I heard bits and pieces of their conversation to know she was throwing me in the mix, like I assumed, which was another reason I hurried.

Grandma Sue would never believe Eugene and me weren't dating based on the simple fact that she was in *my* cabin. No one came to my house. Not even Sue. The old woman knew I didn't help people and would point it out to me later. Honestly, I was just as confused as to how I ended up with Eugene in my home. What made matters worse was my own curiosity concerning my clumsy guest. I was beginning to suspect my annoyance with her came from a sense of fear for her getting hurt since she was clumsy.

I only made the steaks because I knew she hadn't eaten, but I shouldn't have brought her to my restaurant. Grandma couldn't aggravate someone she didn't know about. Yet, it was too late to save Eugene. I didn't want her to think less of Grandma or me. Nor did I want Eugene to feel pressured or uncomfortable by the things Grandma Sue was likely saying about me.

After I brought out the food, I sat beside Grandma.

"It's tough." I knew she'd point it out the second she took a bite. I would have done the same to her.

"It's delicious," Eugene stated as she inhaled hers.

"*Someone* made me rush." I narrowed my eyes at my grandma, but she was too busy watching Eugene to notice. So, I did the same as Grandma and studied Eugene. She was too busy eating to see us staring. She was a fast eater and finished everything. If she thought that was a good steak, which it wasn't, I wondered if she'd ever had an actual *delicious* one. A few red strands fell onto her forehead, and she swept them back. Eugene was pretty. There was no denying that. There was also no denying that she was a walking safety hazard.

Not my type, not my type. Making a sound in my throat, I took a bite of steak, trying to divert my attention from the little red head across from me. Maybe if I thought about those words enough, it might start sounding true. Did I have a type? I couldn't remember what that might have been three days ago. The weird thumping of my heart had me questioning myself.

"*Let's just say, I worked for a shitty man and was foolish enough to think my job was stable.*"

I heard something I shouldn't have. Although it was something not said to me, my curiosity grew all the same. I wish it didn't. Edwin had a stable job, a nice home, and for all that I could tell, he was a decent guy. That was why I caved and allowed his sister into my home. Everything Eugene did made me believe she lacked the things her brother had. Why did I care? Wait! Did I care? I glanced at Eugene, who sipped her drink. Fuck. I was feeling strange and suddenly glad. She might have had some bad luck, but she found me.

Grandma was suspiciously quiet. Her eyes stayed on Eugene for so long that the girl finally noticed. She touched her cheek and asked, "Is there something on my face?"

"Just your beauty, child," Grandma said in a soft voice.

Her kind words made me relax slightly. I knew Grandma meant it, but I wished she'd stop staring at Eugene like she was a school project needing to be tackled.

A blush crept over Eugene's cheeks. Her tangled red locks, wrapped in a messy ball on top of her head, caused more of those loose strands to move as she shook her head. "You flatter me. I look like I just crawled out of bed."

She wore a hoody and some faded jeans. I could tell she had applied some makeup to her eyes, though, because her lashes weren't that long when she woke up. She was pleasing to stare at either way. I didn't know why I kept noticing her beauty. My ears got warm, and I fought the urge to rub them. I looked down at my plate and took a bite of steak.

The awkward woman was making me odd.

"You cooked for us, so I'll clean up." Eugene stood, grabbing her plate.

"You'll sit down," I said sternly.

Apparently, my words weren't stern enough since she ignored me. "I'll come back for y'all's plates when you're done."

I sighed as she disappeared to the back of the restaurant.

"Let her. She clearly wants to help since you cooked," Grandma said.

"I don't expect her to help. I'm the one who offered to make us something." There was a loud clattering sound in the kitchen, and I jumped to my feet. "And I'm positive nothing is safe in that kitchen with her in there."

"How so?"

"She's clumsy."

"Is that so? It must be hard to be pretty. Ah, I remember the days."

Ignoring my grandma, I rushed toward the kitchen.

Eugene yelled, "I didn't break anything. I just dropped the pan."

It's probably dented.

Her shoulders stiffened as I got closer to the sink. "I'm washing these dishes. If you want to help, you can bring me yours and your gran's."

Her cheeks and neck got noticeably pinker the longer I stared at her side profile. I'd already upset her once that day. Strangely, I didn't want to do it again, even for the sake of my kitchen. Rubbing my jaw, my shoulders dropped, and I turned around to get the plates.

After we cleaned the kitchen, I locked up the restaurant as Eugene walked alongside Grandma to the truck.

"I'll take the backseat," Grandma fussed as Eugene opened one of the doors and hopped in.

"I'm already back here," Eugene said. "I'm good. You take shotgun."

"Tell your guest to—"

I cut off my grandmother. "Get in. You're getting older, standing out in the cold huffing."

Eugene's muffled laughter made me suppress my own as I helped Grandma climb into the truck. "These Henderson men all think they need big trucks. Overcompensating if you ask me."

That time, Eugene did a poor job at concealing her chuckle.

It wasn't so funny for me since my manhood was being questioned. "Buckle up."

"Shut the blasted door. I'm freezing," Grandma shouted.

I shut the door, walked to the driver's side, and got in.

It only took about three minutes to get to my parents' house. Grandma lived there, but not by choice. A few years ago, we had to force the situation after her hip replacement. She had too much trouble getting around to be living alone, despite what she thought.

I put the truck in park, keeping the engine running, and looked back at Eugene, who was staring at her phone. "I'll be right back. I'm going to help her inside."

"I don't need your help," Grandma muttered.

It took a few minutes of arguing, but I got her inside in one piece. Mom was the only one at home. I said goodbye quickly before Grandma could let it slip that someone was with me. When I returned to the truck, I frowned at the empty passenger side. I glanced at Eugene. Why didn't she move up front?

"Get up here," I said.

She gawked at me like a deer in headlights before doing as I said. The same silence that fell between us when I upset her returned as I drove, and I didn't like it.

"I hope my grandma didn't offend you. She means well," I said, breaking the tension.

Eugene chuckled lightly. "No. She was fine. Actually, she reminded me a little of my gran." I glanced in her direction, hoping to see Eugene's reaction, but she turned toward the window.

Her phone rang. "Hey... Yeah. I called earlier. As soon as you have the chance, I need your help to get my things from my apartment... Just a futon, some clothes, books—you know me."

The conversation didn't last long, and I assumed it was her brother. When she ended the call, I blurted, "I can help you get your things."

Her eyes widened. "No, no. God. I've already aggravated you enough."

"It's not a problem."

"It's a four-hour drive."

"I said it's no problem. I'll tell your brother I'm taking you."

Her face was red again, and I could feel the heat of her gaze even when I focused on driving. "Don't you need to be at your restaurant?"

I could tell she was trying to find a way to change my mind. "They can survive a day without me. They have before." It didn't happen often, but I've had to take a day off, at least twice since I'd opened the restaurant. Three, if I counted that day with no power.

"Hudson—"

"Why can't you accept my help?" I asked.

"You've already offered me a place to sleep. I don't want to bother you."

"And I told you I don't mind, so it's fine." When she was quiet, I added, "We can go tomorrow if that works for you."

15

EUGENE

WHAT LITTLE WARMTH THAT WAS LEFT IN THE CABIN WAS GONE WHEN WE returned. There was still no power. Max and I were bundled in blankets on the couch while Hudson started the fire.

My stomach was upset. Not as bad as it could be, but... how could I convince Hudson I didn't want him to help me get my things without sounding rude? Or saying it directly? Maybe if I didn't bring it up anymore, he'd forget. I petted Max, then hugged him.

I'd *willingly* lived in that awful apartment for a while and saved a lot of money. That didn't mean I wasn't embarrassed. Of all people, I didn't want Hudson to see how I had been living. With his fancy pajamas, his gorgeous cabin, and his beautiful restaurant and life, he'd likely never understand why someone would live in a mold infested place. I even hid the state of my apartment from my brother because he'd be pissed. But I'd rather deal with his wrath than the utter disgust I imagined would be on Hudson's face when he saw it.

A shudder passed through me.

"Get over here." Hudson pulled me from my dire thoughts. When I glanced up, he gestured for me to come over to the fireplace.

Max got up when I did and followed me as I sat down on the floor with the blanket.

"I'll start the kerosene heater, too."

I was quiet as he disappeared outside. That didn't change when he returned, either. I was too nervous about the idea of him seeing the apartment. There was no pride, just shame.

It was only a little after three p.m. Without power, I was stuck in the same room with Hudson because of the fireplace. What was I supposed to do the rest of the day?

"You're quiet." Hudson surprised me by plopping down beside me. He shucked off his large jacket and tossed it behind us, putting his hands closer to the fire.

I made the mistake of glancing at his lap and averted my gaze just as quickly. Hudson was a large man. Not only was he tall, but he had big arms and legs too. I never noticed his legs until his thighs were right there beside mine. The jeans emphasized the bulk of them, and something told me it was all muscle. Every time he moved his arms, muscles rippled. He must work out.

Suddenly, I was less cold.

"You're still quiet." Why did his voice sound deeper when we were alone?

I looked at him, and of course his heavy gaze was already on me. So, I blurted out the first thing that came to mind. "You're lucky to have your gran, you know."

"She'll likely outlive us all." He outstretched his legs, bumping my knee with his. "What did you do before coming here?"

So, he must have heard bits of my conversation with Sue after all. "I worked for a lawyer. Secretary. Assistant. Whatever you want to call it. That was me."

"You didn't like it?"

"I didn't like *him*. But the work was fine, and the pay was great."

He hunched his shoulders, and every muscle inside me tensed.

Every time he moved; my skin tingled as if I expected to be touched. That was insane.

"There must be more to it than that." Finally, Hudson said what he really wanted to know.

"Turn on the local news. I'm sure his story has made it to these parts, too. He's made headlines the last few days if you're that curious about how I lost my job."

He stiffened beside me.

Max barked, causing us to jump.

"What was that for, Bear?" I asked.

He barked again at his owner.

Hudson narrowed his eyes at the animal and said, "I think *Max* is offended that I upset you."

"You didn't upset me. My situation upsets me. It's like I kept ignoring all the obvious red stop signs and thinking everything would work itself out if I chose to run red lights."

"I knew you looked like the type to get speeding tickets. Knowing you run redlights confirms it."

I laughed. "I knew you were judging me from the very beginning."

He shrugged. "I'm not judging, but watching you stresses me out."

"How so?"

"Actually, I don't know. I honestly don't." His brow furrowed as he watched the fire.

I felt bad that I'd only been around the guy for a few days and stressed him out.

"Actually, *you* don't stress me out, Red, but thinking of your clumsy ass getting hurt does worry me. I don't mind you; you know." He made a sound in his throat as soon as he spoke.

I was glad he wasn't looking at me since I felt my skin heat. Hudson didn't mind me and might worry about me? My heart was starting to pitter patter out of control.

"Ah, I freak myself out, too. It's okay. I judge your matching pajama sets," I whispered.

He threw his head back and laughed, which caused weird flutters to erupt in my stomach. It was a deep, husky sound that made me tingle all over.

"You should treat yourself more. You'll find it quite nice."

My smile waned. "I splurge on my hair and spend eleven bucks a month on digital books. That's how I treat myself." The creases on his forehead deepened, so I added, "I'm saving money."

"For?"

"I suppose I need a home first, but I actually want to start my own business."

I felt embarrassed and silly telling an actual business owner about my ideas. After seeing Hudson's restaurant, my plans looked more like wishful thinking. It took a lot more than just money to start a business.

"Oh? What kind of business?" he asked.

The size difference between us made me nervous. Adding that particular conversation to the mix amplified it, and I swallowed heavily.

I stared at the fire as my pulse roared in my ears. "A book café. I want to open a place with books, coffee, *and* cakes. Any type of sweets, if you ask me, go so well with books and coffee." I sighed ruefully. "But I've been foolish with those stop signs. From the very beginning, I've always needed a home."

More than that dream.

That was never going to change. I couldn't have stayed in that apartment much longer, and deep down, I always knew that.

It's fine. Everything's fine.

"I'm guessing you're in your mid-twenties?" Hudson asked unexpectedly.

"Twenty-nine, actually."

"That means you have forty years, at least, to open a bookstore. Just because it can't happen for you now, doesn't mean it won't happen eventually."

I brought my knees to my chest and rested my head on top of them as I watched him. "How old are you?"

"Thirty-two."

I guessed he couldn't have been much older.

I shrugged. "It's easy for you to say that when you already have your dream."

"It wasn't easy, and it's still not. I work seven days a week. Today would be the third day I've been off since it opened last year." The flames reflected off his light hazel orbs as he studied me. "Tomorrow will be the fourth."

I looked at the fire to avoid his direct gaze. "Today doesn't count as a day off. You chopped up a tree, checked on your restaurant, and fed us. It's not a day off when you have no choice. And don't take off tomorrow. My brother has already agreed to help."

"They already know I won't be there."

"I can't take that day from you. What if you wanted to take off time this summer but used your fourth day to help me. I can't let you." I shook my head vehemently.

"Red..." There was a hint of a smile in his voice, but I didn't look his way to confirm it. "I could take more days off if I wanted. I'm the boss, remember? I choose to work so much because I want to see it succeed."

Since I was curious, I asked, "And you're doing good?"

His lips stretched from ear to ear, crinkling the edges of his eyes was answer enough, but he still said, "Oh, yeah."

Shit, the man was gorgeous when he smiled and laughed.

"Wow. Don't you know you should remain humble despite your success?"

"Answering your question doesn't mean that I'm not."

"No, but your cocky grin says otherwise."

His home was enough proof that he was doing great. Why would he want me to know? I felt silly for even asking.

Of course, he would be proud of himself. I would if I achieved what he did. But meeting him when he was at his best while knowing I was at my lowest...

Tomorrow would be a major embarrassment for me. The reality tied my stomach in knots.

From the beginning, I figured he had a different upbringing than I did. I'd even found our differences amusing, but after a few days, it wasn't anymore. I wasn't sure why.

We were very different people.

My stomach cramped. I stood quickly before I accidentally passed gas and died from humiliation. "I'm going to the bathroom."

16

HUDSON

WHAT HAPPENED? ONE MINUTE WE WERE TALKING, BUT WHEN EUGENE returned from the bathroom, everything changed. She clammed up and pulled out that reading tablet of hers. Why did she choose the couch instead of where we had been sitting in front of the fire? I shouldn't care where she sat, but... Was it something I did or said? I wasn't an easy person to get along with, but I truly didn't mind my house guest. Maybe she didn't feel the same when it came to me.

Shit. I didn't care.

She even turned down a sandwich. I knew she hadn't eaten since I cooked the steak. She had to be hungry, but I didn't press her about it. I should have. She needed more than one meal.

Although I told myself I didn't care, I didn't sleep well. From all of Eugene's tossing and turning on the couch, she didn't either. I ended up browsing the news on my phone, hunting for Eugene's former boss. I didn't have to search in the western part of Kentucky. The man-made headlines here, too.

Danny Hopkins was a prick who conned an entire group of men out of their black lung settlement money. He was also under investigation for his wife's death. I found a bunch of unsettling comments from people trying to include the secretary in the act. People loved trying to solve mysteries. The comments ranged from, *She's his mistress... Of course, she knows he planned this all... To, how could she not have known when she worked for him?*

I turned off my phone. I was fucking pissed. It was as I thought. Eugene was a mess who got herself into trouble. She couldn't take care of herself. Even her fucking feet couldn't do the correct thing. I was surprised she was allowed out of the county during the investigation. Wait. She did check before leaving. Right? Sure, she did. I groaned and tried to get comfortable. Sleep was fitful, and I jumped out of the recliner once to check on Eugene on the couch. Max had watched my every move, so I mouthed, "I'm just making sure she's all right," as if he understood. He huffed and laid his head down. Honestly, I didn't know what was wrong with me either. I fell asleep again.

The sound of the fridge and things rumbling to life woke us up around seven. Eugene said nothing as she scrambled up the stairs. I sighed and took Max out for a bathroom break. The snow hadn't melted at all. My dark mood increased by the minute as I recalled the things, I'd discovered the night before. My last relationship had me questioning whether I cared about anything. Yet, the clumsy red head in my home had me out of my mind with worry. Fuck, I cared a lot—too much about the idea of her seeing those negative words online. I didn't like the idea of her being in such a messy situation either. The people in the comments were furious and needed someone to take it out on. Her being out of that town might be a good thing after all.

In fact, it seemed like fate that she ended up staying with me. I'd be the person she could rely on. Picturing her reading by the fire, happily eating the food I prepared didn't sound bad. It sounded much better than her suffering from our past workplace. When they found the lawyer, I wanted to give him a piece of my mind. I didn't know Eugene long at all, but it was clear she wasn't a con woman. I'd be shocked as hell if she could insult me or anyone without turning red in the face or averting her gaze.

Back inside, I walked up the stairs and knocked on Eugene's door. "I'm going to put the kerosene heater up and check the water lines for leaks. You can use the hot water first. We can leave in about an hour if that works for you."

"You really don't have to take me," she said again.

"I am, so get your ass ready." It wasn't until the words were out that I realized how stern I sounded. A part of me wanted to repeat the words in a softer tone, but then I remembered the comments, and the anger I'd been suppressing pushed through. I took a deep breath as I walked down the stairs because I wasn't just upset. I was furious *for* her. And I wasn't sure what to do about it. In a few days, she'd be out of my life. Instead of feeling relieved, the tension mounted. Her in my cabin, with me, just sounded so much better all around.

"I knew she was trouble as soon as I looked at her," I muttered to myself as I stalked outside and checked the cabin's crawlspace.

The words that should have left my mouth were, *I knew I was in trouble as soon as she smiled at me.*

My breath was visible as I huffed. I barely paid attention to what I should be doing. Instead, I wondered how she'd fix her hair before coming downstairs. It would be in one of those messy buns, revealing her slender neck. If she'd be wearing another pair of leggings, they might rip. I hoped not. I could barely focus, as it was when she was near. If a pair tore again, I didn't think I'd be so good at looking away. The idea of someone else seeing her ass had me gritting my teeth. My thoughts were very telling. More than not minding Eugene, it was starting to seem a whole lot like something else. I wasn't ready to acknowledge that because Eugene wasn't my type. Right?

Eugene was far too lovely to be in such a terrible situation. But saying she was awkward, a mess, and clumsy— those words suited her. Those words also described the perfect example of what I seemed to like.

Shit.

17

EUGENE

HUDSON'S STATURE MADE ME NERVOUS. ACTUALLY, IT WAS MORE ABOUT THE way he scowled at everything that twisted my insides. Generally, he made me anxious as he drove.

Hudson had been nothing but kind to me. Even so, he had a certain aura about him that sometimes screamed *fuck off*. I was getting the same vibes he gave me when I first arrived at his place.

Somehow, I pissed him off. No matter how many times I tried to talk him out of it, he insisted on taking me to get my things from the apartment. It was silly of him to get upset with me when he made the decision.

He was quiet as he drove. The only thing he asked was if I needed to rent a U-Haul. His truck was big enough for my things, so I told him no. My brother said I could drop off my belongings at his place, since he had a spare room.

Everything was almost covered.

I found a job. All I needed was a permanent place to live. My brother would never rush me, but I didn't want to intrude any longer than a month or two. Michael the Ass should be returning to his apartment soon, and I could leave Hudson alone.

Honestly, the thought was the best one I'd had in a while. Get out of the poor man's life and build my own stability. Who knew? When I saw Hudson again, maybe I'd be in a better situation and wouldn't need to feel embarrassed. I liked that idea a lot.

"I'll be out of your hair in a few days," I said to fill the silence.

He turned his head quickly. "What?"

"I'll be going to my brother's soon." I placed my hands in my lap. "The week is almost up."

He seemed even more rigid as he focused on the road. "Right."

I didn't know what I expected, but it wasn't that. My shoulders drooped. Something I said clearly upset him. The night before, he'd been kind and talkative. Then morning came, and I got the grunting, scowling Hudson.

He side-eyed me, forehead crinkling, and then focused on the road again. I tried not to take it personally. "Thanks for letting me stay with you—in your home, I mean." I looked ahead and stopped speaking. The more nervous I got, the more I screwed up and got tongue tied. I didn't like screwing up my words. I loved words. And speaking happily and confidently.

"We should have waited to leave after your hair dried." His hand tightened on the steering wheel.

I touched my wet strands. He had insisted on waiting after he saw I had washed my hair, but I refused. He would be driving for over eight hours there and back. I wasn't going to take any longer. My ears ached in the cold, though. I didn't tell him that. We'd only been out in the freezing temperatures for a minute, and he had heated his truck before I got in.

"I said it's fine." I took the clip out of my hair, so it could dry quicker. "You fuss a lot. Does my wet hair bother you that much?"

He didn't respond. He just shook his head, mumbled something too low for me to hear as he turned up the heat, and pointed the vents at me.

The silent tension between us made the drive worse. He didn't need me for directions since he'd typed the address into his GPS.

Once my hair dried, I twisted back the frizzy mess and clipped it into a bun.

It's fine. Everything's fine.

I didn't care what Hudson thought of me. After the week was over, I wouldn't be intruding on him anymore. Those thoughts kept my nerves calm.

Until he drove into the parking lot.

I bit my lips and looked over at him as he glanced around. He must have felt my stare. He briefly met my eyes before pulling into a parking spot. His eyebrows pinched together. "Is this the place?"

"Yep." I unbuckled the seat belt as he shut off the engine.

"My futon isn't heavy, so we can..." I trailed off as I squinted at the dumpster with black furniture sticking out of the top. I hopped out and ran toward the left side of the apartment building where the trash bin was.

"Eugene!" Hudson hollered.

I ignored him and pushed a random, dirty chair over so I could stand on it and look into the dumpster. My heart hammered against my ribcage. I recognized my cheap, little futon. I still needed to see it closer to believe it, though.

"No, no, no," I whispered.

My chest tightened painfully. It was as I expected. I recognized my belongings. My little coffee table and my fucking TV. The mold on the futon told me it had likely been out there almost as soon as I had been forced to vacate. I shook as my anger intensified.

"What's wrong?" Hudson asked from behind me. "Come down. It's dangerous up there."

If I wasn't so mad, I might have paid more attention to where his hands gripped my hips and lifted me. He kicked the chair away like it had the plague.

"They threw away my things."

But I didn't see my books, DVDs, clothes, or my bed. Without a word, I ran toward the door, up two flights of steps, where my door was cracked open.

I didn't know if it was the anger exhausting me or what I saw when I pushed at the door and entered. Black mold was *everywhere.* Everything, even the fridge and things that weren't mine, was gone. The anger gave way to astonishment as I ran into my room. What upset me, though, was seeing the bookshelf on its side. My books, scattered everywhere, were ruined. Some of them were so wet and moldy that I couldn't even make out the print on them.

My DVDs were nowhere in sight. I hadn't checked my closet yet. Considering the state of the apartment and how quickly it deteriorated, I didn't have much hope for my clothes.

Tears formed, and I took giant gulps of air. *Don't cry, don't cry.* I should have taken my things out right away. Once again, my actions were my downfall. I couldn't be mad at the landlord, could I? I left my things there.

But I had told her I'd come back for everything. It'd only been four days. Four. Fucking. Days.

I crouched beside my broken bookshelf and picked up one of the books. It was a newer copy of Pride and Prejudice. It wasn't a special edition or an old copy. Nothing grand, but my soul ached all the same. It took years for me to build my collection. Just like that, it was gone.

"Hey." Large hands were on my shoulder, pulling me up. "You don't need to be in here."

Hudson was right. The state of my old room was horrifying, so I let him lead me outside. All I could focus on was not crying. I swept my hair off my forehead to give my hand something to do. Instinctively, I went to use the other, but Hudson grasped it. He only let go when he opened the passenger side of his truck. I got in and didn't dare look at him.

"I'm sorry. This is a wasted trip." My voice cracked. "I lost all my books..."

I didn't expect him or anyone to understand, but that upset me most. Some of those books were gifts from Gran. And they were *ruined*.

I took a deep breath, trying to gather my emotions.

"Start the engine. I'll be back." I didn't get to ask what he was doing. He tossed his keys on my lap, shut the door, and ran to the apartment.

As soon as he disappeared inside, I allowed myself to cry big, ugly tears. The sobs echoed in his truck that I didn't start. I told myself I had until he returned to be upset then I had to get my shit together. So, I wiped and wiped the tears from my cheeks until they were tender. I let myself mourn material things. I let myself cry because, no matter how hard I tried, I always seemed to make mistakes.

It's fine. Everything's fine.

After a few minutes, I felt calm enough to stop. I didn't expect Hudson to take that long. I wasn't sure what he was doing, but I pulled myself together by the time he ran out. As soon as he hopped in, he exhaled. "You'll be compensated for your losses."

My eyes widened. Yolanda agreed to that?

Then he glanced at me, mouth parting, brows furrowing, and I looked away. But I still felt him staring, and I was aware of how red and puffy my face got every time I cried.

"Red..."

Since he called me that, I had no choice but to return his gaze. When I did, he dropped his head and rubbed the back of his neck. I didn't know what he wanted to say, but his stalling only made my stomach ache.

"All right," he blurted, nodding as if he'd come to terms with something as he started the engine. "It's as I thought."

"What?"

"You and what I plan to do about you."

I frowned, worrying that I had upset him by making him drive or something. "I'm sorry we came this far for nothing."

He raised his head. "It wasn't for nothing."

But it was.

"It's going to be okay, Red. You'll see." He placed his hand on my knee for a mere second, just enough to squeeze, before palming the steering wheel. I swallowed nervously as goose bumps broke out over my flesh. He tried to comfort me, I believed, but my body was thrumming from the brief touch.

The music filled the silence. I was free to zone out as he drove, and I did until my phone rang. Picking it up from my lap, I felt Hudson's gaze on me as I answered. "Hello, beautiful."

Hudson stiffened and turned the music down quickly.

"Please tell me you're stopping in and seeing me before you head back."

I closed my eyes and held my forehead. Shit. I texted Holly and told her I would be grabbing my things from the apartment. I promised I'd visit her.

"I'm sorry. We're already heading back. I completely forgot."

"What's wrong? Your voice is pathetic."

I scoffed. "Pathetic? Wow. Thanks. Just what I needed."

"Did Michael try something again? I thought you were staying with someone else until he left your brother's."

"It wasn't Michael. I've not seen him since last year." When I kicked him in the sack.

"Then what is it?"

"My things were destroyed. Everything. The washer and dryer Eddie gave me weren't in the apartment or the dumpster. I'm guessing someone stole them."

"Everything was destroyed?"

"*Everything.* I lost my books..." I trailed off when I felt that familiar tingle in my nose. Remembering I was in the truck with Hudson, I took a deep breath. I refused to cry again.

Static hit my ear as Holly breathed into the phone. "I'm sorry, Genie."

"It's fine. I needed a fresh start. It looks like I'm getting one."

"I don't like you being so far away."

"As soon as I get a place, you're going to come see me," I said.

"Of course."

I stole a glimpse at Hudson, who was focused on the road. "Listen, I'll call you later. Okay?"

"You haven't told me much about this Hudson guy, Genie. With your luck, I'm worried."

"*Later.*"

There was a pause.

"Did he take you?"

"Bye, Holly."

I heard her chuckle before I ended the call.

"We still have an hour out, but I can take us to the restaurant to eat. If you want something right now, there's an exit up here..."

"Your place is fine," I blurted.

Honestly, I'd rather not eat his food at all. I didn't think he'd like me paying, and I was feeling uncomfortable with all the free meals.

"Okay. I can pop in the kitchen and—"

"No, I meant your cabin. If you want food, we can stop, but I'm not hungry," I lied. I'd had enough for one day. I would go out and buy my own meal when we got back.

"I can make us something at home, too." Hudson's hand moved to the scruff on his jaw. That was the first day I saw him with any sort of facial hair. The man seemed immaculate when it came to his appearance. Someone should tell him he looked perfect either way.

Something about his words made my heart ache, though.

He must truly like cooking for people because he kept trying to feed me. There wasn't a person who cared about my eating habits since Gran. I didn't think he cared. It was just a common courtesy to feed your guests. Or at least not eat without asking them if they were hungry.

I didn't respond. I simply leaned near the door and watched the vehicles go by.

18

HUDSON

MY THOUGHTS WERE JUMBLED, I HAD A HEADACHE, AND I WAS TIRED AFTER driving all damn day. As I stood at the stove, frying two burgers, I groaned. I recalled the mold infestation in that apartment—*her* apartment. How her mouth gaped as she stood there, shaking from what I guessed might have been disbelief or shock at the state of the rooms. She seemed so tiny beside me as I walked her to the truck. I had trouble imagining *anyone*, especially her, living in that hovel. Her red eyes and face were evidence of her crying while I threatened her former landlord.

Eugene Quillen was trouble, I reminded myself for the umpteenth time. Still, I pulled out my phone and scrolled through the pictures I took. I shouldn't do what I was thinking about doing.

Eugene had nothing to do with me. How she lived, breathed, and took care of herself wasn't my problem. But everything I wanted to do for her proved different. I was trying hard to make her my business. *Fuck.* What was wrong with me? I thought I liked peace, wanted it. It seemed I liked chaos a lot more.

I grinned.

It was settled. The flaming-haired creature lived with me. It made sense that I should help her. I wasn't crazy about her or anything... But it would make sense if she didn't leave the cabin. I liked the idea of her being nearby. How could I help her out if she left? It wasn't because I liked watching her read by the fire, although that itself was no hardship. And Max had grown attached, too, so I'd feel bad if she left. Eugene couldn't go to her brother's. I had to get her to stay. She was practically a woman in distress, so I could work with that.

One thing at a time, though.

Pulling up Gran's number, I sent all the photos to her with a single text.

> Hudson: I know you're going to meddle, so help me find all these books.

When I heard the front door open and close, I walked to the window. Eugene was hopping into her car. Before I could make it to the door, she was out of the driveway. I leaned against the door jamb as the cold air chilled my bare arms. At least, the snow had melted, or her little vehicle wouldn't have made it.

Noticing the spatula still in my hand, I frowned. She knew I was making food, but she left. My confusion intensified my headache.

When I smelled smoke, I ran to the kitchen. My fucking burgers were burning. I never burned my burgers. Since it was just me eating, I suffered through the burned meat. Max plopped down at my feet as I ate at the table. I should have sat in my recliner, put on a movie, and *relaxed*. Instead, I thought about Eugene going to her brother's house if I couldn't convince her to stay. Would she end up in another unfit apartment in the future?

The answer was no. I wouldn't let it happen.

The job Eugene took at Subway wasn't going to work either. I should hire her at Homestyle. It would be beneficial for both of us. I needed more help. Plus, I'd pay her more than whatever Subway offered.

I sighed and put down my burger. Eugene had refused breakfast and left before she could eat, which meant she hadn't eaten anything. Was she embarrassed? She was trying to survive. I understood that. But she didn't have to try to survive. She could live instead.

I just had to show her.

Max wagged his tail and ran to the door, signaling Genie's arrival. He greeted her at the door. From the recliner, I watched her pet his head, a look of happiness softening her features, making her dark eyes brighter, until she locked gazes with me.

Every part of my body begged to move. I stood slowly, then rushed when I saw that she was already walking up the stairs.

"There's a burger in the kitchen," I said to stop her.

"I ate."

She ate?

Eugene bought food, although she knew I was making her something. Why? It couldn't be my cooking. I was a good cook. No. I was a great one.

"Come here for a second, Red."

She froze halfway up the stairs and slowly turned her head.

"Is everything okay?" I asked as I sat down.

When she stopped at the bottom, not bothering to come any closer, I didn't like it. I leaned forward and placed my elbows on my thighs. "Closer, Red."

She hesitated, nibbling on her bottom lip, before she walked to the couch and sat. I wished she'd stop bringing attention to her mouth. I stared at it enough.

"Is Monday a good day for you to start work?" I asked.

She frowned. "Yeah, I start Subway that day, but don't worry. I'll be out of your hair before then."

"No. You're going to stay here with me."

Her eyes widened as her cheeks pinkened. "What?"

I suppressed the urge to smile. She was cute and easy to fluster.

"You'll start work Monday at Homestyle. I'll make sure you're paid well and plus, you'll have tips."

Her nose crinkled. "You want me to be a waitress at your restaurant?"

"Yes. I'd rather you worked with me. I'll know you're getting better pay."

Eugene rubbed her temples. "Did your grandma make you do this?"

What did my grandma have to do with this? "No, why?"

"She offered me a job, too."

I smiled. "Then it's settled."

"I can't accept it." Eugene closed her eyes and stood.

I stood with her. "And why can't you?"

"You've seen where I used to live, and now you think you need to help me. I'll be okay. I don't need your pity."

Yes, I wanted to fucking care for her. But none of what I felt came from pity.

"It's not pity." I scowled. "Why not take advantage of what I'm offering you? You can stay here, work, and get back on your feet. I'll let you choose your hours at the restaurant. Don't let your pride get in the way of accepting my help. Because that's what I'm offering. It's no different getting help from your brother."

I couldn't stand the fucking idea of her getting into the same situation. Her brother didn't seem the sort to allow her to live that way, which meant Eugene suffered in silence. Something I assumed she'd do again. The possibility unsettled me. But that had nothing to do with why I wanted to help her. I just did. And the bonus was helping her kept her with me.

"It's different. We barely know each other."

"That didn't stop me from letting you stay here, and it didn't stop you from coming."

She bit her lip as she threw herself backward onto the couch. She looked to the ceiling and exhaled.

For some reason, her action calmed me. She hadn't agreed to my craziness, but I didn't think she'd completely refuse me, either.

"You'll continue staying here, and you'll work with me."

"What if I don't like working as a waitress?" she asked, still studying the ceiling.

"Then you can be a hostess. I'll find the right position for you."

"You don't seem the type to tolerate people for long. What happens when you grow tired of letting me stay here?"

"If and when I decide you're too much, I'll let you know and give you plenty of time to find a place of your own."

That was never going to happen. I didn't know why I was so sure.

She closed her eyes and said nothing.

I asked, "Why did you agree to stay here to begin with?"

"I didn't want to spend money on a hotel room."

I quirked a brow. "So, why are you letting pride get in the way now?"

She lowered her head and met my gaze. "I can't stay for free."

I crossed my arms. "Then what do you propose?"

"I don't know. How about I pay rent? Your mortgage on this place must be a fortune."

"No to the rent. If you want, you can buy groceries and other necessities for the house."

"Okay. I can do that."

"Then it's settled."

"Shouldn't we put a time limit on it? That way, I know how long I have."

I didn't like the idea. I didn't want to put a limit on her being in that house with me.

"I don't need a timeline. If you need one, then you decide."

"A limit would be good for both of us, so I don't get used to the idea of staying forever." When I met her gaze again, she looked away and said, "You know, it might make me lazy about searching for my own place. I'm not a saint. I'm just being honest. What if this isn't good for me like you think?"

"It's good for you. You'll never save otherwise."

She met my gaze. "You'll tell me when it stops working for you?"

"I never use the upstairs, and we'll see each other more at work than here."

"Are you sure it's a good idea for me to work *with* you then?"

"Red. It's done. We're doing this. When it stops working out for you, it stops. Until then, relax. You have a roof over your head for as long as you need."

She blinked and covered her face. My heart twisted inside my chest when she turned away.

"Are you going to cry?" I asked.

"I'm not." But her shoulders shook, telling me otherwise.

"You are."

One second, I watched her back; the next, she was facing me. She ran straight toward me. All her softness slammed into me. I froze as her arms wrapped around me. "I'm going to be shameful and accept your offer. But I promise I'll be a good roommate." Her hands were hot, pressing against my back. "Thank you, Hudson."

And with that, Eugene ran upstairs, leaving me in the same spot. I looked at Max, and he looked at me. "Got her," I whispered. He clearly had no idea what I was up to. Honestly, neither did I despite the fact that I wanted her to stay and made it happen. And it felt pretty fucking good. I still felt the heat of her on my clothes.

19

EUGENE

I FELT A LITTLE SHAME, BUT NOT ENOUGH TO REJECT HUDSON'S OFFER. I WAS more embarrassed than anything. All that talk of leaving his house, not accepting his food, and bam! I agreed to live there without giving it much thought. The humiliation hadn't lasted long after speaking to him, and I hadn't felt judged. He probably wondered *why* I had lived in that moldy apartment but hadn't asked.

Not weighing all the pros and cons got me into some rough spots. Take my condemned apartment, for example. Living in that cabin was likely a big mistake. But it didn't feel like one. I knew more than anyone that nothing lasted forever. Hudson wasn't hard to live with; granted, I'd only been for there a few days, but I found him pleasant and easy to talk to. Time would tell the truth.

"And just like that, you're going to be living with this man because he said so?" Holly asked again.

I switched my phone to the other ear. "Don't say it like that. I'm not living in the same room with him, Holly. I'm living in the same *house* with him. When you say *with*, it sounds like you're trying to turn the entire situation dirty. His bedroom is downstairs, and he's given me one of the spare rooms upstairs."

"But that's a little weird. He doesn't know you, so that obviously means two things."

"Don't say it."

"He's trying to get into your pants or something."

"Or he's genuinely offering me help."

"So, you don't think it's at all strange?"

Of course, I was shocked and a little wary, but Hudson didn't seem like the sort to be shady. I wasn't afraid of him. But maybe I should be, and that was my problem. "I'm a mess. We all know it, but I wouldn't stay here if I was uncomfortable around him."

"Yes, you would. When it comes to saving money, I know you."

"Shit. You should see him, then you'd know Hudson has no reason to take in a homeless woman if he was trying to get laid. The man is stunning *and* successful. I don't see him having trouble finding women to fuck." I bit my lips and fell back onto the bed. "Although he said it's not pity, it has to be. The dude saw my apartment. Then, he told me I could stay and work at his place. Really, Holly? If he's a creep, he's got me fooled. I think he really wants to help me. I need this to work for a while."

"You're right. I can't help but assume the worst, though."

I smiled. "Because men are pigs?"

"They are." There was some static over the line, like she was doing something before she said, "I'm still calling Eddie. I can't agree with you staying until I know this dude checks out."

"My brother already knows. I called him this morning, and he thinks it's a good idea. Eddie wouldn't send me someplace he didn't think was safe. That makes me trust Hudson more."

"Good, but you know you can come back and live with me, right? I can help you get a job at the hospital."

"I love you for offering, but you know I can't do that." She had a relationship with Roger, but not only that. She had a beautiful one-bedroom apartment. I knew our friendship was solid and could withstand anything, but we enjoyed our privacy. At Hudson's, I could be alone. Whenever he was at work, I could have the entire house to myself.

"Why are you so stubborn?"

I laughed. "I'm not."

"Well, I'll need to drop in soon. I'll give you time to get settled, but I have to check this place out."

I snorted. "You might not want to leave."

"Shit. Is it that nice? Facetime me."

I rolled my eyes but gave her a grand tour of the cabin via video chat.

I wasn't ashamed to admit that I had to use GPS each time I drove to town. Some stops and turns were becoming familiar. Going to Homestyle on Monday was no different. Hudson told me to choose my hours. I'd never had a boss let me pick when I wanted to work.

Restaurant business hours were eight to seven on weekdays. Eight to eleven on Saturday, and twelve to six on Sunday. Hudson left earlier, so I assumed it was to prepare the food. I arrived before eight and had to knock on the door because it was still locked.

A young man wearing a black apron opened the door and smiled. "You must be Eugene?"

I offered him my hand. "Call me Genie."

"Come on in." He ushered me into the restaurant. "Hudson only told us you'd be starting today. I'm Randall, one of the chefs."

"Hi, Randall."

"Red." I recognized Hudson's gruff tone immediately. I found him at the kitchen entrance, holding the door open as his gaze drilled a hole in me. My skin heated, and the weird response only made me more nervous about that day.

Living and being around that man might be harder than I thought.

"I didn't expect you this early," he said.

"You said I could choose my hours?" My words came out like a question. "But if you'd rather me wait until later, let me know when-
-"

"I did say that, but most people would take the opportunity to sleep in or barely show up," Hudson said, wearing a black apron like Randall's. I crinkled my nose. Did he honestly believe I'd choose to work *less* because he'd offered me the chance to pick my hours? He knew my situation. The steady flow of income was perfect for me. "Come on. I have some papers you need to fill out before you get started."

There was something odd in Randall's smile as he looked at his boss. I followed Hudson through the kitchen into a small office. He pulled out the rolling chair behind the desk and gestured for me to sit.

"I need to know how much overtime you'll allow. If any," I blurted. As soon as the words were out, I sucked in a deep breath and fidgeted with my fingers. Asking about work hours shouldn't turn my stomach into knots, but I was all nerves.

"I offered you my home and this job so you wouldn't overexert yourself." He placed a hand on the back of my chair and one on top of the desk, to lean over me.

His woodsy cologne or body wash hit me in the face, and I inhaled sharply. He always smelled so good, damn it. I shouldn't be sniffing my boss slash roommate.

"I'm not going to force you to leave. Ever. So, stop thinking you have to rush to get ahead. You'll make enough money working through the week to save," he uttered the words like it might be a promise.

I swallowed. "So, is that a no to overtime?"

He pinched the bridge of his nose. "I'll allow two weeks out of each month for overtime."

I couldn't help but grin. "Thanks."

"Here." He didn't remove the hand at the back of my chair as he rustled around papers in drawers, so his neck and chest came awfully close to me. I was so close I could feel the heat of him.

My skin felt like a livewire that wanted to latch onto the energy he provided. I leaned into the cushion to get away from the sensation, as if that would help. I felt like I was being consumed by his proximity.

"Fill this out, and I'll introduce you to Loretta," he began. "You'll see her mostly in the mornings. She'll get you familiar with the tables, and I'll get you a menu, so you can familiarize yourself with what we offer. If a customer asks for something that's not on the menu, always check in at the kitchen before you tell them no. Sometimes, we can make what they want, but not always."

I picked up the pen and stared at it. "Okay."

I could feel his gaze on the side of my face.

"You're nervous," Hudson stated.

"I'm always nervous about starting a new job, but it gets better over time. Don't worry."

"Good. Just remember one thing. Pick up your feet as you walk."

My mouth dropped. I flipped off the boss man as he strode out the door, leaving me alone to fill out the paperwork. A woman stumbled a few times around him, and he refused to let her forget.

Loretta was a plump older woman who reminded me of Gran. In those days, everything did, and I hoped it never changed. I kept her alive in my memories.

Loretta was much kinder than my gran, though. Gran said whatever she wanted without caring who she offended. She often indulged me growing up, but still shut me up when I asked about too many things.

Loretta didn't rush or overcomplicate anything, even when I asked silly questions about the tables. The restaurant was divided into four sections. She gave me the tables and booths from sections two and four.

Loretta offered me a pen and notepad, and I began my first day of work at Homestyle. Although I figured Hudson did well with the restaurant, the number of people who came in for a weekday still surprised me. I stumbled a bit when taking orders, but it could have been worse. I just needed to study the menu more, so I could answer questions without hesitation.

I met another worker named Rebecca. She ran the cash register and helped clean tables. She didn't look much older than me. Bits and pieces of her and Loretta's conversation told me she was a mom to two mean boys.

Sometimes, Hudson would bring out my orders for me. It was the only time I saw him. There was a rectangular opening near the kitchen where we placed our orders. Loretta said to just put the order on the board by the window. After I placed the order there, Hudson or another kitchen worker grabbed the paper. One of them would ring a bell when the food was ready.

There was a shift change around two, and Sue limped in. When she saw me wiping down a table, she clucked her tongue. "Ya don't take a job when I offer it, but ya will for Hudson?"

Thankfully, there were only a few occupied booths. I grabbed the spray bottle and rag, then walked toward Hudson's grandma. "We both know you weren't offering me a job. You were trying to give me your grandson."

She shrugged her shoulders. "So? He's still available."

I threw my head back and laughed. "I don't think that's how it works."

"What problem are you causing me now?" Hudson stopped beside me.

He quirked a brow at her, then me, and I smirked. "She's auctioning you off."

"When is she not?" He scoffed and glanced at his grandma. "Come on, menace. You can make the soup since you're—"

Sue held her palm up when he tried to grab her arm. "I'm not cooking today. I'm going to stay out front and look after our new worker."

"Oh?" Hudson asked.

I stiffened and said, "I'm doing all right, thank you."

Sue lifted a brow just like her grandson did. "Yeah, then why have those two pretty ladies been waving their hands at ya the last few minutes trying to get your attention?"

"What?" I turned quickly because I did have a couple of women I was waiting on, but they weren't doing what she said. Even so, I was anxious that I kept someone waiting and hurried to their table.

20

HUDSON

THE WEEK FLEW BY, AND I WASN'T SURPRISED TO SEE THAT MY HOUSEGUEST worked every day from opening until closing. Having another server lessened the burden on all of my workers when the restaurant was packed. Even so, I was glad I set boundaries on how often Eugene could get overtime. I didn't like the idea of her overworking. She'd have plenty of time to do well while with me.

Those days, Grandma pestered Eugene more than me. They put up a Christmas tree at Homestyle the other day. Well, Grandma barked out orders in a chair while Eugene put it together and hung the ornaments. I found it amusing sometimes, but I was worried. Sue wasn't a simple woman. She crossed boundaries she shouldn't had with the things she said. I feared she'd scare Eugene away before I got the chance to help her. Defending Eugene only made my grandma worse. She'd quirk her eyebrow in that insufferable way and say, "My friendship with Genie has nothing to do with ya. Mind ya business!"

The more I responded, the more she'd believe I had feelings for my houseguest. I didn't. Eugene Quillen wasn't my type, but I couldn't tell Sue that. If I did, it would just make her worse.

I was so full of shit. I couldn't stop staring at Eugene. When she wasn't where I could see her, I was thinking about her. I wasn't telling anyone that! If anything, Eugene might think I was a creep who kept her close by if she found out. Yes, I did want her around, but I wasn't being creepy about it. I truly wanted to help by sticking close to her. Just made sense. I liked being able to look at her, too.

Fuck. Maybe I was a creep.

One Friday evening, I found Eugene in my kitchen. Her vibrant hair seemed a little faded as the days went by. Currently, it was drenched, lying against her back. Her shirt with holes in it was soaked through in spots, but it didn't bother her like it did me. She stirred her coffee, hummed, and moved to the sink to clean the spoon she used.

Damn. She wasn't a siren, but something about her kept calling to me.

She hadn't noticed I was in the kitchen or that I walked up behind her either. When I was closer to her, a strawberry scent filled my nose. I lifted a lock of hair off her back. She startled, placed her hand over mine, and met my gaze. Her touch was as chilled as her hair. *But* it didn't bother her like it did me.

"Do you have a blow-dryer?" I asked.

"Not anymore..."

I removed my hand as Eugene backed herself into the counter.

"Have you gone shopping for clothes yet?" I knew the answer. I'd seen her wear the same three outfits since she'd been there. She used the washer and dryer a lot because of it. I wouldn't consider the garments she wore around the house clothes at all because of all the holes in them.

She crinkled her nose. "Clothes?"

"Yes. Remember, you lost all of your clothes?"

"Oh," she said, studying her feet like they were the most fascinating things in the world. "Not yet."

"Why not? If it's money, I can cover it."

Let me fucking take care of you, woman, was what I wanted to say. Then maybe beg her to let me take care of that body of hers, too.

Shit. I was losing my damned mind.

Still, I knew I wouldn't stop worshipping her until she was trembling beneath me.

I needed to fucking cool down.

"What? No," she said. "I have the money. I just haven't prioritized purchasing anything yet."

I looped my index finger into one of the holes in her shirt and pulled at it. She sucked in a breath as I narrowed my gaze. "That's the problem, Red. You don't prioritize yourself."

Her cheeks reddened as she yanked her shirt away, causing the tear to rip more. It was never my intention to embarrass her. I wanted to see her cared for. No, *I* wanted to be the one to care for her. And that body. Fuck. I knew I'd be good to her.

"I better not see you at work tomorrow. Go relax, get some clothes, and a blow-dryer."

She crossed her arms and glared. I knew she was dissatisfied with me, but something about her anger only made her sweeter. With the blush on her cheeks and the wet hair, she looked like nothing more than a gorgeous dessert for someone with a sweet tooth. I had a terrible sweet tooth.

"You said I could have as many hours as I wanted two weeks out of the month."

I stepped away and scratched my neck, trying to process my thoughts and her words at the same time. *Did I just compare my houseguest to a dessert?* "You can, but I want you in new clothes."

"Am I bringing the business down with what I'm wearing?" Her voice got higher-pitched the longer she spoke. "Some of my clothes might be old and ratty, but they're not dirty. I'm just as clean as you are." The last word cracked from her lips.

I didn't have the time to be worried about my sweet tooth or that I might be a creep. Not when she spoke like that, *always mistaking my words for something else.* Stepping close, I propped my hands on each side of her on the counter and leaned into her. The hurt faded from her expression as her lips parted. She didn't know what I was doing. Even I didn't. *You did, you fucker,* another part of me whispered. But it felt good to press some of me onto her. "Saying you need clothes is different than saying you're dirty, Red. If I implied something else, would I risk dirtying myself by being so close? Look at these pj's. You're right. I'm fond of my fucking pj's and now they're touching you."

I pushed away from her right after I said that. I acted on impulse, and what I did began to hit me. Maybe I couldn't be that good guy after all. Maybe I couldn't help her because helping might mean I'd try to consume her. The thoughts were sobering and revealed the truth. It was so much easier to keep telling myself she wasn't my type than to admit the reality. She had me spinning in her clumsy, little orbit since the moment I saw her. That was the truth. Whatever I liked before her, I couldn't recall. All I saw was her.

I rubbed my temple and exhaled. "I shouldn't have gotten into your space like that. I don't like people in mine, so I have no right to yours. I just needed you to see that I don't find you unclean. Not at all. But I do want to see you in new clothes. After losing everything, don't you want to splurge, even a little, on yourself?"

She blinked twice, shaking her head like she had come out of a trance, before replying, "I need to. You're right. I will. But Loretta said the tips are the best on the weekends, so you're asking me to give that up. Of course, I'd rather work and make money than spend it."

"How about you take a *long* lunch break tomorrow and check out some of the stores downtown, grab some clothes, then come back?" I grabbed one of her wet strands, unable to resist.

She beamed, and my body ignited. I felt the heat of her smile at the tips of my ears, my fingertips, and my fucking toes. "That will work."

I jerked my hand away as desire dug into my bones, aching for more than a lock of hair. "I'm allowing thirty-six hours next week."

The smile faded quickly. "That's four hours short."

"Like I said, you only get two weeks to work overtime. I'm allowing no more."

"You work all the time, but you're going to complain about me?" She pouted, and I normally hated when people nagged, so why was she so fucking adorable? "I'm not going to overtire myself. I like making money."

"It's my restaurant."

"So? You have a full staff."

"You're right. Should I work less, too? How about we take some weekends off?"

"Heck no. Loretta said those are the best tipping days."

"Mondays and Tuesdays?"

Eyes widening, she sputtered, "W-why are you asking me? You can take whatever days you want. I'm just saying I'd like to work some weekends."

"How has work been? Are the customers treating you, okay?"

She tucked a wet strand behind her ear. "Yeah. It's been good."

"Good."

We were quiet as I poured me a glass of water at the sink.

"I'm going to bed," she announced.

"Oh, and Red?"

"Yeah?"

"Don't let a man get so close to you like that next time. Knee him in the nuts. Claw at his eyes. I don't care. Just don't stand there. Matter of fact, walk the other way if he approaches."

She snorted. "I'd be turning in circles if I had to walk the other way every time, I saw a man."

She was right, but I didn't like it.

"*But* I understand what you're saying, and you don't have to worry. I don't let anyone get that close."

I smiled as she walked away, but then I frowned. She had let someone that close. She let me.

21

EUGENE

"You have a Merry Christmas," a customer said to me as she exited the restaurant.

"You, too," I said.

I had been hearing a lot of season's greetings since working at Homestyle. Of course, I would, since Christmas was a week away. I walked over to the booth and started to clean it off when I noticed the woman left me an eight-dollar tip. Since morning lunch, I'd made about one hundred and fifty dollars in tips. How was I supposed to leave work to shop when people were so generous that day?

I eyed the kitchen door. Hudson might forget. Pulling my phone out, I checked the time—five minutes after twelve. I bit my lip and groaned. If I wanted to shop, I probably should head out.

"Aren't you supposed to be going somewhere?"

I jumped and turned toward the deep voice. "Sheesh. I didn't hear you. How did you get so close without me noticing?"

Honestly, I had just checked the back for Hudson. For such a large man, he was good at sneaking up on people.

Hudson placed his hand on my waist, tugging me toward him suddenly. My side bumped into his. His palm heated my skin through my shirt as he guided me away from the table and toward the front entrance. "Go buy some nice things."

Turning my head, I had to strain my neck to look up at him; we were so close. I sighed dramatically, which meant I was practically blowing on his neck. He glanced down, one corner of his mouth lifting, and I pulled away.

Whoops.

"I'm going to go blow my money now." I huffed and puffed as I stomped toward the door.

"Are you having fun being dramatic?" he asked.

I looked over my shoulder. "Yes. Thank you for asking."

Shit. He was smiling. My heart did a huge *ka-thump.*

"Here. Take my card."

My eyes nearly bulged out of their sockets when I whipped around. "Would you stop it!"

Glancing around, I saw two women in a booth to the left, whispering and looking. Hudson continued to hold his card out.

"Shit, stop," I whispered, shoving his arm away.

"What? You don't want to spend your money, so spend mine."

I gawked. Was that dude for real? How was he single if he threw his money at women? He gave me a place to live, constantly fed me, and offered me his credit card. I wasn't a materialistic person. I detested shopping because I feared needing the money for something else later.

So, I didn't know how to react to Hudson. For the sake of *getting ahead,* as I called it, I lived under his roof. The reality was that no matter how much I saved, I might not own a bookstore like I wanted. The thought was depressing. Hudson's kindness would spoil me, and I worried I'd get too attached to him. The last thing I wanted to do was take advantage of someone's kindness to help me. Gran's screen door immediately popped in my head, and my stomach knotted.

"Don't worry, I'm going to buy the things I need, so please stop." I met his heavy stare with my own. "I'm grumbling because I'm a tight wad, okay? I have money. The customers are watching."

He put his wallet away and grunted. "Why are you so stubborn?"

"Hmm, maybe because the man who's providing a roof over my head and giving me a job keeps trying to do more." I smiled. "You don't have to, Hudson. You've helped me a lot. So, I plan to get all kinds of yummy food for the cabin. I'll keep us well stocked each week. Tell me what you want, and I'll stop by the grocery store."

His brow slowly lost those harsh lines, and his eyes softened before he cracked a grin. "Get whatever *you* want, Red."

I rubbed my neck as I walked into Walmart. Shopping was so exhausting. A part of me was glad I found some cute pants and shirts in the discount section of several clothing stores, the rest of me wanted to be done with it all.

I figured good old Walmart was the best place to get panties and bras. I could go there and buy an entire pack for almost the same price as a single pair at Maurices. No one but me was seeing my granny panties, so I didn't care. All the same, I grabbed two packs of the bikini-style ones, a few sports bras, and two push-up bras.

They had a few pairs of ugly tan shorts on the discount rack, and I bought all of them to sleep in. There were no T-shirts I wanted to spend money on, so I'd stick with my ratty ones that clearly drove my roommate mad. He should be happy I got me some for work and going out.

I snickered as I imagined the look on Hudson's face when I wore my old shirts around the cabin, then paused at the seasonal section filled with Christmas decorations and trees. Despite being poor, Gran always treated us on that holiday.

Suddenly, the heartache settled deep in my bones. I hadn't celebrated Christmas since she passed. Even when my brother asked me to come visit for the holiday, I always refused. I secluded myself so much after she died. The company of books was better and *safer* than people.

Hudson didn't have a tree up at the cabin. He hadn't put one up in the restaurant either. The other day, I heard his grandma nagging about it, so I told her I'd put a tree up if he had one. She left Homestyle as soon as I said that and came back a couple hours later with one. I put the tree up beside the bar while she complained about every ornament placement I chose. I wondered if he'd care if I put one in the cabin. I didn't know why I was considering splurging on a tree and decorations. It didn't make sense to have a tree in my dumpy apartment. Hudson's home was so big and beautiful, though. It should be decorated.

I gripped my shopping cart as a thrill shot through my limbs. The idea of Christmas lights and a tree, especially in his home, excited me. It would be so cozy to curl up by the fire, read, and see all the lights.

All I had to do was pick out the perfect tree.

22

HUDSON

Eugene didn't return to work that day. I received a text from her letting me know she was going to the cabin instead. It seemed strange. I figured she'd put the groceries up, then head back to work for her tips.

I wondered if she shopped at all. If she didn't come back to the restaurant, something must have happened. Was she okay? Did she get sick? When I asked if everything was all right, she never responded. After waiting for an hour, I tried calling, but she didn't answer.

Unable to focus, I headed home around six. Her tiny car was parked in the driveway. The relief that flooded my chest made my shoulders sag. For some reason, I feared she would leave as quickly as she came. The thought had me staring at my steering wheel for a long time.

Climbing out of the truck, lights shining in the front windows caught my eye. Were those Christmas lights? As I walked to the cabin, I heard, "Bear, no!" Quickening my pace, I opened the door and froze.

"Get that out of your mouth," Eugene said to Max, who ran to me with a green ornament in his mouth.

Eugene had multi-colored Christmas lights in her hands. More lights hung over the fireplace. Bags and opened boxes littered the floor. When she saw me, she looked around at the mess she'd made, then put the lights behind her back. Did she think the seven-foot tree would hide behind her, too?

"Oh, Hudson. You're home early," she blurted.

She blinked rapidly and breathed heavily. Bringing her hands in front of her, she fidgeted with the lights she held. Was she scared I'd be mad that she decorated? Dropping down on one knee, I fought my smile and held out my palm to Max. He dropped the ornament and went back to Eugene, tail wagging.

"I see you went shopping," I said as I stood.

"Yes! Yes, I did." She kicked a box near her, then piled another on top of it.

"Did you get yourself some clothes?" I hung up my coat and slipped into my house shoes, then faced her again.

"I did." She twisted her fingers as she watched me approach.

Her eyes followed my arm as I lifted it and tucked a loose strand of hair behind her ear. "I'm proud of you. That tree probably cost you a good penny."

The breath whooshed out of her. "For a minute there, when you didn't smile, I thought you were upset."

I let my knuckle graze her cheek, and she inhaled quickly before pulling away.

"Do you want me to help decorate?" I offered.

She shrugged. "You can if you want."

"I want to," I murmured.

She averted her gaze, making a sound in her throat.

I watched her hang a few to see if there was a certain pattern she was using before helping. I felt her eyes on me more than once when I turned to get another ornament.

"Why didn't you have a tree up?" she asked.

"It's just me and Max. More trouble than it's worth."

"I haven't celebrated Christmas since my gran passed," she murmured.

I watched her disappear around the tree and frowned. "What about Ed?"

"My brother and Francis invite me every holiday. I don't know. I never feel like doing anything."

"Probably because you don't want to spend the money."

She snorted. "Most likely."

"So, why now?"

"Your home is far less depressing than the apartment I lived in."

I still hated that she had lived in that shithole.

"It's your home, too."

Eugene said nothing until she walked to the stairs and banged her hip on the banister. "I'm okay!"

I shook my head, then chuckled as she disappeared upstairs.

Although it was past my bedtime, I was in my recliner, flipping through channels. Eugene lay on the floor beside the Christmas tree with a blanket wrapped around her. She was reading on her Kindle. I found myself watching her more than the TV. Placing the remote on the arm's chair, I gave up and scrolled through my social media. I found Edwin's Facebook and searched for Eugene among his friends. Her profile was private, so I sent her a friend request.

I rubbed the scruff on my chin as her phone pinged. She opened it, scrolled, then whipped her head up. "Are you stalking me, Hudson?"

"Accept the request," I barked, opening my phone again. "We live together. It makes sense to be Facebook friends."

After accepting, she closed her phone, and went back to reading. I scrolled through her profile, then her pictures, and frowned when I came across a tagged photo of her and a man together. His arm was draped around her shoulders, and they were smiling. He looked like a weasel. She was a brunette at the time, and the date was a few years ago. That had to be her natural hair color. It was pretty, but so was the red. Regardless, the photo's caption ticked me off.

ROSIE BAILEY: LOOK AT THESE TWO LOVEBIRDS! (HEART EMOJI)

I put down my phone and shut my eyes, needing a minute to calm down. My pulse thrummed at my temple. It wouldn't make sense for me to ask who he was. Clearly, he was an ex, but I didn't like it.

Opening my lids, I saw that she was still reading, a slight curve on her lips as she stared at the Kindle. Really? She wasn't even a little curious about me to scroll through my profile?

I grunted, causing her to glance up.

"Is something wrong?" she asked.

"You're up late," I said with a slight rumble in my voice.

She quirked a brow. "So, are you." When I said nothing but continued to stare, she twisted onto her back and looked at the tree. "I forgot how much I enjoy Christmas lights."

The blanket had fallen off her chest as she moved. She was still wearing one of the shirts with holes.

I gestured toward her shirt. "I thought you bought new clothes."

She smirked and yanked her blanket down, revealing her legs.

Well, I believe it was the shorts she wanted me to see, but all I saw was bare skin. I'd never seen so much of her before, and heat spread up my neck onto my face. The absurdity of my reaction to her unnerved me. It was like I'd never seen a woman's legs before.

"See my shorts? I got three pairs of these babies for six bucks. They'll be good to sleep in."

It looked like rough material, so I didn't see how it could be comfortable. "You actually plan to sleep in those ugly tan things?"

She laughed. "They are hideous, but I got them for around the house."

Palming my forehead, I shook my head, which made her giggle again.

"I'm sorry my ugly shorts aren't like your silky pj's."

"They're not all silky," I confessed, dropping my arm. "These are cotton." I gestured to the red flannel I wore.

That time, she shook her head. "I've never seen you mismatched."

"And you never will."

Her eyes twinkled as they crinkled in the corners. "Hmm."

"What?"

"Nothing." She stood, covering herself with the blanket entirely, so I didn't see her legs. "But you know what they say about being around the wrong crowd."

I folded my arms over my chest and tilted my head at her. "What do they say?"

"I reckon anyone can be influenced by the wrong person if they're around them enough."

"You're right. Anyone can be influenced."

In fact, I'd make sure to take a long lunch the next day and *fix* her shirt problem.

She narrowed her eyes, then huffed. "Well, I'm going to sleep."

I stood. "Me, too."

"Goodnight, Hudson. Try not to fall out of bed with your silk."

"I'm not wearing my silk pj's," I corrected her.

"Oh, that's right."

I smirked. "Goodnight, Red. Try not to create another hole in your shirt. You won't have much left if you keep it up."

23

EUGENE

"Mr. Tall Drink of Water keeps staring at you," said Loretta as she nudged my arm.

I glanced toward the kitchen door quickly.

"What are you looking over there for? I'm talking about table four. The tattooed hunk wearing a hat that Georgianna's been waiting on."

"Huh?" I murmured, and my cheeks heated. The first place I thought to look was in the back. Why?

I peeked over at table four and immediately locked eyes with the man Loretta spoke of. I turned back quickly.

She laughed. "See? I told you."

"Stop," I whispered. "We're being so obvious about staring right now."

Loretta was right. The man was handsome. He had brown hair, dark eyes, and tattoos inked all over his arms. He was a book boyfriend come to life. I couldn't believe I had zero response to how gorgeous he was. It likely had to do with a *certain* someone staring at me every night while I read. If I could get used to that handsome man eyeballing me constantly while living around him, I might as well have conquered my libido.

I flinched when something soft swiped my face. Looking up, I saw the back of Georgianna's hair as it peeled off my cheek.

"A loose strand of your hair might fall onto someone's plate," I told her.

She turned around and gasped. "Oh, sorry, Eugene. I didn't see you, but can you blame me? Look at table four. He's totally checking me out."

I looked again, and he winked. Oh, my God.

Georgianna giggled. "See. He just winked."

I averted my gaze quickly. Shit. He wasn't winking at me. That was even more embarrassing!

"He's not winking at you, Georgianna," Loretta said.

Georgianna frowned. "Huh?"

Loretta pointed her finger at me. "His eyes have been on this awkward child ever since he walked in."

I pushed her hand down. "No, he's not."

"Damn," Georgianna muttered. "You're right. He is looking at Eugene." She slapped my arm. "You lucky bitch. Want me to get his number for you?"

"No! Please. I have to get back to work."

"I hope he at least tips good," Georgianna said.

My eyes bulged as Georgianna adjusted her boobs so that they nearly spilled over the edge of her V-neck shirt. Then, she sashayed toward table four.

"Lord, have mercy on that child," Loretta muttered as she walked away.

So, *that* was how Georgianna got good tips.

After checking on my customers, I edged toward a corner in the back and glanced at my plain white T-shirt. I twisted the hem until the shirt tightened and tucked it in. Hmm. It definitely showed more of my shape, but it wasn't enough. Georgianna had ample cleavage, and it appeared to be a powerful tipping machine.

I let my fingers graze over my breasts. Maybe it would be worth splurging on a few low-cut T-shirts. The kitchen door opened, and Hudson stepped out with two plates in his hand. Of course, he glanced in my direction. I dropped my hands quickly, but it probably still looked like I was groping myself.

His eyes widened, and the plates tipped forward, clattering to the floor.

"Oh, no!" I rushed forward to help him.

A mess of shattered plates and food littered the floor in front of him. I reached for one of the broken plates, and Hudson snatched my wrist. "Leave it. I'll clean it up."

"But—"

He pinched the bridge of his nose with his other hand. Glancing at me, he asked, "What were you doing?"

"Thinking!"

His grin was lopsided when he asked, "You grope yourself while you think?"

"I wasn't."

"Oh, let me use a softer term. Were you fondling yourself?"

"Oh, my god. I said I wasn't."

"Then what were you thinking?"

"About tips," I blurted out. "Georgianna makes better tips than me." I elaborated by holding my arms out in front of my breasts, like I might cup them.

He blinked, his jaw tightening. "No. *No.*"

"What do you mean, no? I'm just weighing my options here." He glimpsed down, and I exhaled. "Not literally!"

"No."

Fries and a burger cluttered the floor, along with Alfredo noodles. "That's my table's food, isn't it? I'll go tell them it will be another minute."

My tip was gone, all because I stressed out the chef.

"Hudson wants us all in the breakroom after closing," Georgianna informed everyone as I wiped down a table.

"I wonder what for," Rebecca said as she carried two salads.

"Who knows?" Georgianna shrugged. "I know he wants the first shift to arrive a few minutes early for a meeting about the same thing in the morning."

Did that mean I had to attend both meetings? I'd have to ask him.

After locking the door, we cleaned up and waited for Hudson in the breakroom. He entered the room, yanking at the top button of his shirt. I saw a glimpse of hair on his chest when he unbuttoned the second one. Then he ran his fingers through his styled hair, messing it up, before plopping down in a seat beside us.

The bottom of my stomach tingled. I swallowed and fanned my face. Why was it so hot? Did the AC stop working?

"It's about our dress code," he began.

I lowered my hand.

"It's been a year since we opened. As long as you dressed neatly, I allowed you to wear what you wanted, but we're growing. It's time for uniforms. I need everyone's sizes because I plan to order some shirts. As for pants, we can stick with black or brown. I'm not picky as long as you're clean for the customers."

He stood just as quickly as he had sat down. I crossed my arms.

"That's it. Jot down your shirt size, and I'll get them ordered."

As soon as he left the room, Georgianna groaned. "This came out of nowhere. He's never cared before."

My heartbeat roared in my ears. *Was the change because of me?*

I left the restaurant before Hudson did. Usually, it took him about twenty minutes to get home. While I waited for him, I sat on the couch and petted Max.

When he did, I opened my mouth, then clamped it shut. He had shopping bags in his hand. I straightened my spine when he came my way.

He squatted in front of me and pulled out a black T-shirt and pajama bottoms. "*These* are what you can wear around the house." He took out several more sets. "I ordered you some more."

"You ordered *more*?" He placed seven sets on my lap. I noticed the torn off price tags, which only made it worse. "You shouldn't have gotten me these."

"You were never going to buy them yourself," he explained.

"Thanks, but you shouldn't have."

He hesitated. "Did I get the right size?"

My gaze zeroed in on the silky pink set similar to his. "Yeah."

"You're not happy," he stated.

I met his gaze and let my shoulders droop. "You really shouldn't have."

"It's just a few pairs of pajamas," he said as he removed a blow-dryer from a different bag.

"I'll never use that," I said truthfully. "I never used the one I had."

Determination flashed in his eyes. "It will be used."

Changing the subject, I asked, "Did you decide on the shirts at work because of me?"

"No." When I huffed, he continued. "Now, if you meant I decided to order the uniforms quicker because of you, then the answer is yes."

I rolled my eyes. "Unbelievable."

"I'm keeping you from..." He lifted his hands and mimicked having a pair of boobs. "Doing anything unnecessary."

Hudson was being irrational. If I hadn't been honest when he asked what I'd been doing, he would have never known. I was merely *thinking* about it.

"I have plenty of low-cut shirts I wear. Are you going to confiscate my clothes now, roommate?"

He flicked his gaze over me briefly, and heat stirred low in my stomach.

"Wear them, *please*."

Goosebumps pebbled on my skin at the way his voice deepened. The tingling in my stomach dipped lower, and my clit throbbed.

"I'm sure you'll look nice by my side when you do."

My mouth dropped open as he stood, taking the pajamas from me. I didn't know what to think of the man, but my body sure as fuck did. My libido wasn't as dormant as I pretended it to be.

"I'm going to wash these for you," he stated.

I squeezed my legs together and took a deep breath as he left the room.

It's fine. Everything's fine.

He was *helping* me. My body was getting all out of whack because of him. I fanned my face but stopped when I saw Max staring at me.

"What?" I said to the dog before I stood and ran up the stairs.

24

EUGENE

THE DARK-HAIRED MAN WITH THE TATTOOS RETURNED TO HOMESTYLE TWO days later. He was in one of my booths with another guy. Rebecca informed me that he specifically asked for the *woman with red hair*. I wasn't flattered. That kind of attention from men only made me uncomfortable. I hated feeling more awkward than I already was. Being uncomfortable made me prone to further mistakes and clumsiness.

I could, however, do my job with a smile and hope for a tip. "Hi, guys. I'm Genie and will be your server for the evening. What can I get you guys to drink?"

"Hello, Genie," my admirer said, flashing his pearly whites. "I'll take a Sprite."

His buddy ordered a Coke.

Easy enough. The guy might not be a bad dude after all. He didn't look like a creep, but appearances were deceiving. Waiting on them had been pleasant. They were kind and didn't say anything remotely lecherous, but I felt my admirer's gaze on me everywhere I went.

When they were leaving, he winked and said, "I'll be seeing you again, Genie."

I didn't know what to say, so I said nothing. A hundred-dollar tip waited for me on their table.

"Who was that?" asked Sue.

I turned around as she approached. "I don't know, but they tipped good."

She gripped the table to steady herself. "I'd reckon so with the way that one eyeballed ya everywhere ya went."

Sue seemed to be struggling with walking more that day, so I held her hand and placed my other at her back. "Let's go sit down. I'll get you a chair from Hudson's office."

She lifted her head. "Ya still living with my grandson?"

"Yes."

"I ain't got forever, ya know?"

She must be referring to Hudson, and her need to constantly match him to someone. Only the idea of her setting up my roommate with someone didn't sound so amusing anymore. What happened when she started trying to hook him up with another woman? My stomach cramped.

Despite my weird thoughts, I smirked. "What if he's happiest being alone? Shouldn't that matter the most?"

"That's not being happy. That's being stubborn." Sue shook her head, meeting my gaze and smiling. "Nonetheless, I'm not worried now. I just wish he'd hurry up before I die."

My stomach sank at the thought of Hudson losing that woman. "Don't say that."

She squeezed my hand. "Go tend to your tables. I'll go help Hudson in the kitchen."

After showering, I put on a pair of the pink pajama sets Hudson bought me and headed downstairs for a snack. As soon as I brushed my teeth, I always wanted something to eat, so I might as well get the snacking over with beforehand. Hudson's boots were near the door, so he must have come home while I was in the bathroom.

I didn't see him in the main room. I padded across the floor and then slipped into the kitchen. Hudson was cutting up some tomatoes. There were two plates with sandwiches spread apart beside him on the island. I paused at the door, and his eyes landed on my wet hair.

"I figured you'd want a sandwich before bed, too," he said.

He would know. I believed it was his fault that I needed food around nine or ten each night. The man was always feeding me.

I smiled as I stepped into the room. "I bet I've gained ten pounds since living here," I said.

Seeing him in his black, silky pajamas made me touch mine in response. I liked those the best on him. They weren't tight, but I'd seen his arms enough to envision his muscles. The man had a huge appetite, yet all I saw was a broad, muscular chest, strong arms, and thick thighs.

"How do you stay in shape when I'm pretty sure you eat more than a horse?"

He put the tomatoes on the sandwiches and then added lettuce. "I run on the treadmill in the garage. There are also some weights, but I don't do much lifting through the week."

"You run every day?"

"Yes, before work. I prefer running outside, but the cold is too much for me this time of year. I'll use the treadmill until spring. You can join me. There are a few good hiking spots I've found just behind the cabin that you might enjoy. That is, if you like that kind of thing."

My heart banged out of control against my ribcage. Hudson seemed sure I'd still be there by spring. I didn't know why, but it made my heart go all wonky.

"I used to love that sort of thing," I admitted. "But I haven't been since I was a teen, so you might have to carry me at some point if it's all uphill."

His eyes crinkled at the corners as he pulled out a stool beside him. "Come here."

I didn't think he realized how authoritative his tone was toward me all the time. Then again, maybe he did. My skin pebbled, and my breath quickened every time he used that voice.

As I sat down, he grabbed a strand of my hair. "After we eat, we'll blow-dry your hair."

I stiffened. *We?*

"It really doesn't bother me being wet," I said.

Ignoring me, he walked to the fridge, and my gaze followed. "Want a piece of cheesecake? I brought one home from the restaurant."

"Yes, please."

He froze and turned, his eyes flickering over me in a way that made my skin heat, before looking back into the fridge. I had half my sandwich eaten before he handed me a bottle of water and a slice of cheesecake. He sat beside me on a stool and finally began to eat.

"Your grandma's limp was a little more pronounced today." I slid my empty plate aside and pulled the one with the cheesecake close.

"I know. Her arthritis is likely flaring up, but I told my mom when she picked Grandma up earlier."

I nodded and said, "Good."

He really knew how to take care of those around him. While he was eating his slice of cheesecake, I took the plates to the sink to wash. It was becoming my thing. He always made us sandwiches or cooked something, so I cleaned up even if he never asked.

I could cook, but nowhere near Hudson's level. I'd be embarrassed to prepare anything in front of him. He had a hard time with my walking in front of him as it was. Like a woman could help being clumsy.

"I'll go get the blow-dryer." He walked out of the kitchen.

Shit. We were really doing the hair thing.

My stomach knotted as I finished up the dishes. What did he mean by *we* earlier? Surely, he didn't expect to dry my hair himself.

I'd never seen any man do such a thing for a woman before. I had to be wrong.

"Red!" Hudson hollered. "Get in here."

I gulped and hurried into the living area. I saw him sitting on the floor near the wall, legs crossed, as he held the blow-dryer.

Placing my hands on my hips, I blushed. "Hudson, I'll do it myself."

"No, you won't. You'll leave it hanging on your back like that, and it kills me. Come here." He patted the spot in front of him.

It was like my nerves were lodged in my throat as I ambled toward him. "This is embarrassing," I confessed as I covered my face as if that could remove me from the situation. "No man in the universe would want to do this for a woman."

"Who says? My dad does plenty of things like this for my mom when he's home."

"Really?" I found that hard to believe. Most men I dated thought it was my job to take care of them but didn't want to do anything for me. Unless it was to fuck, and that was always lackluster.

My ex, Jared, was by far the worst, though. He thought I was put on Earth to cater to his every whim. He convinced me to quit my job and wait on him at home. I had just graduated high school, and he had been older. I thought it seemed so sweet to move out of Gran's and have my own place. What I thought would be sweet became a nightmare. He wanted a little maid. It turned out I was far too stubborn to be under the thumb of a man, especially one who thought it was his job to belittle me for a speck of dirt on the floor. Never again would I allow a man to smack me across the face for it either.

Even so, I still carried Jared around in my thoughts when I shouldn't. The damage he did to me stuck around. But as I thought about it, I realized I hadn't gotten too nervous as of late when I made messes around Hudson. Maybe I was learning that not all men were bad, even if it seemed that way.

Besides my brother, I'd only known no-good men. Hudson was proving to be a good guy. I wasn't even his girlfriend, and he did so much. The thought unlocks something inside my chest as I sat in front of him. Like a hidden longing for something I told my heart didn't exist.

"She does the same for him, so why wouldn't he?" he replied.

He was right. If someone cared for you, the same should be given back. The reality was different for most. Some of us were used, either for our bodies or money. Someone continuously gave all their love, patience, and time to their partner while never getting any love back. A person could love you one day, despise you the next. I'd been around enough family members to know that.

I thought of Aunt Cheryl and wondered what sick type of love she let consume her those days. She taught me first with all her lovers. The bruises, the tears, and all the yelling as they chased her to Gran's. My past relationships taught me second how little we could matter to men. So, Hudson's words were like magic. Or his life was a fantasy one. I'd never seen the type of love he spoke about.

As I watched him, I suddenly wanted to believe in the magic of love.

"They sound lucky. That's not the case for most people."

"Yeah, I know," he said in a gravelly tone. "The idea of sharing a life with someone used to seem exhausting to me, but..."

I tensed when he placed his fingers in my hair and turned on the blow-dryer. Warmth blasted against my head, blowing my hair all over my face. Chills erupted on my skin, and I closed my eyes. *Ah.* That was nice.

Abrupt movement near my thigh made me open my lids. Hudson put his legs on either side of me, caging me in.

His soft touch, along with the heat, threatened to lull me to sleep. My body started tipping backward, wanting to lean into the comfort more. I slouched forward to keep myself from laying back and put my hands at my sides. My palms landed on each of his thighs. He was so close.

A tsunami of desire began to swirl and form in my stomach the longer I stared at my hands on his thighs. My body heated inside and out.

I felt Hudson's chest press into my back right before he spoke near my ear. "Am I putting you to sleep?"

My nipples pebbled against my bra. I leaned forward and jerked my hands from his legs as I panted. Oh, shit. How was I getting turned on by something so innocent? Hudson would likely be disgusted if he knew what his act of kindness was doing to my body. It had been so long since anyone touched me. I tried to ignore what his proximity was doing to me.

When the blow-dryer cut off, I jumped up. "I'm sorry. The heat was making me comfortable."

He stood and touched my hair again, which made me look back. "Much better. I'll dry it for you from now on."

Hudson couldn't be serious. I could not survive his kindness! It was turning me into a mess of need. Maybe I should ease off on romance books for a while.

25

HUDSON

"So, Genie lives with you?" Randall asked while making biscuit batter.

Glaring at the man, I scratched my forehead and said, "Yes. How many times are you going to ask?"

"My bad, my bad." He laughed. "I'm just curious about her."

What did he mean by curious? It better not have anything to do with the sappy expression he had on his face that morning.

"Why are you curious about her?"

"Since she lives with you, you must know if she has a boyfriend."

I gritted my teeth. I fucking guessed he liked Eugene. Like he had a chance with her. As if I'd let him get close to her, or any man, for that matter. With a grin, I replied, "She has many."

"What?"

"She sees a different guy nearly every night." At least, that was my presumption. Each night, she sat by the fireplace with her Kindle. I made sure a fire was lit to encourage her to come downstairs so I could watch her. The woman was so animated whenever she read from that device.

I wanted to touch her so badly that I feared my tongue might be hanging out like Max's as I stared each night.

Randall's eyebrows knitted together. "She doesn't seem like that kind of girl."

"I'm joking," I muttered. *Sort of.* "But she is unavailable."

"You're confusing me. So, she has someone, or she doesn't?"

"She's off-limits! That's what she is."

He paused, hands in flour, and looked at me up and down.

I grabbed a bowl of potato soup and a plate with steak and baked potato. "I'm taking these out."

"Why don't you just put it in the window? Or is that for Eugene's table? I notice you take her table's food out for her whenever you get the chance."

Ignoring Randall, I pushed the door with my back and headed toward the dining room. Eugene was smiling at someone in a booth, so I quickened my steps. She glanced my way. "Is that for table six? You could have put it in the window."

Bringing out her orders was an excuse to see her. At least I was helping her out while I ogled her.

"It's not a problem," I said as she took the food from me.

Edwin popped his head out of the booth. "Ah, Hudson!"

Eugene shook her head at her brother before disappearing to tend to her tables.

"Hi, Cuz." Francis waved as I stopped in front of them.

I tucked my hands into my front pockets. "I haven't seen you two in a while."

"Genie hasn't visited us," Francis said.

"If I don't come to her, I'll never see her," Edwin complained. When I smirked, he tilted his head, and his eyes softened. "Thanks for letting her stay with you and letting her work here. She needed a change of scenery."

Eugene eyed her brother as she walked by. "What are you saying to him?" She didn't wait for his reply as she slipped around the tables toward the back.

"How is she?" Edwin asked, forcing my attention away from his sister.

"Clumsy," I blurted out. "Well fed, and she hangs around the fireplace to read."

Francis's eyebrows raised as she grinned, while Edwin's smile was slower to come. Did I say something wrong?

Francis added, "Does Genie seem okay emotionally?"

Emotionally? How would I honestly know that?

Sure, Eugene smiled a lot. She seemed happy, but was she really? It was only two weeks ago that she lost her things and cried over her books. Not to mention the situation with the lawyer. I hadn't looked anything up online since I last checked, and she would never confide in me if something had developed about the case.

My chest burned and fucking ached like I had heartburn. Why did Francis have to ask? I thought I had been doing so well with Eugene. I'd bought her pajamas, got her working with me, and had her under my roof. She had even let me blow-dry her hair—something I planned to do every time she washed it. There was so much more I wanted to do to the little red head, but I was tiptoeing with my emotions. I knew how overbearing I could be when it came to what I desired. Eugene didn't need me pushing what *I* wanted on her, which was her. She'd been through a lot. I could charm her slowly. What the fuck did I know about moving slowly, though? My houseguest had no clue how lovely I thought she was. How much I wanted to consume her.

She was living with me. That was enough. *For now.* Wasn't it? What if I was the creepy guy, staring all the time, who had no chance. It was easy to make Eugene blush, but those reddened cheeks didn't mean interest. Shit. I needed some sort of fucking sign that I had a chance.

Realizing I stood there saying nothing, I cleared my throat. "Don't worry. I'll make sure she's happy."

And I would. Those days, it was clear for me. Her happiness was mine. I wanted all her smiles.

Somehow, the world dropped her, a precious jewel, into a disaster of a life. Edwin chose well sending her to me. No one was going to fuck with her life. Not with me around. She belonged with me. She was the color filling in my gray. I just had to show her how good I could be for her before she decided to leave me. I used to want all my free time to myself. Since Eugene, the idea of her not being in the cabin gutted me.

I was a total sucker for Eugene, and I was fucking okay with that.

"Can you send Eugene our way tomorrow?"

I frowned. "Why?"

"It's Christmas Eve tomorrow." Francis snorted. "Michael won't be there until Christmas Day, so she can't use him as an excuse not to come over."

My frown deepened. "What's with her and Michael? Why doesn't she like him?"

"She once kicked him in the nuts," Edwin said. "I think he was trying to push himself onto her."

My jaw tightened. I wasn't surprised, but the news pissed me off all the same.

"He was drunk," Francis offered.

"That's not an excuse," Edwin stated.

"That's definitely not a fucking excuse," I muttered. "I've got to get back to the kitchen, but I'll bring her tomorrow."

"*You* will?" His forehead crinkled, and his eyes darted all over my face as if searching for something.

"Yeah. Why wouldn't I?"

I didn't wait for his reply.

Fresh out of the shower, I found Eugene in front of the fireplace, reading. Instead of sitting on my recliner, I took a seat on the couch and patted the cushion. "Come here."

She looked up from her Kindle, mouth parting. "What?"

"I said come here."

"What, why?" She pulled her legs to her chest instead of getting up.

With a smile, I got up and plopped down on the floor beside her. When I grabbed her foot, she shrieked. I grinned and placed her bare feet under my legs. "Now how hard was that?" I asked.

"What are you doing?" she grumbled and covered her face with the Kindle.

I took the device from her. "I want to see your face when I'm talking to you."

She leaned forward. Her cheeks and neck had turned red. "Are you happy now?"

I leaned in, too, close enough that I inhaled a strawberry scent wafting from her. My dick throbbed, and my heart quickened. I could see all those lovely specks of brown flickering from the firelight in her eyes. "Are you?"

Her hair was even brighter and untamed. The flames flickered within her dark eyes, and my heart melted under her heat. I realized she was gorgeous—I always had, but it was startling up close. She was everything I never wanted, and yet I couldn't tear my eyes away from her. Again, I realized she had me spinning in her orbit.

I needed to calm the fuck down so my cock could relax. I wanted to comfort her, not freak her out.

She was the first to avert her gaze. Touching her forehead, she murmured, "What do you mean?"

"Tell me about this old job of yours and your boss."

Her brows pinched together. "Why? I don't want to talk about him or the job."

"Danny Hopkins, right? I read the news about him."

"If you read it, then why are you asking me? I know as much as everyone else." Something a lot like hurt flashed in her eyes when she lifted her head. "*You* think I'm hiding something?"

"Hey, hey, hey." I grabbed her hands. "I'm asking because I want to make sure you're okay. If you want to talk about it, I'm here. That's what I was getting at. I don't give a fuck about anything else. I hope the shithead is found, but I care more about what's going on in here." I tapped her head, and she looked down.

"I'm fine. I don't read the comments online," she whispered.

Which meant she likely read every fucking one.

"Those people don't know what they're talking about." I rubbed my thumb over the back of her hand.

"I'd be upset too in their case. Danny stole so much money from them."

"Yeah, but that's not your fault."

"They don't know that."

"*Eugene,*" I said. "Fuck those people. They don't know, which is why they shouldn't be slandering you. Stop empathizing with bullies on the internet."

She bit her bottom lip, and my heart felt like it might pop right out of my chest. Jesus Christ. She was gorgeous. I kept rubbing her hand. I loved touching her. She was soft, but too softhearted. People like Eugene were swallowed up whole if no one looked out for them.

"Yeah. Fuck those people." She nodded, but she had the enthusiasm of a man trying to prepare himself for a prostate exam.

"Red," I said sternly.

"Blue," she said in a serious voice, pinching her brows together.

Fuck. She even looked beautiful, pretending to put up a stern face.

Her mask slipped, and the corners of her mouth lifted before she burst out laughing.

"It's not funny," I said, but I realized she might be trying to change the subject. While she might be cracking up, it might very well be a show for me.

"What?" she asked. "I thought we were calling out colors."

"Mm-hmm. Are you enjoying yourself, Red?"

She pulled her hands from mine, and I immediately missed the contact.

Eugene wiped her eye. "Man, I crack myself up."

I shook my head. Max made a puffing sound. I turned toward him, lying beside my recliner, and pointed at him. "Even Max grunted at you."

When she continued giggling, I gently touched her chin. "Really, how are you? Are you good? Because I need you to be."

She pulled away again. "I'm good, thanks to you." Her sweet expression was soft as her gaze fell to my lips. My throat suddenly felt dry. "Thanks for letting me stay here, Hudson."

I rubbed the back of my neck as my skin heated. "You'll tell me if and when anyone contacts you again about Danny's case? I want to be with you if something comes out of it."

No way would I let Eugene get thrown any further into that mess.

"Sure, but I think I'll be okay."

Slowly, I grabbed one of her feet and rubbed the top. "So, you're happy here then?"

"Of course! I feel like I'm on vacation. Your cabin is so homey."

I felt my ears heat, and I didn't understand why such a simple answer from her made my body warm. Maybe because it meant I might stand a chance with her.

"Why are you rubbing my feet?" She snickered. "You're so fancy that it's odd to see you touching someone's foot."

"This is not someone's foot. It's yours."

Her laughter died, and she slowly tucked her feet underneath her ass, away from me. "I suppose it's bedtime." She peeked through her lashes at me, and desire rolled through me.

Making a sound in my throat, I said, "Oh, I forgot to mention. We're going to your brother's tomorrow."

"We are?"

"Then Grandma will want you over on Christmas Day." I stood

before Genie did, adjusting my cock before she noticed, and headed for my room. I was unraveling. I couldn't have a conversation alone with her without my body responding to her nearness.

"Say what?"

"She'll kick me out if I leave you alone. You have no choice. You're coming to my parents' house with me."

"Do you know how long it's been since I've gone to a holiday dinner?" she asked.

Pausing at the door, I looked back and smiled. "Goodnight, Red."

26

EUGENE

"Michael wasn't supposed to be here," my brother said for the sixth time since Hudson, and I arrived at the house.

Ignoring him, I stirred the mashed potatoes, adding another spoon full of butter. It was just me and my brother in the kitchen. Francis had carried a baked chicken out to the dining room.

"It was just supposed to be us today," he added.

"I believe you. I'm fine."

"No, you're not. You're helping Francis with the food."

"Your point?"

"You don't like to help in the kitchen, which means you're staying in here to avoid him."

"Not avoid." I laughed. "If he leers at my chest one more time, I'm going to punch him in the face this time."

"Is everything all right?" asked Michael in his slimy voice.

My lips curled in disgust. I had no idea how he was Francis's brother. She was an angel compared to him.

I didn't say anything. Scooping up the bowl, I started to walk by him.

Michael held his arm up and blocked my path. "Are you going to be like that forever over nothing?"

"Is the *nothing* you speak of that time you grabbed my tits and tried to shove your tongue down my throat?"

"You were giving me signs to follow you when you stood up that night!"

"*What?*"

Unbelievable. How was getting up for the bathroom a sign to touch a person? As soon as my brother and Francis had gone to bed that night, I should have too. Silly me to think I'd be okay finishing the film with a member of the opposite sex.

"I had to pee."

Edwin swore. "Michael. Just leave it alone. I hardly ever see my sister, and you're always a douche when she's here."

I saw Hudson heading toward us. My face heated from embarrassment.

"I can't stand her acting like I'm the problem!" Michael yelled. "She's a bitch who thinks she's someone special when she ain't shit. She kicked me, remember? Have we forgotten about that?"

Hudson gripped Michael's shoulder and turned him around. "Let's go."

"Let go of me." Michael jerked out of Hudson's hand, stepping backward onto my toes.

I nearly dropped the bowl of mashed potatoes. The veins in Hudson's neck jumped as he yanked Michael's shirt. "It looks like you came here for the sole purpose of antagonizing Eugene just because she didn't allow you to touch her."

"That better not be true, Michael," Francis said from behind Hudson. "You knew I didn't want you here today because we wanted to celebrate with Genie, and you came anyway."

Michael glared at Hudson and said, "You better get your hands off my shirt."

Hudson towered over his cousin. "Or...?"

"Don't hurt him, Hudson," Francis began. "Just make him leave."

Michael snapped his head toward his sister. "Me? I'm your brother."

"Outside!" Hudson shouted, shoving Michael forward and away from me when he tried to jerk out of his grasp again. "I'd rather Red not see what I'll do to you if you don't fucking leave."

"Seriously, Hudson. Don't hurt him," Francis said as she followed them.

My stomach knotted. Turning around, I walked over to the kitchen counter and put the bowl down. "How about I leave instead?"

"Don't do that, Genie," my brother said. "Don't let Michael ruin our time together."

I couldn't believe I had originally planned to live at my brother's. There was no way I could have lasted a day with Michael harassing me. I loved my brother, and I knew he hated Michael bothering me, but he had to think of Francis. She would defend her brother no matter what.

Edwin would have never thrown him out like Hudson did. My brother and his wife would have let Michael go off on his rampage, saying words that didn't help. The truth was sobering. My vision blurred, and I wiped my eyes.

"If Michael behaves this way around me, imagine how he acts toward other women," I said to my brother.

Edwin flinched. "Genie..."

"Thanks for sending me to Hudson." I sniffed. "He can do for me what you can't. And don't think I'm angry. I know Michael is Francis's brother, but just because you two tolerate his behavior, doesn't mean I want to. I love you, Edwin, but I'm going home. All this has done is remind me why I like being alone."

Edwin opened his mouth but shut it when footsteps approached.

"Thanks for not reacting to him," Francis said to Hudson.

"Michael's using again," Hudson replied. "The needles were lying right out in the open in his truck. I know you love him, Francis, but you're not helping him. Red doesn't deserve to be treated that way either."

When they stopped at the kitchen entrance, I met Hudson's gaze, and something in me cracked. My heart roared in my ears.

"Red...?" he murmured.

Tucking my red strands behind my ears, I stepped toward him. "Do you want to leave?"

Every part of my body trembled, and all I wanted was to be done with that day.

"Please don't go." Francis hurried to me. "I should have sent Michael away as soon as he showed up."

"It's fine. He's your brother." I eyed Hudson, who moved his gaze over me once.

"Let's go." That was all Hudson said. No trying to make me stay. No trying to make it better. Instead, he gave me exactly what I wanted—an escape.

Hudson didn't push me into any conversation on the drive to his cabin. If he were any other person, I would have appreciated that space. Hudson was becoming unlike everyone else, though. I wanted to pour out all the words to him. Complain about his cousin and thank him for stepping in where my brother never did.

We remained quiet even after we were home. I only disappeared upstairs to change my clothes and get my blanket. I finally decided that I was done wearing a bra around the cabin. When I was home, I liked to be comfortable. With all those new pajamas, Hudson might never notice. When I returned downstairs, I didn't see Hudson. He might have gone to his room.

Max joined me on the couch, laying within the curve of my legs. I closed my eyes, enjoying the comfort of being back in Hudson's cabin.

I must have fallen asleep because I woke to darkness. A bit of light filtered through the crack in the bedroom door, and that was when I stiffened. The woodsy smell filled my nostrils. I ran my fingers over the bed, trying to make sense of my surroundings. What? How did I end up in bed? Didn't I fall asleep on the couch?

My blanket was still covering me, but...

Standing, I walked toward the door since it was my only source of light. I cracked it open and pulled the blanket over my head. Huh. I was downstairs. Glancing back, my mouth dropped as I ventured further into the main room. I was sleeping on Hudson's bed. Why?

I clearly remembered being on the couch and resting my eyes. Had Hudson carried me to his bed? Again, why? He could have left me on the couch to nap or in my room, so I didn't drool on his pillow.

Oh, shit. What if I really drooled on his bed?

"I was about to wake you," Hudson's husky voice drifted toward me.

I pulled the blanket off my head and glanced around as I walked. He was propped against the kitchen doorjamb, arms crossed, as his lips twitched into an almost smile.

"I made biscuits and gravy," he said before disappearing into the kitchen.

I followed, my stomach grumbling at the thought of food. Considering, I had skipped breakfast for the meal I was supposed to eat at my brother's, I was starved. It was dark out, and I hadn't eaten a thing all day.

"I'm so hungry," I told him.

"Me, too."

I let him prepare a plate for me. The man was honestly too good to be true.

Hudson sat beside me as we ate. "Your brother's been calling me."

I froze mid bite. "Oh?"

Although I pestered Hudson, I didn't want my brother doing it. My living and working with Hudson would eventually stress the man out. Regardless, I found myself really happy to be there with him.

My stomach twisted and churned. It scared me how much I enjoyed where I was. Life was constantly changing, and I'd one day leave.

It's fine. Everything's fine.

"It's going to be all right, Red. Ed and Francis agreed to visit you at my house from now on. So, you don't have to distance yourself from your brother."

The sinking feeling in my stomach dissipated. Hudson continued to eat, unaware of the effect he had on my emotions.

Putting my fork down, I leaned over and wrapped my arms around him. He stiffened, his breath fanning my cheek as he turned. I dropped my face into his neck for only a second, enough to inhale the same woodsy smell from earlier, then pulled away quickly. "Thank you, Hudson."

My skin tingled even after I resumed eating. Hudson was a muscular man, and I found myself wanting to reach for him again. It was like his presence ignited a flame within me and yet calmed my every thought without trying.

I cleared my throat. "So... How hard would it be to get out of going to your family's house tomorrow?"

"I already told Grandma we weren't coming."

"You should go. That's your family."

Hudson shook his head. "I'm not leaving you alone on Christmas Day. Grandma would kill me if I did."

Warmth surged through my chest.

It was so easy to exist in that cabin because of Hudson.

27

HUDSON

I woke to a loud thump. Climbing out of bed, I slipped on my house shoes and stepped out of the room.

"Ow, ow, ow, ow!" Eugene chanted as she rubbed her knees while sitting on the floor. "You're going to kill me one of these days, Bear."

Max, standing beside her, wagged his tail and sniffed her arm.

"Max." They both looked up at me.

Eugene grabbed a giant bag that said Merry Christmas on it and quickly stood. "Merry Christmas!" She held the gift up as she walked.

Again, I had been aware of something about Eugene and myself since she moved in. She was fucking sweet, and I adored her. I loved her awkwardness, her clumsiness, and the way she smiled. I'd never enjoyed anyone's company like I had hers. I enjoyed *her*.

"Listen. I gave you something. You've done so much for me. We didn't talk about gifts, and I'm glad because I didn't want you to get me—"

"Go sit by the tree," I said as I hurried back to my room and retrieved her present. The present I got her wasn't the surprise I'd been working on with Grandma's help. Finding all of Eugene's old books was taking longer than I thought it would, so, I made sure to pick up something else for the holiday.

Legs tucked underneath her; Eugene sat by the tree with the present for me in front of her. Once again, my heart was in a frenzy. She hadn't been in my house for a full month, and yet I couldn't remember what it was like to live with just Max.

What if I had refused all of Edwin's calls until he gave up? What if I had told him no? My throat tightened. I'd still be thinking life was great in solitude with a dog. I'd still be wondering if I was capable of caring for someone. Not only did I care, but I also wanted to get my hands on Eugene. I wanted to unwrap her as if she were my present.

Eugene consumed me with her presence. And for the first time in my life, I had no clue how to approach what I wanted. I'd messed up in a relationship before. I never had deep emotions for Hilary, but I had tried to make her happy. Did I really, though? *No.* I was relieved to be done with her and constantly felt exhausted at the idea of having to entertain her when we were together. Those actions were what led me to wonder if I was capable of loving anyone the way they deserved.

Until Eugene.

I did more for Eugene in the short time I'd known her than I had for anyone my entire life, and it's what I wanted to be doing. Just staring at Eugene while she read every night gave me more peace than all the time I had spent with my ex or any woman before. I was fucking happy, but I was greedy for *more* of her. For touches that weren't so innocent. Kisses that trailed down her neck. I craved to feel her bare skin against mine.

I didn't mind being consumed by Eugene, but I yearned for her on an intimate level. What I felt each day for her... I wished she felt the same about me. I wanted her to find out how well I could take care of her mentally and physically.

"Hudson?"

I hadn't realized I was staring.

Her hair was done in a messy bun on top of her head. She wore the green flannel pajama set I bought her. She looked like I should pick her up over my shoulder and carry her to my bed. The blood rushed to my cock at the idea. That wouldn't work—not yet at least. Eugene's been through a lot recently, and she needed more time to see that life with me was the real deal. I could be her fucking home.

Only she didn't know she was mine yet.

Dropping down to the floor in front of her, I offered the presents to her.

"You shouldn't have gotten me anything." She nibbled on her bottom lip as she looked at the boxes.

"I believe what you meant was, 'thank you for thinking about me'," I said, raising one knee so I could prop my elbow on it.

She rolled her eyes, but there was no mistaking her blushing. "Thank you for thinking about me, Hudson."

"I'll always think about you," I said.

Inhaling sharply, she tore into the presents. The first two were the other pajamas I'd ordered. The third gift was the one I believed she'd like most. As soon as she pulled out the bookstore gift card, her eyes bulged.

"Shit, Hudson," she said. "I can't accept this."

"I believe what you meant was 'thank you'."

Her eyes were glassy as she said, "Seriously, thank you." She sniffed as she wiped her eyes. "I'm going to hug you now."

I wasn't expecting to get another one of her hugs, but I wasn't going to fucking complain. She pushed the presents aside. As I opened my arms, she threw herself into them. Instead of freezing up like the first time, I returned her hug, burying my nose in her hair as she placed her head against my chest. My heart was going to beat right out of my chest. I wondered if she could feel how fast it raced for her. That strawberry scent of hers filled my nose. Unable to resist, I placed a kiss on her hair.

"Thank you so much, Hudson." Her words were muffled against my shirt, her breath heating the fabric. "Losing all my books sucked ass."

All too soon, she pulled away. I devoured her every move with my gaze as she sat in front of me, smiling so perfectly.

"Now it's your turn," she said.

I opened the bag and pulled out several books.

"I saw the books on the coffee table," she said, fidgeting with her fingers. "It seems like you read thrillers or horror?"

I studied the book covers before smiling. "You're correct. Thank you. I haven't read anything in a couple of weeks, so I'll enjoy these."

"You have something else in there," she said before she leaned over and reached into the bag. I found her enthusiasm adorable. She held a silver chain in her hand. "It was cheap, but I thought it suited you and couldn't pass it up."

I grasped the trinket hanging off her fingers and studied it. It was a spatula charm. I grinned and looked up to see her lips parting.

"See! It suits you." She laughed.

"I can't walk around with a spatula hanging around my neck."

Oh, she didn't know I had every intention of wearing the necklace since it was from her.

Eugene chuckled more. "Now you've got to put it on for that comment. I don't see the big deal. You own a restaurant, and you're an amazing cook."

It fucking pleased me to know she enjoyed the food I prepared for her.

I watched as she neared, mesmerized by her beauty, until Max barked. I heard his claws clicking on the hardwood as he ran up behind Eugene. Eugene's eyes widened as she made an *oof* sound, and that was all I saw before she slammed into me. Max barked again. I inhaled more strawberries. My nose brushed against softness. My face was cocooned in warmth. Realization dawned as I gripped her waist and fell backward with her.

"Bear!" she screamed.

Her tits... Her fucking tits were in my face. She wasn't wearing a bra beneath that shirt.

It was over all too soon. She scrambled to get off of me. I lost my grip on her waist.

"I'm sorry. Are you okay?" she asked.

Was I okay?

I sat up slowly, running my hand over my face. There was no guarantee I could mask my expression from her—my ever-growing want. I was trying to be patient with my feelings, but then her boobs hit my face. I wasn't okay. I needed a cold shower. Better yet, I needed her to fall just like that again.

Eugene went on, "I don't know why he jumped my back like that. Do you think he thought we were playing?"

"Who knows." I dropped my hand when I believed my blood had returned to normal. "Are you okay?"

"Yeah."

Wasn't she affected at all? Surely, she noticed where she landed. Getting closer to Eugene was going to be a challenge. I knew that because she didn't seem affected like I was when I blow dried her hair either. She had been falling asleep while I had been fighting not to touch anything else but her wet strands.

The tits in my face might be my final straw.

I wanted to take care of her, but I also wanted to eat her alive. There was no part of her I didn't want to touch and worship. I thought of bringing her to an orgasm over and over. Spreading her legs and devouring her pussy. Placing her on my lap, thrusting into her as she bounced on my cock.

Eugene had no idea that I was a starving man. Seducing her would be pleasurable in itself, but she needed a little more time to see how well I could take care of her.

Finding the necklace on the floor beside my leg, I picked it up. "Are you going to put this on me?"

I hadn't noticed she had stood until then.

"You can. I'm going to clean up our mess."

Hmm. Maybe Max would knock her into me again. A man could hope.

28

EUGENE

My brother called a lot those days. It was the first week of January, and I'd heard from him at least once every evening. He showed up on my day off at Hudson's house, and Max slobbered on him. Edwin said Michael was no longer allowed at his house, but I was.

I appreciated what my brother was doing. For his and Francis's sake, I hoped they stuck to their words. Michael used them a lot over the years, knowing his sister would bail him out of any trouble. Truthfully, it wasn't my place to say anything when I had called, asking my brother for help, too. I would never take advantage of someone's kindness, though.

But wasn't that what I was doing? Taking handouts from Hudson. I hadn't looked at all for a place to live because I liked living there. Hudson told me to stay however long I needed, but everyone had a breaking point. He said to save up while being there. He said a lot of nice things, and I liked them all.

I thought of Gran and that screen door. She kept the door open for anyone. Family, if you'd call them that, used her over and over, like how Michael took advantage of his sister. Oh, God. Was that what I was doing to Hudson? Did I unintentionally become the thing I despised? I never wanted to bother anyone with my problems. The idea that I might be taking advantage of Hudson twisted my insides.

Would it be wrong of me to enjoy his company a little longer? I didn't know if staying there much longer was a good idea. If given the chance, I would let him blow-dry my hair again. Wanting him to play with my hair was the reason I avoided going downstairs after washing my hair. I was embarrassed that he might notice my reaction to him if he dried my red mane. Which was sad since I'd liked the idea of it happening once more.

I still went downstairs and read on my Kindle whenever I didn't have a wet head. Hudson had been reading one of the books I'd gotten him the last few nights, and it had made me feel giddy.

My phone rang. When I saw Holly's name on the screen, I rolled over on the bed and picked her up. "What's my favorite hairdresser doing?"

Holly exhaled in my ear. "Wondering when her friend is going to come visit."

I pulled a strand of my hair up. The red had faded into a light pink. "Hopefully soon. My hair needs you."

"That's not the point." She huffed. "Don't you miss me at all? I'm more than your hairdresser. I'm your best friend."

"I'm sorry. I've just been busy at the restaurant," I said.

"Liar! You live with your boss. It ain't nothing to ask for a day off."

"He forces me to take time off, but I toast my ass by the fireplace on those days. I promise, I'll visit soon."

She groaned, and I imagined her rolling her eyes the way she did when I irritated her. When she gasped suddenly, my heart felt like it launched itself into my throat.

"Hey!" she hollered.

I sat up quickly. "What?"

"You still haven't sent me a picture of Hudson."

"Are you fucking kidding me?"

"What?"

"I thought something was wrong when you gasped."

"Something is wrong. I need to see this man. What's his last name? I'll just look on Facebook."

"Don't you dare," I warned her.

She laughed. "Wait. Do you have him as a friend? I'll just search his name really quick."

"I can't stand you."

"Hold on," she mumbled. "There. I had to put you on speaker. Now let's see... Hudson, Hudson, Hudson. Where are you?" I shook my head as I waited for her to search my friend's list. "Only one Hudson." Click. "Holy...Eugene Quillen!"

I snorted, unable to hide my laughter. I knew she was seeing how handsome my roomie was. Feigning ignorance, I asked, "What?"

"You, dog! No wonder you haven't visited. That man is gorgeous."

"We're roommates, Holly."

"Ain't nothing free in this world, Genie. Either he likes you, as in more than a friend, and wants to get into your pants. Or he simply wants to get into your pants because you're a beautiful woman."

I pursed my lips, letting her words roll through me. She said those exact words before but hearing them again bothered me. "Why do you have to ruin it? I enjoy staying here. In fact, I enjoy his company. You know I don't have much faith in men."

"You swore them off years ago," she said. "Go on."

"But I think he's truly a good person. He's good to me, and you should see him interact with his grandma, Holly."

"Oh, my lord," she muttered. "You like him."

"Of course, I do. If I didn't feel comfortable around him, I wouldn't live here."

"No, you like him, like him, as if you want to sleep—"

"Holly."

"What?"

I was very attracted to Hudson, and that was what made living with him so terrifying and exciting. While I wouldn't allow myself to go after him, I could enjoy being with him all the same.

"I can't go down that road," I said. "This moment in my life will change like everything does, and I'll move on and find my own place."

"Why are you so pessimistic when it comes to relationships?" she muttered.

"Why aren't you more cautious?" I countered. Holly had been through worse than me when it came to men, and she fell head over heels in an instant. The last guy she dated ripped her heart to shreds. "You were so worried about me when I first told you I was living with Hudson. Now look at you the moment you see him."

"Because you were right. That man is stunning. Regardless of what he wants, you should give in and enjoy yourself. You said everything changes, so why not experience life as it comes?"

"Um, because it's not like that. Thankfully, Hudson hasn't shown any interest." My chest tightened at the words. "I want to remain friends with this guy even after I move out."

"Seriously? Nothing at all?"

I thought of him blow-drying my hair, and heat dipped between my thighs. There was no way I was telling her about that night. Hudson's gesture was the sweetest thing anyone's ever done for me. The simple action of him wanting my hair dry, like he needed to see me cared for, made me feel special. I didn't know men could be like Hudson.

"He hasn't made any moves on me," I said, making a sound in my throat. Blow-drying my hair was only sensual for me. There was nothing sexy about it for him, right? If Hudson made the moves on me, I'd be putty in his hands. So, it was a good thing I didn't affect him the way he did me.

"M-hmm," she muttered.

"How are you and Roger?" I asked, changing the subject.

"We're good. Now that you mention it, how about me and Roger come visit you this weekend?"

"I am actually off Saturday, so that day would be great. I'll have to ask Hudson first. This is his house."

"We can hang out elsewhere if he doesn't want us there. No big deal."

"Okay."

On my off days, Hudson was home by four p.m. I wondered if he worked shorter hours when I took time off. There was no way it had anything to do with my schedule. When he refused to let me work too much, he probably noticed how little time he gave himself to relax.

He brought home lasagna and salads from the restaurant. As I ate in the kitchen, I told him about Holly wanting to come visit. The words weren't completely out of my mouth when he said, "I have three more spare rooms. They're welcome to stay over for the weekend if they'd like. If that doesn't work, I can drive you to see her."

I dropped my fork and nearly choked on the salad I ate. "Lord, no, Hudson. Are you insane? Allowing them to visit for a few hours is more than enough. This is your house, and I just wanted to make sure it was okay."

"This is your home, too. While I'm glad you let me know, I wouldn't refuse you."

A tingle formed in my lower stomach. My growing desire for Hudson slipped between my thighs, causing my clit to pulse. My body was confused. I averted my gaze because his stare made me feel like I was about to be swallowed up. He was too good to be fucking true. Yet, I couldn't hide my smile as I picked up my fork again. He was my roommate, boss, and *friend,* who I believed secretly pitied me. I wished the butterflies in my tummy would get a grip.

Placing his elbow on the island, he leaned forward and watched me eat. Hudson had a problem when it came to staring. It took everything in me not to squirm under his gaze. I couldn't remember what we were talking about.

Oh, right. Holly was going to visit.

29

EUGENE

The weekend arrived. With Hudson's approval, Holly and Roger decided to stay Friday night. I got off work at four that evening and met up with them at a steakhouse. A huge part of me wanted to bring them to Homestyle, but I felt like it would be too much to bring my friend into Hudson's workspace, too. Hudson was allowing Holly and her boyfriend to stay over, so I'd wait to introduce them at the cabin. I might make it obvious that I wish he were with us if I showed up at Homestyle.

A small voice in my head said I could stomp all over Hudson's territory, and he'd let me. That thought would lead me into hopeful expectations if I allowed it, but I wouldn't be in his home forever.

It was the first time I met Roger, but he seemed like a decent guy. If he was willing to put up with me and Holly together, he must care a great deal for her. After we ate, we caught a movie at the cinema. Halfway through the film, I received a text from Hudson.

> Hudson: Where are you guys?

> Me: Movie theater.

I kept checking my phone for the rest of the movie, but Hudson never responded. It was hard to focus on anything happening on the screen. I forced a smile when Holly gushed about the film as we exited.

We were walking to our vehicles when I heard a husky voice. "Red."

I spun around, my mouth dropping, as Hudson strode toward us. The white hoody he wore looked snug, like it was forced over his chest and arms. His blue jeans were loose, yet they looked far too good on him. I swallowed nervously as my heart raced. What was he doing there? He couldn't possibly be out there for us.

"Hudson," I mumbled, glancing at Holly, who continued to ogle my roommate. "Holly, this is Hudson. Hudson, this is Holly and her boyfriend Roger."

Holly extended her hand. "It's a pleasure to finally meet you. Thanks for taking care of my girl."

"Taking care of her is easy," said Hudson.

My skin pebbled and my stomach fluttered with a million butterflies. It was like he touched me physically with those words. I was speechless as he shook Roger's hand next, and the two men spoke. Holly peeked over at me, batting her eyes purposefully while gesturing with her head at Hudson.

I mouthed, "Stop it!"

She smirked.

If Holly kept that up, I'd murder her.

"What did you guys have planned next?" Hudson asked, looking at me.

I checked the time on my phone. "It's late. We were going to head to the cabin."

"Good. We can heat up the chili I brought home." Hudson reached out and snagged my fingers with his, rubbing gently. "Be careful. It's dark, and a deer might run out in the road." He released my digits all too soon.

My skin felt electric as I whispered, "I will."

After Hudson said bye to Holly and Roger, he walked toward the parking lot. Holly nudged my shoulder, leaning close. "How long do you think he waited out here? It's freaking cold!"

I shrugged. "I don't know."

"Maybe he wanted to hang out with us. Didn't you invite him?"

Of course, I hadn't invited him. Hudson was still working when I left. I didn't want to push too much by asking him if he wanted to hang out when he saw me all day long. Could he have wanted an invite? Was that why he showed up? The idea seemed crazy to me, but I wished I had invited him out with us.

Hudson must have loved feeding people. Why else did he feed me all the time? Roger and Holly devoured the chili he brought home from the restaurant. When it was me and Hudson, we always sat at the island and ate. With company, we ate at the table.

Holly patted her stomach and leaned back into her chair. "That was the best chili I've ever eaten."

"There's nothing Hudson can't make," I told her. "Everything he cooks tastes yummy."

I caught Hudson staring with a smoldering gaze. He let those hungry eyes roam over me before smiling. What. Was. That? My heart raced. I blushed and focused on my friend.

"I believe it," Roger added.

Hudson said, "I don't know. Red isn't picky about her food, so she might not be the best judge."

His smoky eyes were hooded as he watched me. *Still?* I squeezed my thighs together.

"Hey," I said, swallowing nervously. "I know good food from bad."

"Speaking of red..." Holly pointed at my hair. "If Hudson wants to keep calling you Red, we need to redo your hair. Luckily for you, I brought the dye for you. I can get it done before I leave tomorrow."

I reached out for her across the table, thankful for the distraction. "You are a beautiful soul. Did I tell you how stunning you look?"

Holly lunged forward and grabbed my hands. "No, but you can right now." When she winked, Roger groaned, and we laughed.

I didn't know which was worse. The constant creaking of the bed or the steady thud of the headboard hitting the wall. Throwing the pillow over my head, my feet started bouncing in tune with Holly and Roger's screwing in the room beside mine.

"Right there! Right *there!*" Holly moaned.

Oh my God! I groaned and shot out of bed. My hair was still wet from the shower and clung to the back of my shirt.

It wasn't the first time I'd heard the woman get it on with a man before. Long ago, I found it amusing. The cabin was so quiet at night. If I could hear them, I feared Hudson did too. How embarrassing!

Even so, I laughed. I wished I had my best friend's confidence. She genuinely seemed to enjoy sex. Me? I liked the *idea* of it. In reality, the act was lackluster for me. I didn't know if it was because I stayed in my head too much or because men just sucked, but it had always been a struggle to reach a climax with any of my partners. When I was alone with my vibrator, that was a different story. It was fabulous, and so much more enjoyable than having a man with me.

Unexpectedly, I imagined how Hudson might be between the sheets. My thoughts froze. There was no reason I should be going down that road, but the thuds hitting the wall had my brain a fucking mess. He was a very attentive person. Something about the way he took care of those around him made me think he'd probably be an incredible lover. He'd likely know how to meet a woman's needs.

I thought of the way he was practically devouring me with his eyes at the table. Had I imagined that heated look? My toes curled as my clit throbbed. *Stop it,* I told myself. If I kept going down the slippery slope of thoughts for Hudson, there would be no going back. I'd obsess over it.

I wiped my brow and inhaled deeply. Reading would be good. Anything to take my mind off the wicked thoughts I had. I grabbed my Kindle and headphones. Slowly, I opened my bedroom door and tiptoed downstairs. Yeah. I could still hear them, so I hoped Hudson was sleeping heavily.

There was no cozy fire to sit by, and I'd already taken the tree down, but I'd make do with the couch. Once I picked out a playlist that matched the mood of my book, I began reading. I wasn't there for a couple minutes when the cushion dipped beside me and one of my earbuds was yanked out.

I looked over at Hudson. The light off my Kindle was the only reason I could make out his features.

"Hudson..." I was about to ask what he was doing awake when Holly moaned again. Trying hard not to smile and feeling my cheeks heat, I said, "I'm sorry about this."

He cocked his head slowly. "No, you're not."

I laughed and pointed at the earbud still in his fingers. "I'm trying to drown them out."

"You started smiling as soon as your friend moaned. Why is your face so red, Red?"

"What?" My mouth dropped. "Don't you know people laugh and smile when they're feeling awkward or embarrassed. It's very uncomfortable to be sitting here with you while they're up there bringing down the house. So, I'm going back upstairs. Give me back my earbud."

"I'm teasing you." He smirked. "Stay down here and read."

I huffed just when Holly cried out. Looking upstairs, I groaned and fought the urge to hide my face from Hudson. "Still going? Ain't no way."

The bed hitting the wall said otherwise.

"Oh?" There was humor in that one word. "It could be the second round."

"Hmm," I mumbled. "I hope your wall is okay."

Hudson burst out laughing.

"I can't believe they aren't being quiet in someone else's house," I went on. "She's going to be so proud of herself tomorrow when I tell her."

Hudson remained quiet as he placed his arm behind me. "Does sex make you uncomfortable?"

I could feel his body heat, he was so close. A tingle formed in the pit of my stomach, and I tried to ignore it. "It doesn't."

"Then why are you getting embarrassed?"

"I'm just a private person. I wouldn't want anyone to hear me with my partner," I said. "Besides..." I let my words fade. There was no way I'd admit to not having great sex. I'd had decent sex, good sex even, but nothing earth shattering.

I spent the majority of my time with the same man every day. Being around Hudon constantly was turning me into someone who was needy and hopeful. I swore off men a couple years ago because I didn't want to become like Aunt Cheryl or end up with another guy like the ones I dated. Hudson wasn't like any of my exes. He was not someone I was sleeping with. In all likelihood, that was why things between us were so nice. I didn't know why, but that possibility twisted my stomach into knots.

He was a good guy. Why couldn't I trust that? I desperately wanted to trust in the peace Hudson brought into my life.

"Besides...?" His voice was oddly deeper. No, he was closer. I hadn't noticed he'd leaned toward me until I turned, and his breath touched my cheek.

I inhaled his woodsy scent, flexing my fingers when I craved to reach out for him. "Why are you so close?"

"I couldn't see you." His voice was definitely huskier.

I shivered and turned my body so that I faced him, and we were no longer so close. His palm found my shoulder, rubbing my shirt. "I should go back to bed," I whispered, but I didn't want to leave his side.

Shit. Hudson had no idea what a needy little creature I was becoming for him.

"No, read. I'll leave you alone," he replied.

My skin heated beneath my shirt. His hand moved to my back and stilled. When he pulled up a strand of my damp hair, he murmured, "I was beginning to think you didn't wash your hair anymore."

I scoffed, yanking the lock from his fingers. "Of course, I wash my hair."

"I haven't seen you with wet hair since I blow-dried your hair weeks ago."

The man had sat right beside me and touched me like he had a right to. If he had been Michael or any other man, I would have told him to stop rubbing my shoulder. Honestly, I didn't believe my roommate had any idea of the wild thoughts he was causing when he caressed me so innocently. Was that why I allowed him to touch me so freely? Because he didn't have indecent images of me like I had about him? Or was it because I felt safe with him. I anticipated each word and touch when it came to him.

I clicked the power button on my Kindle, plunging us into darkness. There was a small bit of moonlight peeking through the curtain, but not enough to see Hudson.

My heart raced as I breathed slowly, waiting.

"I'll go get the blow-dryer," he said, standing and walking away.

The longer I stared into the dark, the more I could make out the objects in the room. A door creaked upstairs, and I heard someone walking. Holly or Roger must be going to the bathroom. I stood deathly still until Hudson flipped on the lamp. I blinked as my eyes adjusted to the dim light. Hudson dropped down on the floor and beckoned for me to sit between his legs.

My pussy clenched. It was obvious my body was getting the

wrong idea when it came to Hudson. There was no way the man could be around me all the time and not feel anything, unless he wasn't interested. His body must not feel like it could melt like mine did every time we touched. That was what he was doing to me. Melting me with all his compassion toward me. If he finally admitted everything, he did for me was out of pity, I might cry.

"What's wrong?" he asked as I plopped down.

"I'm sleepy," I said, which wasn't a lie. The actual truth, I was freaking myself out when it came to the man behind me. "Holly and Roger will probably hear the blow-dryer, right?"

"Good. Aggravate them for a while instead."

I laughed as he hit the power button. The heat blew into me, and I moaned. He ran his fingers through my hair, and it felt so nice. Hudson shouldn't be playing with my hair.

His chest pressed into my back. "Am I putting you to sleep?"

Closing my eyes, I nodded. There was no point in denying it. I wondered if that was what being spoiled felt like. If so, it was *perfect*.

I let the heat seep into my bones, and a soft, warm touch pressed against my forehead.

I woke to warmth and a delicious, woodsy man smell. The heat I felt wasn't from my cover, though. And that familiar scent belonged to the man of the house. A man I shouldn't be touching. I stiffened, my eyes slowly opening to darkness. The source of my comfort was the man I was snuggled against. A large arm was draped over me. When I moved my face, I froze again. Great. I was pretty sure my nose had been in his armpit. He smelled so good.

Would it be weird to sniff him?

Yes, yes, it would.

I pulled away, and his arm tightened around me.

What happened? Did I fall asleep while he dried my hair? Oh, my God. I groaned as my heart raced.

Wait a minute!

He took me to his room *again,* and he was in bed with me. Why?

He could have put me on the couch, if he didn't want to carry me up the stairs. My heart couldn't handle that sort of proximity to Hudson. He was a lethal drug to my system, and I knew I'd become addicted. I had to be careful, or I could trust that he wasn't like the men I'd seen all my life.

I wanted to lock up his goodness and throw away the key, so that no one else could have it. But Hudson wasn't mine. *You swore off men, remember, Genie?* I couldn't recall beyond that sensation rocking through me. I feared becoming more attached. I knew I had to leave him one day. I couldn't play so dangerously with my feelings, especially when the emotions were about the person offering me a roof over my head.

God, I was so conflicted.

Hudson putting me in his bed only confused my heart and body more.

Pushing at his arm softly, I climbed out of his bed and tiptoed to my room. Hudson was my friend. He might be becoming my best one right along with Holly. When I left his home, I wanted to keep that ease between us. I wouldn't take advantage of Hudson like I saw so many family members do Gran either.

30

HUDSON

Eugene left my bed before my alarm went off, and somehow, I hadn't noticed. *Fuck.* Was I being too obvious about my intentions? Did I make her uncomfortable when I laid her on my bed? That was the last thing I wanted to do, but I couldn't resist putting her there when she fell asleep. She had fallen back onto my chest while I dried her hair. It was difficult to finish, but I tried to get it as dry as I could before carrying her to my room.

I hadn't let myself pull her close when I joined her on the bed. I had hoped I'd awaken with some part of her body draped over me, so being alone that morning was a bitter disappointment.

When she asked about her friend visiting, I made sure to take Saturday off, which shocked Randall and Daisy. Eugene had plans with Holly and Roger, and I included myself when I prepared breakfast. Eugene called them out about the previous night, and Holly chuckled, clearly pleased with herself.

Eugene didn't bring up what I had done, and the disappointment deepened. If she had asked why I put her in my bed, what would I have said anyway? I knew I wanted her. I'd been ensnared by her the second she started calling my dog Bear. Despite how hard I tried to tell myself she wasn't for me or my type, I knew the truth. Patience wasn't something I excelled at when it came to what I wanted. When I finally realized I'd rather own a restaurant than be miserable at my father's company, I put all my time and energy into making it happen.

My yearning for the woman currently getting her hair color touched up in my kitchen grew each day. I loved my restaurant, but fuck. Whenever she clocked out, I found it difficult to stay and finish my work. I was afraid I'd miss the opportunity to watch her read by the fireplace. For her to do so, I had to start the fire. That was how I justified leaving work early every day.

Then I wondered what she'd do when spring arrived. Would she want to read on the porch? Would I need to update my patio for her? Or would she prefer me to build her a reading nook in the cabin?

My world arrived in that ugly Kia last month. Every beat of my heart knew she was mine. *There is no point in denying a heart, because when it knows, it knows.* Mine had recognized hers as forever.

"Are you sure you'd rather not be at work?" Eugene's voice pulled me from my thoughts.

I hadn't really noticed her enter the main room until she spoke. She had a cap over her head as she stared down at my legs while I sat on the recliner. I hadn't noticed how furiously I tapped my left slipper on the floor until I followed her gaze.

I stopped bouncing my leg. "Are you trying to get rid of me, Red?"

Her cheeks reddened. "No. You just seem restless." She pointed to the leg, I continued to bounce.

I was fucking restless. Looking at her all day, every day, was maddening. It only made me want to claim her more. I couldn't help but stare. I'd rather die than not see her at that point.

I was losing my damned mind because of Eugene. She didn't seem to notice me at all, either. I put her in *my* bed. My fucking bed. Wasn't I being obvious about my feelings?

I told myself I wouldn't rush. I convinced myself I wasn't being creepy. But I was doing both for someone I deeply cared about. The last thing I wanted was to make her uncomfortable, like she couldn't be safe in my presence. I was losing control and didn't know how to behave anymore.

Dragging my hand over my face, I rose from the chair and stretched. "What's the plan for today?"

"Bowling, I suppose," Holly answered. "Roger and I want to head home by five, so we figured food and competition." Eugene groaned, slouching in her seat, which made Holly laugh. "Let's go wash out the dye so, we can get this show on the road!"

No wonder Eugene groaned. She was terrible at bowling. Every ball she rolled went straight into the gutter. "I'm just warming up," she said after we started the third match.

They decided on playing in teams. I had Eugene, of course, so I was losing. I didn't like losing, but it was okay. Seeing her brows pinch together and her tongue dart out as she tried her best made my heart slam against my ribcage.

But hope dwindled for Eugene. As another ball rolled into the gutter, her shoulders drooped. She returned to her seat with her head lowered.

I stood and picked up my ball. "You know, Red, you're impressive." When her eyes narrowed, I grinned. "I've never seen someone hit the gutter every single time. It must be a world record."

Holly nudged Roger's arm with a grin. "They can't beat us, babe."

Ignoring them, I rolled and hit a strike. I would never make enough of them to outdo their points combined. At that point, though, I was determined to help Eugene score *any* point. When it was her turn again, I stood. She paused as I came up beside her. "You're favoring your left. How about you aim for the right gutter this time?"

She huffed. "Look." She swung her arm forward while holding the ball. "My arm is completely straight. It should go down the middle."

"Yeah, but maybe your arm is swaying from the weight of the bowling ball?" I offered. "Before you let go, just move your arm a little to the right. It can't hurt."

Eugene nibbled on her bottom lip. "Show me?"

Show her? She wanted me to touch her. I'd let her hit me with the fucking ball for the opportunity. I nodded. Before we were close to where she needed to be, I placed one hand at her waist and the other at her wrist. She let me lead like that, and I hoped I didn't look as smug as I felt.

Eugene impressed me. She started hitting the right gutter after that. Since my coaching hadn't helped her score points, she denied me the chance to show her again. Just before we called it quits, she finally managed to knock down some bowling pins.

We cheered for her, and she waved her hands in the air.

"You guys can go ahead to the parking lot. I'm going to use the bathroom." Without waiting for a reply, Eugene headed toward the restrooms.

As soon as she was out of sight, Holly faced me with her arms crossed. "You like Genie."

"Of course, I like Eugene."

Holly's eyes widened as she studied me. "You don't deny it."

"Give me the chance to tell her in my own time. If you say anything, she might leave the cabin." *Leave me.*

"I won't say anything if you tell me what your intentions are with my best friend."

Roger, resting his hand on Holly's shoulder, said, "Babe, maybe you should leave this between them."

"No. Genie's been through a lot. I love Eddie, but even he does her wrong when he comes to Michael. So, I want to know why you're offering your home and time to my best friend."

"I want to help her," I said.

Holly smirked. "You want her?"

"Yes, I want her. I want to keep her in my life. She needs to be right where I can see her."

"You mean as more than a friend?"

"Fucking hell." I ran my hand through my hair. "*Yes.* I want her in my bed, but that's none of your business. I plan to thoroughly spoil Eugene. She's safe with me, mentally and physically."

"Okay, then. I'll hold you to that, but know I love her to death. If *you* hurt her, it won't be hard for me to ruin your restaurant's reputation."

Holly's threat gave me some peace of mind. Before Eugene landed on my doorstep, *someone* cared about her. I could tell her brother loved her, but he let too much shit slide when it came to Michael.

I smiled. "I'm glad we're on the same page."

31

HUDSON

Waiting sucked.

I was cooking at the restaurant. The quicker I prepared the order, the sooner I had an excuse to venture up front to where Eugene was.

It had been a few weeks since Holly and Roger stayed the night, and things were good with Eugene. She smiled a lot, which sent my heart into a frenzy. Nothing had changed between us, though. In fact, there might be some distance. Eugene still read downstairs and ate the food I cooked. We talked about work, Max, and food, but nothing to ease the distance. She hadn't been telling me anything personal lately.

I was a starving man.

Being near her wasn't enough. I wanted to peek inside her brain and discover all her secrets. Her smiles were slowly killing me. She was a sweetheart, giving that beautiful beam to everyone. I wanted her to give me something, *anything* to claim as mine. A secret beam with a wink or slipping her fingers between mine when no one was around. Even better, her being completely mine. How did I make her love me?

That's what I truly desired. For her to see how perfect we were together.

I sighed.

"You're going to scorch the milk!" Grandma yelled, knocking me out of my thoughts.

Glancing down at the pot, I saw the milk bubbling over and swore. After removing it from the burner, I stirred the milk, but it was ruined. "Fuck. It's got to be thrown out."

In my peripheral view, I saw Grandma put a hand on her hip. "What in tarnation are ya sighing about? You're wasting ingredients."

Daisy and Randall peeked across the kitchen, snickering until I scowled.

"I don't know what I'm doing wrong," I said low enough that only Grandma would hear as I dumped the milk in the sink.

"What do you mean ya don't know? Ya let it boil too long."

Ignoring her, I rubbed my neck and glared at the burnt milk at the bottom of the pot. "Maybe I'm not doing enough," I said. "She's not coming downstairs when her hair is wet again."

"Huh?" Grandma stepped closer. "I take it you're not talking about the milk."

I narrowed my eyes at her. "Aren't you supposed to be meddling? What happened to the whole I-need-a-wife-and-you-need-grand-kids thing?"

She quirked a brow. "Ya get mad when I say anything."

That was true, but only because I didn't want her bothering Eugene about me. The situation had changed. I was contemplating sending Grandma to speak to Eugene. Did Eugene like me at all? Maybe Grandma could convince her that I was a great fucking man. Shit. I had no shame. The clumsy creature in my home was melting away at my resolve to give her time. Our friendship was amazing, but I wanted more of her. My fingers itched in her presence. I wanted to touch her so damn badly all the time. It was hard to find excuses to get close to Eugene.

Fuck. I was a total creep for her. Maybe she wouldn't mind. Or maybe I should have admitted I might be in love with the beautiful woman in my home and didn't know how to act on it.

"I don't want you to try to hook me up with any woman that crosses my path," I admitted.

"I haven't tried lately," she fired back. "I've been too busy helping you find all these books for Eugene."

Grandma had no idea how much I appreciated her for helping with the search. Any time I found one of Eugene's old books, I'd let Grandma know so she could cross it off the list. She'd do the same when she found one, so we didn't end up getting the same book twice. "How many do we need before I'll have them all for her?"

"Just a few more."

Good.

I ran water into the pot, scratching my ear and shifting my boots. "...Do you still nag Eugene about me?"

Grandma laughed. "I might as well give up. She won't budge at all. I don't know how much more I can help when she refuses to claim ya as hers. No matter what I say or offer, she doesn't seem to want ya."

Sue cackled worse when I frowned.

"Oh, yeah. That's the reason I came into the kitchen. I forgot to tell you."

"What?"

"Poor Eugene. This handsome devil keeps coming in at least once a week and flirting with her. He tips well too. Where are you going?"

"Is he out there, now?" I asked over my shoulder as I stalked toward the door.

"Yes."

I rushed out of the kitchen. Eugene's laughter caught my attention, and I turned toward the sound. She was really out there treating everyone to her smile. Betrayal pumped through me. My blood felt like it was boiling as I took in the man, causing her to chuckle.

Fucking Jeremiah.

I went to school with the guy, and never had a problem with him in all the years I'd known him. Not until his wandering gaze roamed over *my* woman. Eugene noticed me walking toward them, and her laughter died down. We seriously lacked that around each other lately because of the god-awful tension between us.

My eyes swept over Eugene, landing on Jeremiah. I crossed my arms. "I haven't seen you around in a while, Jeremiah."

"Hudson," he said. "Good to see you. If I had known what you were hiding, I would have visited your restaurant much sooner." When his gaze locked on Eugene, my anger spiked.

Eugene backed away, and then hurried to another booth. I watched her work for a second before returning my attention to Jeramiah. "If you're coming here to see her, you're wasting your time."

"Oh?" His eyebrows shot up. "Is Genie seeing someone?"

He called her by her nickname. What the fuck!

"She lives with me," I informed him.

He placed his arms on the table. "You're dating one of your waitresses?"

I didn't want to lie, so I evaded the question. "Is there a problem?"

Eugene was my future wife. She just didn't know it yet. In that case, perhaps the fib would be okay.

"My bad," Jeremiah said. "No wonder she wasn't taking the hint. I've been here several times. I'm glad you told me. I was about to ask for her number before I left, fucker."

So, Eugene ignored his attempts at her affection as well. I didn't know whether to feel better or worse. I didn't want to compare myself to the dude who tipped her well, but it got me wondering, how did she perceive me? Just the guy who wanted to blow-dry her hair? The man who cooked her meals?

Wait!

Did those things make me seem like a weirdo? I only wanted to care for her. She didn't do it enough on her own. Fuck. I was beginning to overthink every little thing when it came to her. I *never* questioned myself.

"Don't do that," I warned him. "Don't make Eugene uncomfortable."

"Eugene?" His brows furrowed. "Is that Genie's name? Weird."

Randall popped his head out of the kitchen entrance in the back, probably searching for me. I rubbed my temples. "It was good seeing you." Not really. "I've got to get back to the kitchen."

"Thanks for letting me know I've been wasting my time," Jeremiah muttered as I turned.

I paused and said, "It's not a waste. I'm a damn good cook, you shit. Make sure to tip my waitress well." I put the emphasis on the word *my*. When his jaw tightened, I smirked.

A few minutes later, I finally had a pot of mashed potatoes ready when Eugene burst into the kitchen.

Her eyes locked with mine, and her cheeks puffed as she moved toward me.

"What did you do?" Grandma muttered in her chair behind me.

Eugene glanced at her before bringing her gaze back to me. "Can I speak to you alone for a minute?"

"Sure. My office," I told Eugene, then pointed at the new batch of potatoes. "One of you finish this up for me."

Eugene followed me into my office and shut the door behind her.

She placed her arms over her chest, which caused her breasts to push upward. Even with the new uniform shirt she wore, her shape couldn't be mistaken. "What did you say to table eight?" she asked.

I scratched my ear. "What do you mean?"

"You approached his booth and called him Jeremiah, so you know him. I also know you said or did something because he left before he even ordered more than a drink. The man always leaves a tip, and I didn't get one."

Good. Jeremiah understood me. "It's probably because he left before he ordered food."

"Why did he leave?"

"He had bad intentions for you."

She threw up her hands. "Most men don't have good intentions. Show me one with my best interest at heart, and I'd be—"

"Me. I have the best intentions when it comes to you."

I could love the shit out of her. The woman who showed me how much I could care about someone other than my own wants.

She lowered her hands, a blush taking over her cheeks as she averted her gaze.

I crossed my arms. "He knew your nickname."

She scoffed and pointed at her nametag. "Genie is on my nametag. Besides, I greet all my customers by introducing myself."

That made sense since he didn't know her name was Eugene. I still didn't like the idea of him flirting with her. "I don't like him, or any man, calling you that. Maybe we should remove your nametag altogether."

"What?"

I swept my gaze over her as I frowned. "Would ma'am work best for our customers? No. Actually, some young punk might enjoy saying that."

"Hudson!"

My eyes widened when I realized what I said. Holy shit. She was going to figure out I was planning our wedding if I didn't ease up. Still, I cleared my throat and went back to Jeremiah. "Jeremiah's not a bad guy, but he would have pushed for your number or something else."

She eyed me up and down. "And I could have told him no if he asked."

"You're right." I grinned, not ashamed in the least, about what I did. "But I didn't like the way he was looking at you when I saw him."

Her nose crinkled. "How was he looking at me?"

There was no way I was going to explain what I saw in that man's gaze. "Tell me when another man flirts with you because I don't want you uncomfortable."

"I know you try hard to be my knight in shining armor since I've moved in. Honestly, my life has been easier since I moved to Senkins. I'll never be able to thank you enough for offering me a home and a job, but I'm so glad you did. You can put away the cape, though, because nothing terrible has happened. I rarely deal with rude customers." She smiled, and that small reward had me feeling like I was on cloud nine.

When I saw my desk behind her, my thoughts spiraled. I could lift her up, spread her out, and yank those pants down. Show how good I could make her feel. Show her how well I could take care of her. Or *the wall...* I could pin her to it, shove my hand down her pants, and reward *her* for gifting me with one of her smiles. She held those hostages from me lately. My patience was splintering. I could be so good to Eugene, and I fucking would, but damn, I was ready to devour her. I swallowed down those thoughts and lost myself in those pretty brown eyes instead. I could behave a little longer.

"I'm always going to take care of you, Red," I said truthfully. I would take really good care of her when I finally got my hands on her.

Her smile waned as she looked at the floor. "I'm going to head back to the front."

Why did she seem so sad? My words were meant to reassure, but they seemed to do the opposite.

32

EUGENE

On my day off, I was surfing the Net when an unknown number called. My heart felt like it had dropped to my feet, thinking it might be the police finally calling me about Danny. They didn't believe me when I said I didn't know anything. I would pay for his wrongs instead of him.

Swallowing nervously, I answered. "Hello?"

"Genie?"

It was Sue. My shoulders sagged in relief as I smiled. "How did you get my number?"

"Hudson." There was another woman talking in the background. "Listen. We'll be there to pick you up in about an hour, so get dressed."

"We?"

"Hudson's mom, Kelly, and me are going to pick you up."

I frowned. "What for?"

"To shop for your dress."

"Why do I need a dress?"

"Our family company hosts a small Valentine's Day event for the single folk and couples. You know, so you can mingle and find partners if you don't have someone special."

"I don't want a partner, so I better not go," I uttered.

"Nonsense. The food is worth the trouble. Besides, when are you going to have another chance to dress like a princess?"

"I'm terrible in heels and not really the princess type."

Sue laughed. "Be ready, child."

The second she hung up; I dialed Hudson to tattle on his grandma. Although I didn't expect him to answer while working, he did. "Everything okay?"

"Your mom and Sue are on their way over!" My voice cracked near the end.

I could hear the hesitation and confusion in his voice when he asked, "What for?"

"Apparently you guys host a Valentine's Day event?" I questioned.

"Oh, yeah, we do. I forgot. I don't have anything to do with the family business now."

"Sue's making me buy a dress," I whined.

"Make sure to buy a nice one—maybe black or red. Stop by the restaurant and grab my card if you need it."

My cheeks heated. "I'm not a charity case, Hudson."

"I know, but this might be fun. We can go together."

My heart skipped a beat, and I swallowed nervously. Together? That sounded a lot better. "I swear... If I go to this stupid thing, you better stick with me and not leave me alone. My armpits are getting sweaty thinking about it. There won't be any dancing?"

He laughed. "Yes, people dance there, but you don't have to. Besides, I won't leave you, Red. I would never leave you to fend for yourself."

I huffed. Despite my jitters, I was oddly pleased. "I need to get ready."

"Have fun."

"Try this long-sleeve dress. Oh, and this blue strapless is gorgeous!" Kelly yelled before lifting two more dresses over the stall I was in. "Let us see that green one before you try on the next one."

I felt like I was in another dimension. Gran never took us shopping. I hadn't tried on clothes in dressing rooms until I was an adult shopping with Holly. Gran gave us whatever she could afford. Most of the time, our clothes were way too big so we could grow into them.

So, I felt weird every time Sue and Kelly gushed over a dress I tried on. I knew they meant well, but I felt like a three-headed lion on display at a circus. It was bad enough that they brought me to a freaking shop that looked like a bridal store. The price tags made me cringe. Just how fancy was the event? I assumed Hudson was fancy —I called him that, but I was beginning to see *why*. His family must be rich. The cars, the clothes, and everything they owned seemed so nice—like Hudson's belongings and his home.

I stepped out of the dressing room, so Kelly and Sue could see the green dress. The hideous gown hid what little curves I had, but they wanted to see the garment on me.

Sue flinched as soon as she saw me. "Oh, good Lord. That's dreadful."

"Grandma." Kelly laughed. "It's... something."

I smiled. "You're completely right, Sue. It's ugly, and *you* made me try it on. You knew it looked awful on the rack, too."

She tossed her hand up. "I thought it would look good with your wild hair, but instead ya kind of look like a watermelon."

"Oh, dear. She's right." Kelly placed her fingers on her chin. "Try on the blue one!"

I loved that Hudson's mom had only met me a couple hours ago and didn't mind telling me what to do either. It must run in the family since it killed her son to see me walk or keep my hair wet. I smiled and tried on the next dress.

I stepped out of the stall and spun around for them.

Sue shook her head. "No. Just no."

"Here. How about this one?" Kelly asked.

When I saw the simple black dress in her hand, I reached for it. "I'll try this one next."

It wasn't as simple as I thought, though. Once I put it on, I saw that there was no back piece. The strap wrapped around my neck, and the material was loose, plunging between my breasts. I kept my bra on for the try-on, but I'd have to go without one for a dress like that. I studied myself in the mirror. The gown hugged my hips nicely.

I stepped out and turned for them.

"Now, we're getting somewhere." Sue nodded. "It's almost like we want to seduce someone."

"Who are we seducing?" I asked. "Do you have another single grandson or someone?"

"I do. Hudson's brother, Finnick, will be there. You'll like him. He's funnier than his brother."

I mock gasped. "Just wait until I tell Hudson."

Sue smiled. "Tell Hudson what?"

My body heated as I realized what I had said. Tell Hudson what exactly? Why would he care if his grandma was trying to set me up with her other grandchild? Why did I have such an absurd thought?

"Hudson said we were going together," I said. "*Not* like that, so stop smiling. I'm just saying I can't abandon him like that. He already promised to stick with little awkward me at the event since you forced this upon me."

Kelly narrowed her eyes at Sue. "You said she wanted to attend."

Ignoring Kelly, Sue smirked. "Ya called Hudson as soon as we got off the phone."

"Well, yeah—"

"That's good, right, Kelly?" Sue glanced at her daughter-in-law. "I'm sure Hilary will be there. I bet they haven't spoken since they broke up."

"Hilary?" I asked.

Hudson had an ex that would be there. Suddenly, my stomach cramped.

"Grandma." Kelly crossed her arms. "Those two broke up on peaceful terms. Don't be starting stuff to get your way."

Sue shrugged. "I'm not doing anything."

"Hilary likely won't be there," said Kelly. "So, don't worry."

"Oh, that's none of my business," I said far too quickly, and then pointed to Sue. "Despite what this one says, I'm not dating Hudson." The words felt so awful leaving my mouth that I coughed, but it was the truth. "But... I do think he's my best friend, so I do want what's best for him."

"Oh." Kelly's eyebrows shot up to her hair line. She looked at Sue, who grinned, and then everything about those two got even more suspicious. "Well, if that's the case, maybe Hilary will see Hudson and want to rekindle things."

That was not what I meant. I gawked at Sue. How could she smile as Kelly said that? I thought Sue wanted *me* with her grandson. I'd gotten so used to her trying to set me up with Hudson every day that I felt betrayed. The woman was evil.

33

HUDSON

LIFE HAD BEEN TEACHING ME SOMETHING AS OF LATE. MY RESTAURANT could survive without me. Since Eugene arrived, I took at least once a week off and often left before closing some nights. Randall and Daisy ran the kitchen well without me. Not only them. The rest of my kitchen staff worked well.

I had no intention of slowing down so soon, but life happened. Eugene happened. I loved the idea of Homestyle branching out, and I saw the opportunities. I thought of Eugene's hopeful dreams too. I had the funds to make that book café a reality. The wheels were turning inside my head, and I tried to slow myself down.

I hadn't told her my feelings. Yet, I couldn't stop planning all that I wanted to do for her. My father wasn't home much growing up, but there was one thing I remembered when he was. He doted on Mom. A part of me thought he constantly praised her due to the guilt of being gone so much. That might have been part of it, but the fact was, he probably liked spoiling her.

It was like I saw my entire childhood differently, all because I couldn't stop wishing to do all those absurd things for Eugene. Was that love, like I believed? I cared so much that I felt like I might split in half. If it wasn't love, I didn't want to know what it was because I never wanted to escape the rush in my veins that came when someone spoke her name.

Max nudged my hand. I glanced down and petted him. The stairs creaked, and I quickly sat up as Eugene descended. She'd been upstairs when I got home, so I hadn't been able to ask her how dress shopping went. As soon as she told me about it, I called Mom and told her to behave. Mom had promised she would be nice, but she was laughing too much for me to feel assured.

A loud thump had me bolting out of my recliner.

"Mother trucker—" Eugene groaned.

Rushing over, I found her sprawled out on the floor in front of the stairs, holding her knee. I bent down beside her. "You, okay?" I asked.

"Yeah, but my knee seems to have taken the brunt of the fall."

I shook my head. "Here I thought you were finally learning to walk."

"Shut up." She held out her hand. "Help me up."

Her hand was soft, fitting perfectly into mine as I helped her.

She hissed as she stood, hopping. "Ow, ow, ow."

Worry tugged at my chest. "Do we need to make a trip to the ER?"

She shook her head, and that's when I noticed her hair was wet. "It's fine. I can bend it, but it's going to be sore."

I barely focused on what she was saying. *Her hair was wet.* She avoided me and stayed upstairs when she washed it because she knew I'd make her dry it. So, her being downstairs meant only one thing. She wanted me to dry it. I refused to believe anything else.

"What am I going to do with you?" I asked as I grasped a strand of her wet hair with my free hand.

Her lips parted. Slowly, she tugged the hair from my grip.

Smiling, I let go of Eugene's hand and scooped her up in my arms.

She squealed. "Hudson! What are you doing?"

She wrapped her arms around my neck. Ecstasy took hold of me, shooting through my limbs and stomach. Eugene didn't have a fucking bra on again. Even with the pajamas between us, I could feel her left boob smashed against my chest. I noticed she hadn't been wearing a bra around the cabin. It was killing me slowly, but it could very well be my undoing one of those nights. The simple thing she did finally made me crack and kiss the fuck out of her.

God. I could kiss her—I *should*. My arms shook, and I gripped her tighter.

With a ragged breath, I walked to the couch and sat her down. "You know what we're doing, right?"

She bit her lip, and I had to look away.

"But first, let me see your knee." Pushing up her polka dot pants leg, I rubbed my fingers over the bruise forming. "Can you bend it?"

Despite the bruise, her kneecap looked normal, but I still wanted to be sure. She nodded, bending her leg in and out for me. I sneakily ran my palm down her legs during the process, thankful for the opportunity to touch her skin. All I had to do was lean down, and I could make my way up her leg with a trail of kisses. I just fucking knew her skin would pebble for me.

She inhaled as I grabbed her heel and pulled her pants leg down. "I'm fine, Hudson."

"Be right back. I'm going to go get the blow-dryer," I said, knowing the distance was needed to let my thoughts cool.

I went to my bathroom, retrieved the blow-dryer, and came back to her sitting on the floor in our usual spot. Something about her *wanting* me to dry her hair was setting my body ablaze. So much for trying to calm down. My heart was beating out of control. One would think I'd never touched a girl based on how excited I was because the flaming-haired woman living with me was letting me dry her hair.

As soon as I sat behind her, I had to adjust my cock in my pajama pants. She smelled like fucking strawberries again. She scooted back, and I closed my eyes, savoring how close she was. Did she not know what she was doing to me? She seemed to trust me so blindly that I should be ashamed of the hard-on I had.

"How did the dress shopping go?" I asked, trying to steer my thoughts to something safer.

"I found a dress," she answered. "Your mom was sweet."

"I hear a but in there."

She tensed. "I believe your mom and your grandma are up to something with this Valentine's Day event. Don't be surprised if they try to hook you up with someone—maybe even a past someone."

When her shoulders drooped, I asked, "Past someone?"

"I don't know," she whispered.

What did she mean? Grandma knew my intentions with Eugene, so she wouldn't try to set me up with other women. But Grandma would try to rattle the one in front of me by bringing up others, which seemed to be the case.

I smiled. "Well, I've got a date to the event, and she's already claimed all my time there, saying I must stick by her side. Grandma will have to stick her business elsewhere when it comes to me."

Eugene looked back, beaming at me as if my words made her happy. "I try to tell her to leave you be, but she's so determined that you give her more grandbabies."

"Grandma will be fine. Don't you worry."

Hitting the power button on the dryer, I catered to my woman, who didn't know she was mine yet.

I stopped in my tracks as I walked by Eugene's car the following morning. Was that a spare tire she was using? I couldn't believe I hadn't noticed sooner. It was a little after six. None of the stores in town were open yet to buy a new tire. I'd have to take a long lunch and get it changed for her.

Since Eugene entered my life, the world became so fucking

strange. It bothered me to see her using a spare. I knew she could afford it, but she likely didn't bother. Didn't she realize she lived with me? Why wouldn't she use me? I wanted to be *her* person.

Eugene had me wrapped around her fingers and didn't know it.

I ran my fingers through my hair and glared at the cabin where Eugene slept. That woman... Knowing her, she likely forgot or didn't care.

Staring at a tire, I decided I was done tiptoeing around her. Valentine's Day was two weeks away. There was plenty of time for me to ease into something more with her. An extra touch, or my lips grazing her neck... A kiss. One of those hugs she liked to give me when I did something for her, but I'd slide my hand down her back.

Fuck. I had to get to work before I needed a cold shower.

34

EUGENE

Homestyle was jam-packed the following evening. My legs were killing me from the constant running back and forth. Although the boss man hadn't worked that day, I couldn't wait to tell him how bad my feet hurt. I wondered what he would do or say after I complained.

I smiled as I parked my car in the driveway. Max was on the porch and ran to greet me. His fur was chilled when I petted his head. "How long have you been out here? Come on. Let's go in."

He hiked his leg up and peed on my tire. When I saw the tire, I remembered I was still using my spare. I shouldn't have forgotten about that. How did the smaller tire hold up so long?

Walking around the vehicle, I expected to see the spare, only to find it had been replaced. When I popped open my trunk, the spare was inside.

I looked toward the cabin. Hudson must have noticed the tire and taken care of it. He was the only one with access to my vehicle. I was never going to be able to repay the man for everything he'd done for me. My shoulders slumped. I was tired of being the charity case, but I didn't think I'd ever be on equal footing with Hudson. Compared to him, I was clumsy and forgetful. My sore, bruised knee was proof of that.

I still had a limp when I walked, but the pain was much better.

Max followed me inside. When I entered, a loud banging sound caught me off guard. Was Hudson using a hammer or some other equipment? The constant thuds made me believe so. Max barked and ran up the stairs in the direction of the noise.

Curious, I followed the dog. When I got to the room beside mine, the door was open, and the banging intensified. My jaw dropped when I spotted Hudson drilling a large wooden board into the wall without a shirt. My body heated. I'd never seen the man without a shirt. There was so much muscle to stare at. Oh, *oh*. How was someone so masculine yet absolutely beautiful? My tongue darted out as my gaze trailed over the sparse hair on his chest. I pictured running my hands over his dark nipples and placing a kiss on his neck. My thought was so inappropriate that I looked away and breathed deeply. I lasted a few seconds before staring again.

Shit, shit. I was so attracted to Hudson. *Please, Genie, don't make it awkward.*

He turned and did a double take when he saw me in the hall. His eyes darkened as they roved over me.

"What are you doing?" My voice sounded hoarse to me.

The room used to have a bed, nightstand, and dresser. At that moment, only boards of wood filled the space.

"I decided this room would make a good little library." He placed the drill on the floor, then stood up, hooking his thumb in his pants.

My breath quickened.

"What do you think?" He must be talking about the room, but I couldn't look away from that thumb and the way it pulled at his jeans, revealing more flesh.

Clearing my throat, I glanced around the room and saw the shelves he was attaching to the walls. Having a room dedicated to nothing but books was a booklover's dream. Smiling, I asked, "So, you're turning all the walls into bookshelves?"

"In the future, if you ever need more room, more bookshelves could be installed in the center." He laughed, but something about it was husky and thrilling. "I think it will take a while for you to fill these shelves, though, but it will be all yours."

As I processed his words, my heart stopped. He included me again. My throat burned, my eyes tingled, and my chest felt like it was swollen. I walked away before my emotions got out of control.

Stepping into my room, I quickly undressed and slipped on the black pair of pajama shorts and spaghetti strap shirt. There was a knock on my door a second before Hudson opened it.

Thankfully, I had just finished tugging on the shirt. "Did you get an eyeful barging in like that?"

"What's wrong?" he asked. Hudson looked around and then inhaled sharply. "Damn. It smells like you in here."

"What?" Did I have a weird body odor?

"You smell like strawberries."

"Oh." I sighed in relief. "I use strawberry-scented lotion."

He stepped in, shutting the door behind him. "What's wrong, Red?" he asked again.

"Nothing," I blurted. "Why would anything be wrong?"

Hudson took one step, then stopped. "You looked like you saw something you liked at first. Your eyes were glassy, and your lips were parted. And you were looking at *me*." His voice deepened as he told me.

Holy shit. He was actually calling me out.

"Then the heat faded from your gaze, and you got this sadness in your eyes the second you walked away," he finished.

Hudson in my room made me flustered. The fact that he was pointing out my reactions to me made it worse. Fuck. It was taking all my focus not to fidget, but I couldn't help rubbing my hands down my bare thighs. I couldn't take another second in that room with him. The hot pulse sparking through my veins would give me away. There was no hiding it. Not when he said he was making me a library. No, I believed he already knew what I felt for him from my gaze.

"I didn't look sad," I lied as I hurried toward the door. That was a mistake.

He blocked me. "Where are you going, beautiful?"

My heart raced as I met his gaze. It was like a fire was lit within his eyes as he placed his palm at my back, letting his fingers tease my skin at the bottom of my spaghetti strap. The same desire trapped inside me might be leaking out of Hudson, too. Did I dare hope? Or was I too afraid to act on what I felt?

"Beautiful?" I whispered.

"Yes, you are," he murmured before dipping his head near my neck, placing a single kiss there. "Put your hands around my neck. I'm taking us to bed."

My clit thrummed like it had its own heartbeat. I did as he said, inhaling his woodsy scent as I buried my face against his shoulder.

Gently, Hudson lifted my ass, and I hooked my legs around his waist.

I was quiet as he carried me to the bed and sat down with me on his lap. Caressing my thighs, he parted them slowly, allowing me to adjust to the snug fit around his waist.

"Now tell me," he said. "What's wrong? Why did you have that look when you walked away?"

My face burned as tingles spread through me. His bare chest was so warm. I didn't want to let go, but it felt inappropriate to keep straddling him. I pulled away from his shoulder. When I lifted my hips, Hudson guided them back down. My pussy clenched as I felt his thick thighs beneath me. I covered my face when I started to tremble. The desire dipped between my thighs, and I was helpless against it. I was ready to crash into Hudson and consume him, but I still tried to hold myself back. All the adoration and attraction I had for my roommate was pouring out. I never meant for him to see how easily I'd crumble if he held me in his arms.

"Red." His raspy voice had my pussy clenching on nothing.

"It made me feel weird." I whispered. His presence overwhelmed me. All those moments of trying to behave, trying to see him as nothing more than a friend, went up in smoke. I unraveled as he rubbed soothing circles up and down my arms.

"What did?"

"Your words."

He grabbed my hands, pulling them away from my face, so I looked down, still too embarrassed to face him.

"A bad weird... Or a good one?" he murmured.

"A sad one," I admitted. That gloom crept in, and the tears escaped. I tried to wipe my face, but he caught my wrists.

"Why are you sad, baby? I thought you would be happy about the room."

My skin tingled as I inhaled. *First beautiful, then baby?*

"Everything is temporary," I mumbled, lifting my hips again. "I won't always be here..."

My words died out when Hudson urged me back down onto his lap. An undeniable hardness pressed against my ass. Hudson was erect. My nipples pebbled. The tension inside me kept mounting. Soon, I'd combust.

Hudson grabbed my chin, lifting my gaze to his. "Nothing about this is temporary. Nothing that's been building between us has been so simple."

I trembled, waiting for what he'd do or say next.

His eyes were glassy and full of what might be longing. I must be imagining what I hoped to see.

"Hudson," I said breathlessly.

He traced my bottom lip with his thumb. "Just a peck."

I held my breath as he leaned in. His lips brushed across mine. I trembled as he pulled back to meet my gaze again, as if to make sure what we were doing was okay. My heart fluttered as I saw the desire pooling in his appraising stare.

"Just a kiss," he said before placing his mouth against mine.

My lips parted as I exhaled. I was so turned on that I could hardly breathe.

He pulled away just enough to say, "Mm. Now just some tongue..."

Then he pressed his way into my mouth, swiping his tongue against mine. Ecstasy danced across my skin as I tasted him. I wrapped my arms around his neck, pulling him closer.

He groaned, and his hands tangled in my hair. Every time my arm grazed his bare chest, I wanted to rub myself against his tented pants, but I didn't. Despite him so thoroughly kissing me, I felt timid. I didn't know how to fully plunge into intimacy with him, although I desperately wanted to.

He broke the kiss and pressed his forehead against mine, panting. "I'm sweaty, baby. I've been working in that room for a while."

Did he say that because he was worried that I was bothered by it?

"I don't care," I said in case he needed to know, kissing him once before pulling away. I waited for him to make the move again.

He groaned, and the sound was full of desperation. "Then... just a peek."

Desire had my stomach fluttering as he hooked his finger beneath my shirt strap. He glanced at my face. "Are you going to let me see you, baby?"

He kept calling me that. It was making my heart beat out of control.

"*Yes,*" I whimpered, dropping my arms to my sides and surrendering to him.

Returning his attention to my shirt, he tugged the straps down. The material grazed over my hardened nipples. Goose bumps rose on my flesh. He drank me in with his gaze, letting his knuckle graze the side of my tit.

"You know how badly I've wanted to touch you?" he asked in a raspy voice.

Was that actually happening? *How* did that happen? Hudson's hands were on me, his eyes on my breasts, and I felt like I was floating in clouds of ecstasy.

"Just a taste." Hudson dipped forward, covering my nipple with his mouth.

"Ah!" My clit throbbed as a deep ache settled in my stomach.

The cool air kissed my breast when he removed his lips, only to flick his tongue against the sensitive nub. My pussy clenched, and I rocked against him, gripping his hair as his tongue swept over my other nipple.

A delicious thrill raced through my veins.

He cupped my heavy breasts, fondling them as his teeth nipped at my neck. When he pinched a nipple, I cried out and arched into him.

"Look at you," Hudson murmured as he kissed the spot below my ear. "You're so fucking beautiful, skin flushed, sitting on my lap. I bet you'd look just as good sitting on my face, riding out your release. I bet you'd love to take pleasure from me because I will fucking worship this body." He pressed our foreheads together as I rocked into him. "You know I will. I can take care of you, baby. Take care of you *so* well. It's what I'm here for. What I've been waiting to do."

Oh, fuck. His words shocked me in a delicious way. I was so turned on that my panties were damp. He kept talking to me, keeping me in the moment with him instead of letting me get too deep into my head. I loved it so much. No one had ever taken the time to speak to me during sex.

"You do t-take care of me." My words were shaky and unsure, but I desperately wanted to reach him. I didn't know how to properly express how good he made me feel. I felt like I might scatter into dust if he didn't finish what he started. I might die if I didn't get more of him. "Need more, Eugene." Hudson's hands slid down my back, gripping my ass through my shorts. "Just another taste—a different one."

My eyes rolled back as his words stirred all the pent-up desire that I'd kept dormant for him the last two months.

"Need these shorts off." He helped me to my feet, grabbing my waist quickly when I swayed.

The man had me a trembling mess.

"What am I going to do with you?" He made a tsking sound. "Can't even stand."

"*Hudson...*"

It wasn't my fault that I was a mess that time. He was to blame.

I got a little nervous when he tugged at my shorts. He pushed the material down my legs, and his mouth parted. As soon as I moved my thighs, I could feel how wet I was. Hudson didn't take his eyes off me, which made my skin heat. I squirmed slightly before climbing into his lap again, so he couldn't look anymore.

Hudson laid back, pulling me along with him. My breasts smashed against his chest. I whimpered as my nipples rubbed against his hard muscles. The sensation was incredible, but when he placed his palms on my ass, I moaned as pleasure shot through me.

He pushed my ass forward. "Come on, baby. You know where I want you."

I blushed as embarrassment set in. "I can't..."

"Why not?"

I buried my face against his neck. "I've been working all day. I need to shower."

Hooking his arms beneath my armpits, he pulled me upward a little, pressing his lips against my neck and breathing heavily. "You smell fucking good to me. I need to taste you." His fingers delved between my ass cheeks, briefly rubbing my opening once.

Lifting my head, I watched him bring that hand to his lips, tasting me.

"Hudson, fuck," I whimpered. My pussy clenched as his gaze burned into mine, searing me with its intensity.

He brought his hand right back to my ass, sliding his fingers into the slickness between my legs. "This pussy is going to be so good for me. So, get up here and let me make you come on my tongue."

Oh, shit. My core throbbed as my stomach fluttered. I'd never been so turned on in my life.

My thighs were shaking as he nudged me up his body until my opening was right over his face. The man didn't waste time. He urged me down. When his mouth covered my clit and sucked, it was like being doused in bliss. I would have shot off the bed if he hadn't been holding my waist. He flicked his tongue over my swollen flesh, then made swirling motions. His breath fanned my sensitive skin and my stomach fluttered. He probed my entrance with his tongue then sucked my clit again.

"Ah! Hudson, please." I panted.

An inferno had taken root inside me, claiming me from tip to toe. I gave into the urges and wiggled myself over Hudson's face.

He groaned and swirled his tongue. Fireworks burst through me. I came alive from his touch. I worked myself on his face, letting the magic spread into my lower stomach. The pleasure was building, building, and all I wanted to do was come on his face. My stomach tensed and fluttered as I got closer.

When he sucked my oversensitive bud again, I exploded. My thighs quaked against his ears as I tried pulling away from the intensity of the release, but Hudson gripped my hip with his arms, locking me in place.

"Please, Hudson. Oh shit—I'm still coming." My words slurred as I twitched. "I can't handle it anymore."

My body tingled. Every time he flicked his tongue over my clit, I saw stars. I was so sensitive.

When I tried to get away that time, he let me. I crawled down his body before collapsing on his chest. I'd never orgasmed like that. I felt so thoroughly spent, and he hadn't fucked me yet.

I panted, my eyes opening as I breathed in his sweaty chest. *He hadn't fucked me yet*, I thought again.

One of his arms caged me in. When I heard the clanking of his belt, then the zipper, heat bloomed inside me. He was going to take it further. I lifted my head to meet the fire in his eyes. "Just the tip?" I guessed.

He smirked. "No, baby, you're going to take the whole damn thing."

I couldn't help but blurt out, "I was going by what you've been doing. Just a peek, just—"

"I know what you were doing," he assured me as he grabbed my hips and raised my ass in the air. I lifted my upper half off his chest to look between us. His cock slapped against his stomach, and I moaned, wiggling my ass in the air instinctively. I'd no doubt be sore after taking him, but I didn't care. His grip on my hips tightened. "You're killing me."

My cheeks burned as I watched him fist his cock between us. Anticipation built, and I started to shake as I lowered myself. Palming one ass cheek, he urged me down and teased my entrance with the head of his cock. I panted as I waited.

"Look at me," he ordered.

So, I did. I got sucked into the intimacy of his stare as he pushed into me. Pleasure bloomed. Hudson was inside me, stretching me as he went deeper. My pussy began to clench as another orgasm built.

"Fuck!" Hudson groaned. His cheeks flushed, and his eyes were still on mine. All too quickly, he jerked me off his dick and cum spurted on his stomach. I swallowed heavily as he grabbed his erection and gave a few heavy pumps to finish himself. "I'm sorry. I didn't ask about a condom and didn't want to do something you were uncomfortable with."

Oh, shit. I never forgot to use a condom. Another rush of desire hit me. Hudson had been bare inside me for a few seconds. I had refused that level of trust with anyone before, which pissed a lot of my old boyfriends off. But I had also never been so turned on in my life that I didn't even think of protection.

Shame crept in. Still on top of him, I rose to my knees. "I'm so sorry, Hudson. I'm never this careless. I've never—"

He rubbed my arm. "Don't apologize."

"But you apologized."

"Yes, but only because I don't want to do anything to make you uncomfortable. I, on the other hand, will take whatever I can get from you. I'm fucking starved, Red."

Tingles spread all over my body.

Even so, the reality of what I'd done with Hudson was creeping into my thoughts. Fear slithered in, and I climbed off him. "I'll let you clean up," I said as I ran to the bathroom.

That encounter with Hudson only proved how painfully attracted I was to him. My body was still humming. I'd never been so *present* during sex. Hudson made it impossible to slip into my head. Which it wasn't really sex yet, the man had only eased inside me before pulling right back out.

Shutting the door, I rubbed my face and took a deep breath. I was scared that we had just screwed up. I really, truly liked Hudson. What if we ruined the friendship? Was it ever friendship? It had been so easy to get attached. Nothing lasted. I always knew one day I had to leave him, but...

Everything was fine. *It's fine.*

It was like someone wedged a knife in my chest, though. It didn't feel fine. When I thought of losing my friendship with Hudson, I felt like I was losing home.

I heard the thud of boots approaching. I began to tremble as need took root deep inside me again.

35

HUDSON

Just the fucking tip. Eugene cursed me when she said that. She had me so out of my mind. No wonder I didn't last—I knew I wouldn't because I had been so turned on after eating her pussy. If I had known I would have lost control, I would have jacked off before she came home from work.

I should let her retreat. Out of nowhere, I pushed us into something more, but I was so tired of behaving. Tired of seeing her look dejected about something when the bookshelves should have made her happy. When she saw the room and what I was making for her, I figured she would understand my intentions. Instead, she said, *"Everything is temporary."* She didn't get it. I would try my hardest to make her see that her home was with *me*.

When I put her on my lap, that was the smartest thing I'd done. Before the sadness dimmed the heat in her gaze, I caught her checking me out. The *chance* of her wanting more from me was all I needed.

I wiped my stomach with Eugene's shirt. Tucking my aching

cock in my boxers, I left my pants unzipped as I walked to the bathroom. I tried the doorknob. She left it unlocked, so I opened it without knocking. She stood, completely naked, in front of the mirror. My heart recognized her. The organ went into a frenzy any time she came near me. I wanted her to be mine.

With her wild hair and her reddened cheeks, I swore I'd never seen a more beautiful sight.

"You said the fucking tip, and you got it," I said with a smile. "Does that make you happy?"

Her mouth twitched, but she said nothing as she averted her gaze.

"Come here." I held out my hand. "We're not finished. I can make you feel even better, baby. I can show you I can last longer than that. Eating that delicious pussy of yours had me about to blow my load before we began."

As soon as she stepped toward me, I picked her up. She wrapped her legs around my waist. Her hot pussy pressed against my stomach as I carried her downstairs. Max stepped in my way, and I told him to go lay down. I kicked my bedroom door shut and placed her on the bed. Her gorgeous tits jiggled as she sat up. I took off my pants. Eugene's gaze dropped to my bobbing cock. I loved that her eyes stayed on me as I walked to the dresser and pulled out a condom.

"Yes or no?" I asked, knowing I didn't want a barrier between her and me, but I wanted her to trust that I would look out for her.

She hesitated, looking between her legs, and closing them. "I'm on birth control. But if you'd rather—"

I dropped the condom back in the dresser and closed it shut.

Heat engulfed me as I moved over her on the bed. She leaned back, and her red hair tumbled over my black sheets. Dipping my head toward her tits, I covered a nipple with my mouth, letting my teeth graze her slightly. She moaned.

Raising my head, I stared down at her. "You know what you look like?"

"What?"

"Mine." I kissed up her neck until I reached her lips, then I devoured her, delving my tongue into her mouth. She wrapped her hands around my neck. My arms shook with the restless need to be inside her. Parting her knees more, I slipped between her legs until my cock nudged her entrance. She squirmed, and I continued to kiss her, wanting her to feel my desire as I thrust into her. Fuck. Her pussy clamped around me, and my skin heated as pleasure surged through my stomach.

She felt exquisite.

She moaned into my lips, and I breathed it in, needing everything I could get from her. She put her legs around me.

Once I was completely inside her, I remained still for a moment, letting myself feel Eugene's pussy wrapped around me before I pulled out halfway, then thrust back in. I continued fucking her, moving at different angles until I found the spot that made her breath hitch.

"Hudson," she whimpered, and I sucked along her neck.

"That spot?" I asked, pressing against that place halfway inside her.

Fuck. Pleasure zinged down my spine.

"*Yes!*" she shouted. "Please."

She kept squeezing around me, and it was driving me fucking mad. My ball sack tightened. I wanted to ram into her, but I wanted to savor her so much more. But the desperation to get her to under-stand she was mine was slowly eating me alive.

I kept plunging into her, sliding against her G-spot, until she shattered beneath me. Her pussy reverberated around me, and I let out a ragged breath as she came. "I already knew it, but I need you to know, too." My arms shook as intense pleasure shot down my spine, rushing to my cock. "You're made for me, baby." *Thrust.* "Look at me."

She opened her eyes. "Jesus," she whimpered.

"Fuck, you feel good," I rasped as I increased my pace, slamming into her hard enough that her tits jiggled against my chest. "I want you to come again."

I placed my hand underneath her ass, squeezing her heated flesh, and groaned. I thrust all the way in and held myself inside of her for a few seconds, wanting her to feel me fucking deep. *Fucking home.* She was my home. Her body was my sanctuary. One I'd planned to worship.

"I think I can," she yelled. "For you I can—fuck, Hudson, I'm..."

I stroked her deeper, loving the way Eugene's legs twitched and her stomach quivered. The pressure at the tip of my cock kept building. Her sweet pussy gripped me like a vice. My breath quickened. Eugene kept eye contact, which made the moment more intimate, and I fucking ate that up. The second she came undone, I buried myself to the hilt and joined her.

Panting, she lowered her arms to the bed. I stayed there, watching her for probably too long, but I couldn't help it. I wanted to memorize how she looked after being thoroughly fucked.

"Do you realize how gorgeous you look beneath me right now?" I asked. "I could fucking eat you up."

Opening her lids, she smiled. "You already have."

"Mm..." I leaned forward and kissed her cheek. "You know what kind of appetite I have." She laughed and pushed at my shoulder. I eased out of her slowly, but she still winced, causing me to frown. "Are you okay?"

"Yes. It's just been a while." Tucking hair behind her ears, she said, "I'm going to go clean up."

When she started to leave my room, I pointed toward the bathroom. "I have a bigger, *nicer* bathroom down here," I told her.

"I'm going to go use mine," she said, and then slipped out of the room.

My smile waned. I rubbed my forehead as I groaned. "Fuck." Did I push her too soon? Maybe I revealed too much. No. She fell apart for me every time I touched her. Eugene was attracted to me as much as I was to her. It was okay for her to use the bathroom upstairs. It was the one she always used, but she called it *hers*. I feared she was establishing boundaries, which was going to be hard for me.

I wanted her in my bed, underneath my blankets. The reality wasn't so simple, though. Even if we were dating, I wouldn't have her in my bed every night so soon. Just because she lived with me didn't mean I could start keeping her in my bed. Clearly, she never stayed every time I put her in it.

I could be patient with her. No one could be better for her. Worry tugged at my chest. I didn't want to lose Eugene.

Max walked to the entrance of my room, stopped, and cocked his head at me. I pointed at him. "I'm doing my part. You're not even trying lately. Be cuter or something."

He turned right back around and left.

36

EUGENE

"You look super cute today," Georgianna said, picking up a red strand of my hair and smiling. "You added more makeup. It makes your dark eyes pop."

Eyes widening, I pulled the hair from her hold. Shit. Did I put on too much? If Georgianna took notice, everyone would, including Hudson.

"I only added a touch more."

The words rushed out like I tried to explain myself. A woman didn't need to justify applying more makeup to her appearance. I was allowed, and it had nothing to do with what went on upstairs and downstairs in the cabin the night before.

My clit pulsated just thinking about it.

After speaking a few words with Georgianna, I checked on my tables and helped Rebecca clean one of her booths. Busy, busy, busy. I tried to be anyway, but Hudson carried out my orders for me, so I had one less thing to do. That was my job, but he *always* did it. I couldn't pretend his attention didn't make me happy. There was no ignoring the not-so-little thing it did to my heart. How tight my chest clamped up because all those feel-good emotions were smacking into me, forcing me to pay attention.

I really liked Hudson. Maybe more than like. We weren't on an even playing field, though. What I lacked; Hudson likely had his whole life. Vehicles, a home, and the ability to reach his dream had come so easily for him. Meanwhile, I smooched off the man who was becoming the most important person in my life. That scared me. I was nobody, and I didn't like how much I depended on him. The idea that I might be exactly like the so-called family who took advantage of Gran growing up made me sick.

No part of me wanted him to see me as less than.

How could I be more? Maybe I should have finished college after all. I had gone to a community college for a year but had quickly dropped out. A business degree would have been nice when I opened my book café—*if* I ever did. In the middle of rural Kentucky, who would want to visit my bookstore? What were my odds of doing well?

It's fine. Everything's fine.

I had plenty of ideas to make the store interesting. Women were busy creatures. We didn't have time for much, but I could offer a haven for women to host book clubs. Start my own club. Maybe see about adding a gaming section or computers for teens. If I could create a steady flow of traffic into my place, I would have a better chance of succeeding. The idea of getting people to see the beauty in reading was exciting. But all of it was intimidating.

The other night, I finally looked and found a small apartment complex with rooms available, but I hadn't put in an application. I didn't want to leave Hudson's. But I had to, didn't I? Hudson took care of me. It was more like he babied me, and that terrified me. I liked the way he made me feel just by being in the room with me. He never once made me feel less than, even when he complained about my clumsiness.

All the fear and doubt were my past clinging to me. *Don't be a bother to Hudson. Don't use him like Gran was used.* It wasn't only that. The idea of him changing scared me. What if his sweetness was pretend and he got upset, like Jared, over one dirty dish in the sink?

Stop, Eugene!

My heart believed Hudson was different. He never expected anything from me. Every smile, laugh, and conversation, even with his sighs thrown in, were beautiful. But my brain still ran the past in a loop in my head.

Placing two Coca-Colas on a table, I turned and locked eyes with Hudson, who was carrying plates. He paused, his gaze devouring me head to toe, and then he smiled the sweetest of smiles. My cheeks heated, and my heart snagged in my chest. It was like all the negative thoughts ceased in that moment.

Hudson Henderson was one of the good guys. I needed to stop projecting my past onto the man heading my way. That didn't mean what happened between us meant anything to him. Maybe he comforted every upset woman with his penis. The thought spiked anger inside me, and I swallowed it down. He never brought anyone home. I never saw him with anyone at the restaurant. He was always with me when he wasn't working. Why did we have sex? I didn't know intimacy could be that good. Of course, I knew it was good for a lot of people, just not much for me.

What did Hudson think of me? What did I want him to think? Did he think I was dirty for letting him come inside me? I was a careful person when it came to my body, but... If he tried touching me again, I'd let him spill inside me again. My nipples pebbled, and I looked away, trying to control my wanton thoughts.

The truth was crystal clear. I knew what I felt for the man I lived with. It was the reason I was sad when I saw the bookshelves he was building. I wasn't going to be in his life forever, and that caused me a great deal of heartache. I believed I might be in love with Hudson. My feelings kept growing, and I was scared I was doing a terrible job of keeping my feelings to myself.

When he approached me, I lifted my chin. "Is that for one of my tables?" I asked when I knew he only brought out my orders.

"Table ten," he answered. "Two steaks and baked potatoes."

"Thank you." My words were soft and rushed all at once. "I'll take it to them."

His throat bobbed as he swallowed. "You did your eyes different," he said. "Looks good. I like it."

My skin tingled as I looked at his chest as I took the plates. I couldn't meet his eyes because he had already complimented me three times since morning.

The makeup was so freaking obvious. How embarrassing!

"Thank you." My words came out chirpy as I hurried away.

I caught Georgianna's gaze, and there was a huge smile plastered on her face. As I tended to a few of my tables, she bumped hips with me.

"I knew it!"

"Knew what?" I asked.

"Hudson is crazy about you." She laughed. "The man has been waiting on *you* hand and foot since you started working here two months ago."

My stomach clenched. "It's not like that."

She stopped smiling, then shook her head as if I had disappointed her. "Hey now. There's nothing wrong with seeing him if you are. The man is stunning, but too much of an ass. Well, to me, anyway. I see that you get the princess treatment. I'd eat that shit up if I were you. If the man had given me any of the looks he gives you, I would have folded right away." She nudged my shoulder. "You lucky bitch."

"It's not like that," I said again.

All I needed was for the workers to start gossiping about us. If Hudson believed I was telling everyone we were a thing, he'd be furious.

37

EUGENE

I brushed through my wet hair on my bed. Knowing Hudson worked until closing, I went ahead and washed it. A part of me, the biggest part, wanted him to touch me in some way. I didn't know how I was supposed to act, though. Did I pretend everything was the same? Would Hudson?

I had to leave. Being comfortable was dangerous. I'd rather walk out before those feelings got any bigger. But I didn't want to. I wished my brain would shut up.

The second Hudson touched me, it marked my doom. From the briefest of skin contact, I melted. No matter what I said about being done with men. None of it mattered when I encountered Hudson.

Shit. It was already too late. I truly loved him.

My shoulders drooped. I missed him and couldn't wait for him to be home. My confused thoughts didn't matter much. No matter how much I fussed at myself, or how scared I got, I didn't think it was going to make a difference in the end.

I couldn't leave him unless he made me.

God. That made me insane.

Even if he wasn't home, I should take care of my hair. He would be happy if I told him. Jumping off the bed, I hurried to his bedroom, thinking the dryer might be in the bathroom. As soon as I entered his room, I froze, my heart racing as steam poured out of the bathroom.

Hudson was home. Why? It wasn't even six o'clock yet! He must have returned while I was in the shower. Embarrassment seeped through my pores as I tiptoed backward. As soon as I turned, Hudson's deep voice called out, "Eugene?"

"I didn't know you were home yet." My voice came out squeaky as I faced the bathroom again. "I was going to grab the blow-dryer."

Hudson stood at the entrance of the bathroom, dressed in his pajamas, and with a wet head. My heart still warmed. I loved how easily he could come home and make himself comfortable. I found his habits endearing.

His gaze flickered over my hair before settling on my face. "Get on the bed. I'll take care of you."

My pussy clenched. I knew what he was talking about. My hair, right? But fuck, my body was scalding hot. My clit steadily throbbed as I slipped onto his bed and folded my legs beneath my butt, waiting for him to come back from the bathroom.

He returned with the blow-dryer, and disappointment crept over me. I already knew he wanted to dry my hair. But I was *aching* from the idea of getting something more from the man. Leaning over the nightstand, he plugged the cord into the wall before settling in behind me. He was radiating heat like a furnace behind me, and all I wanted to do was mold myself into him. Instead, I sat ramrod straight.

I tensed when his palm touched my waist. I moved my head slightly and watched the way his fingers flexed over the blow-dryer. It was like the breath got trapped in my lungs as I waited. He lifted his arm, then lowered it like he was stalling. He repeated the motion once more before his grip on my waist tightened, and he finally put the blow-dryer on the bed. Since he was behind me, I had no clue what expression he had.

My breath quickened. Hudson moved his hand upward, and my nipples pebbled before he cupped a breast. He squeezed, molding me in his hold, and groaned, setting off an explosion of desire inside me. "I like that you don't wear a bra around the house. Even if it kills me to see you prance around the house with your nipples hardening beneath your shirt."

I caressed my other breast like he was doing. His touch was better, but I was needy and wanted him to see what I was doing to myself. As soon as he noticed, he placed his other hand up my shirt, tugging at my wrist until I moved my arm. He massaged both breasts, kneading them in his palm as a steady throb built between my thighs. Pressing his chest against my back, he kissed along my neck, ignoring my damp hair.

"Ah." I panted as tiny bursts of pleasure spread from where his lips touched me.

He grazed my ear with his teeth, and goose bumps rose on my skin. When he pulled back, I tried to chase the high he gave me. He dropped his hands to my waist and lifted me. "Rest your head on the bed, baby, and lift your ass."

Leaning forward, I placed my arms in front of me and laid my head on them. Then I got on my knees in front of him. My ass was the only thing in the air, and the lights were on. Slowly, he tugged down my shorts.

"Jesus, Hudson." I wiggled my ass as he pulled at the shorts until they were off my legs.

"You have a beautiful pussy, baby. And that ass...." He slid his palm down a butt cheek. Delicious tingles spread from his caress, dipping lower.

"Would you stop looking and do something?" I whined. "Don't be mean." My complaint turned into a moan as Hudson covered my clit with his mouth. He flicked his tongue out, then sucked. *Oh!* I cried out as he dipped his tongue inside my pussy. "*Yes.*"

"How about this?" he said before pressing two fingers inside me.

My legs shook as delight sparked inside my stomach.

"You're trembling," he murmured before circling my clit with his tongue.

"Ah, I'm so close," I whined.

When he curled those two fingers inside me and sucked my clit, I exploded, screaming to the top of my lungs as he continued to lick and finger me. My hips would have buckled if he hadn't held them in place. I felt like a perfect, fucking beautiful noodle all strung out on the bed.

One second, his lips were on my pussy, and in the next, his thick cock slipped inside me. I moaned at the exquisite burn of him filling me. I was sore from the night before, but that pinch of pain was only a reminder of how good the man could please me. And he could. My insides clamped around him. Just knowing who filled me was going to make me come again.

Hudson had complete control of my body because he consumed my thoughts just as much.

"You were *made* for me. You can't tell me otherwise." He palmed an ass cheek. "Fuck. I'm going to have so much fun taking care of this pussy."

My insides fluttered, and my heart raced. All I heard was *taking care,* and my heart wanted to take it for something else. The words were lewd, and I loved them, but he meant during sex. But I liked him taking care of him in and out of the bedroom *so* much.

Oh, shit.

I cried out when he hit a sweet spot, rotating his hips, and holding himself inside me. Intense pleasure bloomed, and my pussy clenched as the first wave of an orgasm edged closer.

"I'm about to come," he said through a groan. "Fuck. You feel so good, baby."

He slipped his thumb into my ass, and his cock jerked inside me. Ecstasy burst through me, shattering me to pieces as I felt him come.

Pushing my hips forward, Hudson urged me to my belly before pulling out. "Want me to get you a washcloth?"

"I'll clean up in the bathroom," I said, but made no move.

I was so relaxed. No part of me wanted to leave the bed, but I knew I had to go clean up.

He smacked my ass lightly, and I squeezed my butt cheeks together. "Go wash up, beautiful, so I can get that hair dry."

"Okay, okay."

I shivered when he pressed a kiss on my ass. Jumping out of bed quickly, I dashed to the bathroom, closed the door, and freshened up. When I opened it, he patted the spot in front of him. Warm tingles spread over me as I sat in front of him.

I was positive that nothing could be better than spending every moment with Hudson.

Coughing a few times, he turned on the blow-dryer and played with my hair.

I awakened in a dark room. A heavy arm was draped over my middle, and hot breath blew into my nape. Hudson held my hips snug against his. How did that happen? Did I fall asleep? Of course, I fell asleep while he played with my hair, especially after he gave me the most delicious orgasms.

Why did he keep letting me sleep in there? He couldn't be... Was he intentionally allowing me to sleep in his bed? As soon as the thought took root, my heart raced. What were we doing? If I hadn't been living under his roof, if I wasn't so paranoid of *why* he took care of me, I would have asked him. Did his heart pitter patter out of control when we kissed? What about when we were together? Did everything feel perfect and sweet, like coming home?

Or was I the only one who felt happiness when we were together. Was I setting myself up for heartbreak?

God. I'd never felt so consumed by someone who I was dying to know their thoughts but terrified at the same time.

But if I left him alone in that bed, would he find another reason to get me back into it?

The idea had me twisting out from beneath Hudson. Slipping upstairs, I was hoping, wishing, and waiting for what he would do next.

38

EUGENE

I was up before Hudson. That rarely happened. Most of the time, he'd already left for work. As I stumbled down the stairs, I saw him slipping on his boots. He swayed, nearly smacking into the wall, before he righted himself, and then grunted. Flinching, I hurried over. "Are you okay?"

He grunted again, rubbing his head. Did he have a headache? When his greenish-brown orbs met my gaze, he pouted, his brows pinching in the middle. "Where did you go?"

I crinkled my nose. It took me a second to realize he must have meant when I left his bed again. "I went to sleep in my room," I admitted.

He rubbed his forehead, rising to his full height. "Always leaving."

I couldn't help but notice how pale he looked. Hudson had dark circles under his eyes. Most days, he rarely left the stubble on his jaws. I thought he looked yummy with it, but I'd learned that

Hudson liked to be immaculate in appearance. He was always grumpy, but normally he had a pep to his step in the mornings.

"Are you feeling, okay?" I asked.

"I'd feel better if I had awakened beside you."

I averted my gaze as my heart pitter-pattered out of control. "Are you sure you're all, right? You look pale."

When I turned my attention back to him, he shrugged before coughing and rubbing his chest. "Just a little under the weather..."

My heart pinched as he coughed again. Reaching out, I placed my palm on his forehead. He felt hot, but I couldn't be sure. "You're warm. Do you have a thermometer?"

He shook his head.

"You're sick." I pulled at the jacket he had on.

"I don't get sick."

I snorted and yanked when he wasn't helping me take the garment off. "You can't go to work."

"I can't miss work."

That made me chuckle because I'd noticed him leaving work early more and more. "Yes, you can. You're the owner. Besides, I need to check your temp. If you have a fever, you can't go spreading your germs everywhere."

Hudson moved closer until he towered over me. "I'll stay home if you stay with me."

"I'm off today and already planned on staying in." February was too cold for me to do anything else but stay in and read.

He smiled, then bent down and slipped off his boots. "I'll call Randall."

When Hudson coughed and stumbled, worry tugged at my insides. "Go lay down or something. I'm going to get a thermometer and medicine in case you are spiking a temp."

He turned and gave me an honest-to-God pout on his perfect lips. "You said you were staying here."

I couldn't help but giggle again. "We need medicine."

He reached for his boots as if he hadn't just taken them off. "I'll go with you."

The man was impossible. Did he think I couldn't do anything myself?

"I can handle going to the store," I said, stepping in front of him and rubbing his arms. "You take care of me all the time, so let me do the same for you."

"It's likely a cold. I'll be fine, so there's no need for you to trouble yourself."

"Go lay down," I said to Hudson, but it was Max who walked away and plopped himself near the couch.

Hudson slouched forward suddenly, planting his forehead on my shoulder. He had to be running a fever. I patted his back, inhaling his scent. "It won't take me longer than an hour."

"Okay, baby."

Something about that huge man being such a baby while calling me one had butterflies fluttering in my stomach. Hudson Henderson was a giant teddy bear. No matter how cranky I saw him get with his workers every day, he was so good to me.

I wanted to return the favor.

When I returned, I found Hudson shivering on his bed. Ripping the thermometer out of the box, I put in the batteries and checked his temperature—101.4 Fahrenheit. I knew he was running a fever.

I left the room and grabbed him a Gatorade from the fridge before I hurried back.

"Hudson, I need you awake a minute," I told him as I tore into the Tylenol box and put two capsules in my palm. "Take this medicine for me, please."

His eyes fluttered a few times before he managed to open them. Grumbling, he sat up and took the medicine. Frowning, I watched him rub his temple.

"Body aches?" I asked, and he nodded. "It could be the flu. Do you want to go to the doctor?"

Hudson shook his head. "I'll be fine, but if it is the flu, I don't want to give it to you. You've already been exposed enough..." He let his gaze trail over me slowly. Despite the sickly droop in his eyes, I could feel the heat in them. "Especially after last night. I don't want you to get sick."

We didn't kiss the night before while we screwed, and I didn't think he had a fever at that time. But as I thought about it, I was sad that our lips didn't meet at all during that encounter. "Don't worry. I'll be okay."

"I am worried," he went on.

"Rest," I instructed. "How does your stomach feel? Do you have an appetite?"

"No."

"I'll try to cook something that will be light on your stomach later." The key word was *try*. I wasn't an excellent cook like Hudson, but I was sure I could whip up homemade soup of some sort. There would be no guarantee of how it might taste. It didn't really bother me because I wanted to do that for him.

I didn't like him feeling bad, but I couldn't help being slightly giddy at the idea of doing something for him. Maybe that was the answer. If I started behaving like him, helping in some way, maybe I wouldn't feel so guilty for sticking to him like glue.

39

HUDSON

I felt like I'd been hit by a truck. Fuck. The last time I had the flu was in my early twenties. It had been a long ass time, but the body aches, fever, headache, and coughing all pointed to it.

Of course, I'd get sick when I was trying to impress Eugene. Being weak couldn't have come at a worse time. She was finally letting me touch her. Instead of being sick, I'd rather have her in my arms, yet I needed to put distance between us, so she didn't get whatever I had.

Why did she keep leaving my bed? What was I doing wrong? I was a greedy man when it came to her. I would beg on my hands and knees to get her to stay in my damn bed *after* I got better.

I coughed, and pain filled my chest. Sitting up, a cool washcloth fell off my head. Eugene must have put it there while I was asleep. She was going to end up sick because of me. I rubbed my chest as I coughed a few more times.

Eugene could do whatever she pleased. After all, my home was her home. If she needed a spot away from me or a moment to herself, she could do that there. But the idea terrified me. I was crazy about her. I didn't know what I'd do if she picked up and left one day.

I didn't know what made me feel worse—the fever or my thoughts.

"You're awake." Eugene stepped into my bedroom carrying a steaming bowl. "I made you some potato soup, but be warned, I'm not a great chef like you."

I smiled despite the throbbing in my temples. "You didn't have to make anything. I'd rather you keep your distance until I'm feeling better." The words felt wrong coming out of my mouth, but I didn't want Eugene to get sick.

Ignoring me, she sat beside me on the bed, handed the bowl over, and placed her palm on my forehead. "You need to take more medicine after you eat. Even better, you need to go to the doctor. You know Tamiflu has no effectiveness if you wait longer than a day. Or is it two? Regardless, if you wait too long, you're stuck feeling bad."

"I'll be fine, Red."

"Even if you don't feel like eating, take a few bites."

I didn't have an appetite, but my stomach wasn't queasy. So, I ate the whole thing for her. The quicker I got better, the quicker I could go back to making her see how perfect we'd be together.

"Hudson... Hudson..." Soft hands nudged me. I opened my eyes and saw Eugene sitting on the bed beside me, holding more medicine for me to take.

My head felt like it was going to explode as I sat up. Eugene was so fucking pretty. I wished I didn't have to keep closing my eyes because of the headache. I wanted to keep staring at her. "Sorry, Hudson. I hate to wake you, but we need to try to keep your fever down. Here."

I took the Motrin from her. "You need to start calling me something else, baby."

Her gaze shot to mine. "Huh?"

"I call you baby, even Red, and you still say Hudson—which I don't fucking m-mind," I slurred as I gripped my head. "I love my name on your lips, but I want a pet name. Please."

When I could focus again, her face was slightly red. "Your fever has you talking like this."

"No. I know what I want, and it's for you to call me something, anything. I'll be your baby, too, okay? Or if you want to call m-me *hubby,* I'll eat the shit out of that."

Her eyes widened. "I can't call you that."

"Why not?"

I knew the answer. We weren't married. I wasn't her husband, but that didn't matter. When I started admitting to myself what I felt for Eugene, my heart got lighter. I wanted her to be a part of my life. I wanted her to remain in my cabin and be mine. I was already hers, even if she didn't realize it yet.

"We will talk about this when you're feeling better," she said.

I swallowed the pills and then said, "What are you going to call me?"

Her red hair swayed as she shook her head. "I need time to think about it."

"Leave now," I urged. "Before I decide I don't care that I'm sick and scoop you up. It doesn't matter that my brain feels like it's about to squirt out my ears. I still want to hold you close, so go, baby. I'll set the timer and take my medicine through the night, okay?"

She pouted. I wanted to lean forward and kiss her. Instead, I laid back and tried not to think of my achy limbs.

"You should have gone to the doctor," she said.

"It's okay, beautiful. It's okay."

I woke up at four that morning feeling like a new man. The headache, body aches, and fever were gone. It was probably a twenty-four virus. I believed the flu would have lasted longer.

I yanked the sheets off my bed sheets and carried them to the washer. I had sweated a lot and wanted to get rid of all the germs if I wanted Eugene in bed with me. Before showering, I guzzled a Gatorade and ate a few bites of ham. The hot water was heaven. I brushed my teeth while I stood underneath the spray. As I lathered soap over my chest, I recalled one small detail from the night before and stiffened.

I asked Genie to call me hubby.

Holding my head beneath the spray, I sulked. I truly believed Eugene would be my wife one day, but that didn't mean I should scare the fuck out of her by bringing up the word 'hubby'. She might not like clingy people, and I felt like I could hold her hand all day if she let me. Fuck. I shook my head. I haven't recognized myself since Eugene entered my life. But the changes were good. I liked how she made me feel. I liked having someone to care for. It made me happy to see how she wanted to care for me while I felt bad, even if it worried me, she'd get sick. She might think I was crazy, but it was who I was becoming around her. For her, I cared more than I ever thought possible.

Her being my wife was the future I wanted. But it was hard enough to keep her in my bed. I had to make her fall in love with me if I wanted her to one day be my wife.

I loved Eugene. I fucking loved her. I might die if she left me.

The question was, what did Eugene feel when she was around me?

40

EUGENE

Since working at Homestyle, I discovered most customers and their orders blurred together after a while. The only faces I remembered were our regulars, and that was because they visited frequently. Except I'd never encountered a man quite like the older gentleman in booth eight. Loretta said he asked for me, so she put him at one of my tables. She had smiled and told me, "He asked for you. I bet you'll get a good tip." I didn't get that vibe from him. The way he scowled at me put me on edge. The hairs on my arm stood on end every time I went to his table.

I didn't know why. He didn't seem out of the ordinary. Nothing screamed dangerous about him besides the way he continued to glare.

I stood in the corner, wiping down one of the back booths, when a hand came up to my forehead. I jumped and spun around. My shoulders sagged when I saw Hudson crowding over me. "You scared me," I whispered, glancing around to make sure no one paid attention to us.

He bent down and pressed his forehead against mine. I let my eyes close briefly, enjoying the contact even though I knew he was fussing. "Do you feel like you're getting sick?" he asked.

He'd been asking that for two days. Hudson hadn't invited me to his room, and I hoped it had something to do with the fact that he was making sure he was better. He had just returned to work that morning, but the man had constantly checked on me.

When he pulled away, I smiled. "I told you I don't get sick much, but when I do, it's normally bad, so be warned."

"I'll make sure you're taken care of," he promised, tucking a strand of hair behind my ear.

"You do take care of me. Probably too much."

"Not enough," he corrected.

"That's how spoiled brats are created, Hudson." The second I spoke his name; I remembered the conversation we had had when he'd been sick. He had asked me to pick out a pet name for him, but he had also said it could be hubby. He was probably out of his head because of the fever. He hadn't brought it up again, but my body heated at the memory. I had thought about what I could call him and came up with something. I just wasn't feeling brave enough to say it yet.

"You can be my spoiled brat." He grinned. "I like that idea a lot. But I still don't want you to get sick."

My heart pounded out of control. I didn't know it was possible to be so happy. Gran would likely call me a fool for being swept up in those feelings for Hudson, but she wasn't a romantic. If she saw him, even once, I believed she would tell me to stop filling my head with doubt and just live.

"Everyone gets sick," I said.

He groaned. "Don't remind me." He glanced toward the back of the restaurant. "Let me know if you need me, okay?"

I laughed. "You're crazy."

"Crazy for you." His fingers grazed my cheek.

Butterflies danced in my stomach as he sauntered away. As soon as I turned, I locked eyes with Sue who sat in one of the front booths. When she wanted to pester me, she sat around and made comments as I worked. Her grin stretched from ear to ear. She totally caught me with her grandson.

"Genie," she practically sang my name.

Damn it.

Groaning, I walked over. "What is it, Sue? I have tables to check on."

Her brow arched. "Is that what you've been doing?"

I smiled. "I'm trying."

Sue crossed her arms. "Ya going to put that poor boy out of his misery or what?"

"What?"

"Don't play coy. The entire restaurant sees the special treatment Hudson gives ya."

"What are you talking about?" I knew exactly what she was talking about, but I enjoyed aggravating her too.

"Tell me, do ya struggle to carry your plates out?"

"Now that you've said it..." I waved my arm around, pretending it hurt by pinching my brows together. "I do struggle."

When I smiled, she smirked and then shook her head.

"I need to check on my tables," I told her, and she shooed me off.

I hesitated as I ventured back over to the weird old dude's booth. He followed my movement with his gaze as I stopped in front of him. He'd already ordered food and dessert, but I kept returning every so often to offer more drinks. When he refused everything, I asked if he was ready for his bill.

"This is a nice set up you have here." I frowned at his odd comment while he glimpsed around the restaurant. "You can fool some people, but not everyone." He glared at me.

I stepped back, confused. "Excuse me?"

He adjusted his ballcap. "I'll take that check now."

I nodded, my stomach feeling queasy as I hurried to print his receipt. The quicker he paid, the faster he left. Returning to his booth, I placed the paper in front of him. "Here you go, sir. I hope everything was to your liking."

"Oh, it was," he said with a hint of malice. "I definitely got what I came for."

I didn't understand the man's attitude, and it made me nervous. There was no way I was going back to his table. I asked Loretta to pick up the cash from him, but he still caught me by the door as he was leaving. "Enjoy it while it lasts, Eugene."

My heart froze in my chest as I watched him leave. My nametag said Genie.

Could I have a stalker? Did he have something to do with Danny's case?

I could be overthinking the way the old man had been looking at me. But how could I mistake someone's obvious hatred? That was the first day in a while that I'd had to run to the bathroom because of my stomach. My nerves were on edge the rest of my shift, which only caused the grumble in my belly to worsen.

Home.

No, the cabin might be where I laid my head down, but home was—

My door creaked open, so I peeled my blanket off and sat up on my bed.

"Every light was off when I came in." Hudson's brows knitted together. "What's wrong?"

"Stomachache," I said, which wasn't a lie. It just wasn't the whole truth. A huge part of me wanted to confide in Hudson about what happened. But the little voice in my head convinced me otherwise. It reminded me how much Hudson did for me. I didn't want to add one more thing because that might be what finally made Hudson see how much trouble I could be. I didn't want to be a pain for him. All I wanted to do was cuddle with him, talk about our days, and let him bury himself deep inside me. My feelings were impossible to ignore. There was no denying them. I was wholeheartedly in love with Hudson.

He was good. There is nothing like the men from the past, especially Jared.

But just because Hudson was a good man shouldn't mean I should bother him constantly. In my head, I pictured the screen door at Gran's old trailer. I remembered how often it opened and closed. Every visit from a family was for something. No one came to see Gran otherwise. My heart ached at the idea of treating Hudson or anyone the way I watched Gran be treated. I refused to be a burden or ask for anything. All I wanted was to be near him.

Besides, the old creep might not be anything to worry about. If he showed up at Homestyle again, I'd let someone else take his order. There was no point in annoying Hudson.

I smiled as he hurried over and dropped down beside me. "Fuck." He put his hand on my forehead. "Did I get you sick, baby?"

Laughing, I took his hand and hugged it to my chest. "No. I'm not sick. Just..." I huffed and finally said, "I get gassy and stomachaches like the rest of the world, okay?"

He cracked a smile. "Did you eat something? I got some Tums downstairs."

"It's my anxiety," I admitted.

"What happened?"

I wouldn't speak of the man, but I would honestly tell Hudson about my mental health. "That's the thing about anxiety. It doesn't need a reason to appear. It just exists inside me. Sometimes, I'll have days where I feel like the walls are closing in, and I don't know what to do. Nothing bad happens, but it feels so ominous like something terrible is coming." I shrugged, trying to brush off my feelings. Unless someone lived with anxiety themselves, it was hard for most people to grasp. "It's hard to explain."

"What helps you get through it?" he asked, and I kind of liked the fact that he didn't try to say he understood or make me explain it more.

"Hot baths, music, sleep..." I started naming things that helped me. "I've gotten better at working through my thoughts when the feeling is there, too. I just wanted you to know I have an anxious stomach. So, I'm bound to fart in front of you." He laughed, so I continued, "I need you to be prepared."

"You know, Red, I find myself lucky in that case."

I gasped dramatically. "How so?"

"If you're warning me of future farts, you must be planning to stay here with me."

His words held magic. My chest felt warm and fuzzy. While he didn't erase the anxiousness inside me, he brought bigger feelings to battle against it. Soft and lovely sensations spread through me, eclipsing the negative.

I brought my legs to my chest and rested my head on my knees. Moving my gaze over Hudson adoringly, I whispered, "I believe I've found a new weapon against my anxiety."

He brushed my hair off my shoulder. "What's that?"

"You."

His cheeks reddened right before he leaned in and kissed my forehead. "I'm going to run you some hot water in the tub downstairs, prepare some strawberries, and fucking feed them to you while you relax. How about that, baby? Your anxiety and stomach are no match for me."

I burst out laughing as he climbed off the bed. "Thank you, Blondie." My stomach fluttered as I tried out the nickname. My cheeks felt hot. Since he called me Red due to my hair color, I figured I'd give him the same treatment.

He paused, his mouth curving to one side. "Blondie?"

"My hair is red. You're a blond." I brought the blanket up to my face, stopping at my nose. "You don't like it?"

He ran his hand through his hair. My body buzzed to life as more color appeared on his cheeks. "I do, Red, I really do."

41

EUGENE

The past few mornings, I awakened to a large arm draped over my middle and my back plastered to Hudson's chest as he held me. He slept in my room. I sat up until ten, waiting for him, and he hadn't shown up. So, he must have snuck into my room much later.

My clit throbbed before I was completely awake, like my body was aware of who lay beside me. Even though I was burning up from his body heat, I remained there, soaking in how good he felt crushed against me. The last time he'd touched me sexually had been the night before he got sick. I didn't understand. It had been a week, and the man slept with me every night. He didn't wake me. He simply held me. I should be happy, and I was more cheerful than I ever have been in my life. But I was also hornier than I'd ever been before. Hudson had created a needy little monster the moment he touched me. His caresses never led to sex, and it was driving me insane. Why wasn't he? He had the perfect opportunity to sex me up the other night when he got me in the tub and fed me like he said he would. But the man didn't.

I wanted to take him inside me *every* night.

My shirt pressed against my sensitive nipples, and delicious tingles spread from the spot. There was no light shining through the window, so I didn't know what time it was. Unable to help myself, I wiggled my hips until I was snug against the curve of his hips. When he stirred and his arm tightened around me, I froze.

Then his phone alarm blared. Hudson removed his arm, turned off the alarm, and then replaced his arm over me. He thrust against my ass, letting me feel his erection. A vicious torrent of desire took root inside of me.

Hudson pressing his dick against me was all the encouragement I needed. "If you're not inside me in the next minute, I'm going to—"

He yanked down my shorts and panties, wrestling them off my legs. Still on our sides, he lifted my thigh, rubbing his fingers between my pussy lips. I moaned.

"What are you going to do?" His voice was deeper, fucking sexy as hell from sleep.

"I don't know," I admitted, because I didn't. "Please Hudson."

Seconds later, his dick pressed against my opening. He kissed my shoulder, then slammed into me. Tingles spread through me as I cried out. He didn't get all the way in due to our positioning, so he lifted my leg more as he pulled out, and that time I took him deeper when he thrust. My tits bounced as he fucked me. He strummed my clit until I saw stars and came all over his cock. He grabbed one of my breasts and molded it in his palm as he jerked twice before groaning. Only then did he lower my leg.

Still inside m e, he slid his hand down to my ass and smacked it lightly. "You're going to sleep in my bed, baby."

"Hmm?" I spoke.

Hudson stayed inside me. I didn't mind feeling him becoming soft inside me. It just felt good to have him there. I was satiated.

"Listen, Eugene."

I opened my eyes when he said my name, looking over my shoulder.

"You're going to sleep in my bed," he said again.

"Okay," I whispered.

"I'll keep coming up here if you don't."

"I don't mind that either."

"My bed is yours, Eugene. Do you understand? I know I should give you space. Let you be you, but now that I've had you, I don't know how to wait. If that's really what you need, I'll figure it out, but I fucking need you to know I want you in my arms each night."

"I don't want to ruin anything," I confessed. Truthfully, I wanted the same thing he did, but I didn't want to destroy the friendship we had.

"Do you like being in my arms?" he asked. When I nodded, he squeezed me tight. "That's all that matters. As long as you want this, nothing's wrong. This is right between us, baby."

When he finally slipped out of me, I couldn't hide the delicious shudder that swept over me. I already wanted him back where he was. I smiled as he leaned over me and kissed my arm.

"Why did you wait so long to touch me again?" The words came out more like a grumble than I intended.

His lips stopped moving over my skin. "I was waiting for some sort of sign that you wanted me to touch you again. When I think back, every time I took you, I did just that. I *took*."

"No, you didn't," I told him. "I wanted you just as much."

"I know. What I should have said from the beginning is that you have a home here, whether I'm between your legs or not. I don't want you to be afraid of what's happening between us. Trust that I'll take care of you, baby. It's all I want to do."

I laid on my back and touched his cheek as he looked down at me. "I trust you, Blondie."

"Good."

"But I need you to touch me every night," I said. "I like it when you take control. When I don't feel like having sex, I'll tell you. Just *please* don't wait a whole damn week again."

I felt his cock hardening against my side when he said, "I'm not going to work out before work, am I?"

I smiled. "No."

I jumped in the shower after Hudson left for the restaurant. The bed sheets had to be washed too, so I stuck them in the washer. But from the sound of it, I wouldn't be sleeping in that room anymore. I smiled as I petted Max. Before I left, I always tried to give him plenty of pats on the head.

Being so happy was a foreign feeling. Even when Gran was alive, worries about money and her health bogged down all our potential sweet moments. I enjoyed every second I had with her, but the bliss I experienced with Hudson was new.

I should call my brother and thank him. The only reason I met Hudson was because of him. Maybe I could invite Edwin and Francis over that week.

"Be a good boy, okay?" I told Max as I walked out of the cabin.

There was a yellow note on my car window. It was the first thing I noticed. I laughed as pleasure bloomed in my chest. Hudson must have left a note for me. When I unfolded the paper, my heart felt like it was yanked from my chest.

Living a life of luxury while the rest of us are struggling to make ends meet.

Enjoy it while it lasts.

I swallowed and spun around, glancing left and right before hurrying into my vehicle. As soon as I was inside, I locked the doors. Oh, God. Hudson would have noticed the letter when he left, which meant whoever put it there did so after he was gone.

Was it the man from the restaurant? I tried to think of who I could have upset, but there was no one. Maybe it was someone who knew I worked for Danny. Someone who assumed I helped him with his con. Could it have been someone Danny ripped off from the settlement money? I'd been cleared by the police, but people still wouldn't let things go. All because I worked for the jackass.

I spent fifteen minutes on the phone with Huntingsburg police, only for them to tell me they could do nothing. Since I didn't live in their district anymore, they couldn't help me. They told me to file a complaint with Jefferson County.

So, I went to the police station, only to be told there was nothing the police could do either. No suspect. No name. And if I were honest, I didn't believe the police took me seriously.

"Ah, I'm sure it's just someone trying to scare you," an officer said.

Shouldn't that be an issue, though?

When I asked what was going on over Danny's case and disappearance, they still didn't care. I didn't know what I expected, but the police shrugging me off wasn't it. At the least, I figured they'd go check out Hudson's cabin.

They told me to keep them updated if anything changed.

One of the officers said, "If anything else happens, we'll check it out."

But I didn't want anything else to happen. I wanted peace.

I was a few minutes late for my shift at Homestyle. A part of me feared that ominous letter, but another part was terrified of being a pain for Hudson. Everything was going great. I didn't want to ruin anything. If the old man showed up again, I'd tell Hudson, but I hoped it didn't come to that.

I refused to believe someone would terrorize me over something I didn't do.

Once more, I felt completely overwhelmed with the idea of being a problem Hudson had to take care of.

I knew what a burden my brother and I were to Gran growing up. If she'd let *Child Protective Services* take us, she could have lived her life a lot more peacefully. I always wondered if she regretted keeping my brother and me, despite how much she loved us.

I thought of Hudson, and my heart filled with warmth. *Don't be Hudson's burden now.* I refused to be anyone's problem anymore. I didn't want his affection for me to turn to anything like regret.

42

EUGENE

My arm jiggled, and the bed dipped.

"Baby?"

A hand rubbed my arm that time before giving it another shake.

"Baby, wake up."

Awareness trickled over me as I registered Hudson's voice. Turning away from him, I buried my face in a pillow.

He chuckled. "Come on. I want to show you something."

"Not right now," I murmured. Hudson's bed smelled fantastic, just like him. Since I'd been sleeping in his room, I found it harder to get up in the mornings. Something about being in his space and breathing in his scent was satisfying. The fact that he wanted me there made me extra happy, too.

But I told him I would tell him if I wasn't in the mood for sex. That morning was one of those times. My pussy was sore from all the screwing we'd been doing. He'd been insatiable after I told him I wanted more sex.

He squeezed one of my ass cheeks. "Not that. I know you're sore.

There's something else I want to show you besides my dick, Red. And it's not my cooking. I know how much you love that, too."

I groaned and lifted my head. "You're having a whole ass conversation with yourself this morning."

He laughed as he rose off the bed, holding his hand out for me. My chest warmed at the sound.

I took his hand and walked behind him, rubbing the sleep from my eyes.

"Don't trip her, Max," Hudson warned as the dog stepped in beside us. "She has trouble enough with her feet without you."

He turned back to grin, so I glared. When I saw him leading me toward the stairs, I frowned. "What are we doing? It's too late to make me sleep upstairs now." I tried tugging my hand out of his, but he held firm. "You'll never keep me out of your bed, Blondie. *Never.* That's my bed now."

"It's *our* bed," he corrected. Bending down, he scooped me up and carried me up the stairs. "It took a while to find them all. Some editions are different than what you had, but I'll keep looking."

I had no clue what Hudson was going on about until he brought me into the room with all the shelves he built. My heart knocked against my ribcage as I took in the books organized on one of the left bookshelves. He set me on my feet.

As I got closer, I started seeing all the familiar titles I once had. *Pride and Prejudice* and *Persuasion.* The editions were different than what Gran had, but still. I swallowed the ball of emotions in my throat. God. *The Hunger Games* trilogy and the *Twilight* saga were there from my teenage years. My favorite paranormal romance series was there, too. I covered my mouth. How was that possible? How could he have known all the books I used to own?

I'd like to believe I was a simple person. I didn't dwell on the bad things, or else I'd never be happy. The day I lost all my belongings, especially my books, I allowed myself to cry. After that, I told myself to move on because I could start over.

But seeing those books made me realize what Hudson had done

for *me*. I bent over and started bawling like a child, as if a dam burst inside me. Hudson's hands were at my back as he murmured, "I didn't want you to cry, baby. You were supposed to be happy."

"I am happy," I said.

"There's a few books I couldn't identify because of the mold, but I'm sure you can remember what you had so we can get them again."

I lifted my head, wiping my face with my hands. "How did you know what I had?"

"I took pictures of your books before we left the apartment."

"Why?" I had only been staying with him for a few days at that point.

"Why else?" He wiped my eyes. "So, I can find them for you."

"Yeah, but why? We were practically strangers."

"You've never felt like a stranger. I kept telling myself you and your red hair weren't my type, but the truth is the opposite. You're everything. It's like life slid into place, making sense and becoming perfect because you were there. Do you understand? You're my home."

I started crying again. The warmth and affection couldn't be contained inside me, so they needed to pour out in some form.

"Shh, don't cry," he whispered, wiping my tears and kissing my forehead.

"Then stop making me," I said. Max nudged my legs, whimpering, as if he sensed my distress. I reached down and petted his head. "It's okay, Bear. These are happy, emotional tears."

Hudson shook his head as I stood up, but it seemed he wouldn't correct me for calling his dog Bear. Wrapping my arms around my man, I hugged him tight. "Thank you, Blondie."

He cocooned me in his embrace. "Anything for you, Red. Anything for you."

Later at Homestyle, I was wiping down a table, humming, when Sue stepped in beside me.

"Ya seem awfully happy these days," she said as she plopped down in one of the chairs.

I smiled. "There's a lot to be happy for."

Her lips curled as she arched a brow. "Hudson told me he showed ya the books this morning."

I froze, eyeing the old woman. "You knew about the books?"

She huffed. "Who do ya think helped him find them?"

"You helped?"

"Of course."

Sitting in the seat beside her, I wrapped the old woman in a bear hug before she could object. She stiffened as if I caught her off guard before slowly melting into the embrace and patting my back. "Thank you. You guys are too good to me."

"Never settle for less," said Sue. "Hudson is plenty capable of this and more, but if he acts up, tell me. I'll correct him."

I laughed as I pulled away. Instead of confirming or denying my relationship with Hudson, I said, "I'll make sure to threaten him with you if he misbehaves."

She nodded, seeming satisfied. "That a girl." She glanced toward the kitchen, smiling suddenly. "I see Hudson a lot less around here lately, and I know that's because of ya."

"I don't—"

She held up her hand. "Thank ya for showing up out of the blue and teaching Hudson there's more to life than this restaurant. I'm proud of him, but the men in this family are terrible when it comes to balancing life and work. I'm happy that he's achieved this much, but I've always wanted him and his brother to experience more than the careers they chase."

I thought back to how Hudson had told me he'd work less with me around because he didn't want me working overtime. Warmth spread through me as I smiled back. "I like that he's career driven."

"So do I, but there's nothing wrong with balance. That's all I've ever wanted for him and his brother."

"I can agree to that."

"Hudson's dad is a great man, but he spent a lot of time away from home due to his career. I wished to see him slow down too, for Kelly. Now Finnick's doing the same thing with his life. They built an empire, so you'd think they'd know when to relax. What am I going to do with these men?"

I got the feeling Sue meddled in everyone's affairs. She had to know that sometimes people chose careers over other things in life. Life was a different adventure for every person. But I could see her point. If there were other people in your life to think about, there should be some sort of balance.

"I'm sure you'll figure it out," I said.

"Enough about the boys. Are ya excited about tomorrow?"

Sue was talking about the Valentine's Day event for the Henderson Company.

"I don't know what to expect." I gave her a sheepish grin. There was no way I would tell her how anxious the entire thing made me. I wasn't a fancy person. The fact that I was wearing a dress made it seem extravagant. Even if it were a simple occasion, it would be a big deal for me. It was so obvious Hudson came from a wealthy family, and I didn't know how I'd fit in at that event. "Look at me, Sue." I opened my arms wide. "I hope you know what you're getting into when you invited me."

She observed me. "What's wrong with ya?"

"Nothing. I'm just..." I let my arms drop. "Nervous. I don't want to embarrass, Hudson."

"Why would ya embarrass him?"

"Because I'm me. I can be so awkward. What if I fall on my face and bust my nose trying to walk in heels?"

Sue lifted a single brow, smiling. "Then ya fall and hurt your nose. Hudson will take ya to the doctor to make sure you're okay."

"You know, I expected a different sort of pep talk," I admitted. More like, *you're not going to fall tomorrow, so don't worry.*

"It's not a big deal. Just a place for adults to mingle while some investors chat. It's fun for us women because we get a reason to wear gowns."

The truth of why I was so anxious about the event set heavy on my stomach. Hudson's ex would be there, and I didn't want the trailer park to come out of my mouth if she looked at him.

"Be ready around two. Kelly and I will pick ya up." When I frowned, she added, "So we can get our hair and makeup done."

43

HUDSON

I arrived at Henderson Enterprise without my date. Mom and Grandma stole Eugene away so they could get ready for the Valentine's Day fundraiser, so I wasn't sure what time they'd arrive.

My dad started the company by building homes. Those days, the company dealt more with major companies, building and repairing franchises from the ground up. He never studied architecture, never went to school past eleventh grade, and still succeeded through hard work.

The entrance to the company was a giant oval-shaped room with a fountain in the middle. The walls were nothing more than an artistic display of black glass and mirrors.

Soft piano music played, and people mingled in the room in separate groups. No one noticed me entering the building, and my shoulders loosened. My father did something amazing with his life, but as I stepped into that world again, I knew I had made the right choice in carving out my own path. Finnick would do better there than I ever could.

As soon as I turned, I spotted a young boy sitting on a cushioned bench near the wall and smiled. Finley had a gaming device in his hand as he slouched forward, elbows on his knees. He wore a black suit, and his light-colored hair was unkempt. I walked over and sat beside him. "Long time, no see, Finley."

He looked up, sighed, and then went back to staring at his screen. The shithead had his dad's attitude.

"Not even going to say hi to your uncle?" I asked.

He never once looked up. "Can I truly call you my uncle if I only see you once or twice a year?"

I frowned. The kid was right. I was surprised to see him there. Finnick was a teen when he got Finley's mom pregnant. With a baby on the way, Finnick hopped right into the business. Sadly, his relationship with Finley's mom didn't last beyond that first year. Since Finley lived with his mom and she refused to let him visit, the family barely saw him. Finnick's work required frequent travel. That killed Grandma and my mom, of course, but there wasn't much we could do about the situation.

"You do remember I have a restaurant now? I don't travel anymore, which means you could come and stay with me any time you wanted. Grandma Sue would like that." He lifted his head at the mention of Grandma. "At the very least, come see her at the restaurant."

"Do you have burgers?" he asked quietly.

"I can make whatever you want," I said. "There's someone I want you to meet, too. This is between me and you." When I nudged his shoulder, he arched his brow, his mouth curving upward to one side like *I* was a kid. "She's going to be your aunt one day. You'll know her when you see her. She's got red hair."

I mentioned Eugene's hair because I figured it would make me seem cooler to the ten-year-old that my woman had bright-colored hair.

"Grandma Sue doesn't care that she has red hair?" Finley asked.

"Why would she care?"

He looked down quickly. "I don't know."

"What are you two talking about?" Finnick interrupted.

He stepped in front of Finley, who stood and walked away instead of answering his father. Finnick, looking exhausted, rubbed his beard and frowned. He might be wearing a suit and even share some of my features, but he always looked untidy. His blond hair was tousled, and his beard needed a good trim. Since he worked out in the sun, he was darker than me, too.

"Mom and Grandma will be happy Finley's here," I said as Finnick plopped down beside me.

"The kid hates me."

"He barely knows you."

"He and his mom want for nothing because of me," Finnick said, rubbing his temple.

That was true, but Finnick's absence in the boy's life had done its damage.

"Dad's retiring." When my eyes widened, Finnick grinned and said, "Mom's going to cry tonight when he tells everyone."

I smiled. "She doesn't know."

He shook his head. "He's finally stepping aside, Hudson. Are you sure you don't want to return?"

I patted his back. "You're going to be fine, but... there's something I discovered recently. I like taking time for myself. I'd been working every day since the restaurant opened until a couple of months ago."

"Why are you telling me this?"

"Because it's fucking nice to relax. Everything's still going to be there after I take a day or two to rest."

He grimaced. "If only it were that simple."

"It is."

The very next second, he whistled. "Who's helping Grandma?"

Finnick stared toward the entrance. I spotted Eugene holding the door open for Grandma as she waddled through. Mom was walking a few steps behind them, but my gaze rushed back to my woman.

No wonder my brother whistled. The black dress she wore molded to her body, revealing every curve, and her cleavage was practically spilling out the top. She was absolutely stunning and had to be cold since she wore no jacket. I could fucking eat her in front of everyone in the building. Well, I wouldn't behave that way in front of my mom or my grandma, but everyone else was fair game. I needed her by my side, so everyone knew she belonged with me.

I smacked Finnick's back as I stood. "Show some respect to your future sister-in-law."

He quirked a brow, laughing. "Well, I'll be damned. I better go introduce myself."

"Keep what I said a secret," I told him.

"Why?"

"Why else?" I glared at my younger brother like he was a moron. "Because she doesn't know she's my future wife yet. I've got to convince her first."

He kept laughing as we walked over. When Eugene finally noticed me approaching, our gazes locked. As soon as I was within reaching distance, I grabbed her waist and pulled her close. After kissing the top of her head, I gestured to my brother. "This is my brother, Finnick. Finnick, this is Eugene, my better half."

"Hello," Eugene said, taking his outstretched hand and shaking it.

Finnick let his eyes rove over her before he said, "You are indeed his better half."

"It's about time ya two stopped pretending." Grandma Sue piped in as she stopped beside Eugene. "How long were ya two going to wait before ya told me you're together?"

As if Grandma didn't know from Eugene and my interactions at work.

"Wasn't it obvious?" I held Eugene tighter as if to say *see*.

"Okay, okay. I'll take him off your hands," Eugene said, tucking her arm beneath mine and hugging it as she leaned into me. "Does that make you happy?"

Grandma sniffed. "I expect grandbabies by next year."

Eugene didn't even flinch when she replied, "Maybe I don't want kids. Maybe I want to hog him all to myself." She looked up at me, and she was so fucking beautiful that I had to lean down and kiss her nose.

Grandma muttered, "Do ya hear this, Kelly?"

Ignoring Grandma, I continued to stare down at Eugene. "Eugene's the boss, Grandma. What she wants, she gets. If all she wants is me..." I looked at Grandma. "I won't deny her."

"So, you're saying if she wants babies, you'll want them?" Grandma eyed Eugene.

Grandma was no doubt planning how to convince Eugene we needed babies as she smiled.

Yes, I would be happy with kids one day. The idea of children had once seemed repulsive, but with Eugene, I knew I could love our child. I'd find pleasure in life with her, regardless of what we chose.

Eugene laughed. "I'm not sharing him, Grandma. Not for a long time."

The word Grandma coming out of Eugene's mouth had a good effect on the old woman because she stood straighter, nodding, until she saw Finnick. "And you! If I don't get to see Finley soon—"

"He's here," Finnick blurted out.

"Well, why didn't anybody tell me?" Grandma swiped her hands out at her sides as she stepped forward. "Move."

"Don't you love me anymore?" Finnick followed behind her.

"No."

"You handle Grandma well," Mom said to Eugene.

Eugene pointed at me. "She's been offering this one up to me like he's a meal ever since we met, so I'm used to it. She kind of reminds me of my gran." Eugene sucked in a breath instead of continuing.

Mom must have understood that Eugene's grandmother had passed because she patted her shoulder. Mom spotted how tightly Eugene hugged my arm and grinned. "Well, I'll leave you two to mingle. I'm going to go find your father, Hudson."

As soon as Mom disappeared, I said, "You wore that black dress for me."

"Why do you say that?"

"Because I said get black or red. You got black."

"It was the only one that looked decent on me."

"Are you kidding me? This dress is more than decent. You look like you want me to sling you over my shoulders and find someplace where I can shove my face between your thighs." She pressed her ear against my arm. "Are you going to admit the dress was for me? You were thinking about me too, weren't you? Before I got between your legs the first time, you were. Tell me what you feel for me, baby. It'll make me happy to hear that you're all crazy for me like I am for you."

"Yes, Blondie. I got so turned on when you dried my hair, so I tried to avoid it altogether. There. Does that make you happy?"

My chest became fucking warm. "Yes, it does."

"Attention everyone!" My father's voice boomed over the microphone, pulling our attention toward the fountain where he stood. The room was more crowded compared to when I first arrived, which probably had something to do with the news Dad was about to share. I was sure the shareholders wanted to know where the company stood when he left.

Eugene tugged on my suit. "Who is that man?"

"Speaking?" I studied her side profile as she looked at Dad talking. "My father."

It was like she recognized the old man.

44

EUGENE

LIFE WAS FULL OF SURPRISES. SOMETIMES, INSTEAD OF JUST BEING SHOCKED, it seemed strange. Out of all the chances, *that* man was Hudson's father. The same man who stopped and checked on me beside the road when I had a flat tire. The same man offered up his son to me. Much like Grandma Sue had.

I could do nothing but gawk as he spoke to the crowd. Everything felt bizarre, yet so perfect. It was as if the world had finally aligned for me, and I was right where I was meant to be. If the universe was trying to tell me something, I would be a fool not to listen.

My skin tingled, and I got a scratchy feeling in the back of my throat.

"What's wrong?" Hudson cupped my chin, turning my head in his direction.

I started laughing as two tiny tears leaked from my eyes. It wasn't sadness spilling out. I was just so overwhelmed and ridiculously happy.

"Baby..." His brows pinched together.

"It seems Grandma wasn't the first to offer you up after all."

He cocked his head to the side as he studied me. Before I could say anything else, everyone started clapping, and Kelly was in tears as Hudson's dad hugged her.

I frowned, realizing I missed something major during my shock. "What happened?"

Hudson smiled. "Dad retired."

Then Hudson's younger brother walked up beside his parents and started discussing his future with the company.

A few minutes after the big reveal, Kelly ushered her husband over to us. When he looked up, he did a double take. I couldn't help but grin like the creepy cat from Alice in Wonderland. His dad had been amusing the brief moment I spoke to him, and I knew he was also surprised.

When he smiled back, Hudson asked, "What's going on?"

"Well, well, well," Hudson's father began. "Honey, remember the little red head I told you about?"

Kelly gasped and then said, "You're joking."

I felt myself blushing. "It's such a small world."

"No, it's not," he said. "Life doesn't work out that way. You've come full circle, darling, and wound up right where you needed to be."

I didn't dare blink my eyes for fear of crying.

"You know my father?" Hudson asked.

"I don't know his name," I admitted.

"Landry," Hudson's dad said.

"Eugene, but everyone calls me Genie," I replied.

"Well," Landry began. "I saw a young lady changing a tire along the side of the road. I figured I'd stop and check to see if she needed help. It was Genie here."

"Your father told me he had sons," I said to Hudson, squeezing his hand.

"When she said she couldn't cook, I thought of Hudson and his weird obsession with cooking. I knew right then he'd do well to have someone like that."

I cringed, pinching my thumb and index finger together almost to demonstrate. "I can cook a little."

Kelly and Landry laughed, but when I glanced up at Hudson, he was smiling at me softly. He rubbed my cheek. "See? You were meant to come to me."

"How did you two meet?" Landry asked.

Hudson gave his parents the details, leaving nothing unturned. I expected myself to be embarrassed or ashamed, but Hudson was so animated and happy as he talked about me living with him. Even when he spoke of my hardships with the apartment and job, he spoke highly of me. There was no room for me to be uncomfortable. Instead, I watched him, mesmerized, as he gushed over me. Suddenly, I realized I was in *my* moment. Things were only going to get better. Hudson was making it clear I was a part of his life.

The place was jam packed with people, and music played. As Sue said, most of them seemed to come to dance and have fun, while others chatted in groups throughout the huge building. I was too enamored with Hudson to notice the older women at first. But I had to pee so badly, and the moment I stepped away from Hudson, my attention snagged on everything. The way people eyed me. As I walked to the bathroom, a hateful-looking woman said loudly, "Hudson's really dropped the bar for taste in women when my daughter broke up with him."

"Was a good idea on her part," added another woman. "Hudson walked away from the company to *cook*."

I felt my anger boil to the surface. Forget what she said about me. Was she looking down on Hudson for choosing to cook in *his* restaurant? Were they idiots? Had they not visited Homestyle? Hudson was very successful.

"Look at that hair," the first one muttered. "She's begging for attention with that color."

I stopped and fisted my hands at my sides. Turning their way, I saw they were looking to their left and didn't notice me. "Hilary has made her way to Hudson."

The second woman laughed. "I bet he's filled with regret."

I looked toward Hudson and Finnick. A gorgeous brunette stood beside them. Was that Hudson's ex? She placed her hand on Finnick's shoulder, who kindly shrugged her off. I smiled. Regardless of what she once was, I didn't care. Hudson wasn't paying attention to her. Even when she kept looking at him, he gave her a nod and went back to his conversation with the man next to him and Finnick. There were no staring or interactions on his part. I was getting a bit irked that she kept ogling my man, but she finally withdrew and went back to chatting up the other brother.

"Oh, look!" a young voice called out beside me. I turned to find a young boy—maybe about nine or ten—standing beside me. He had dirty blond hair and familiar eyes, but when did he arrive? "It seems Miss Hilary is onto the next Henderson brother."

Hilary's mom turned bright red as she glared at the boy. He smiled, holding his gaming device up as he waved at the two gawking women. With a huff, they turned away, and the boy said, "Just so you know, she didn't break up with Hudson. Hudson ended things because she was giving him a hard time when he wanted to open a restaurant. Grandma told me. She likes to gossip."

Grandma Sue?

"I wasn't worried. I mean, have you seen my hair." As I picked up one of my red curls, I spoke in the same snooty tone the women spoke in, causing the kid to laugh.

He nodded. "It's cool."

"And you are?"

"Hudson's my uncle."

That was Finnick's son. I should have known immediately. The kid looked like the Henderson men. For a second, I believed I might be staring at my future if I ever allowed such a scenario. I couldn't believe my thoughts! Sue was rubbing off on me.

"I'm Eugene, but you can call me Genie."

"Finley." Even his name was like his father's. So cute.

"Well, thanks for scaring them off. The trailer park might have come out of me if they kept talking."

He laughed. "That's weird."

"Hold that thought," I said. "I have to use the bathroom so bad! Both of your grandmas kept me at the salon all day, and then dragged me here. I've barely had time to do anything."

He laughed again as I hurried to the bathroom. As I wiped myself in a stall, I heard the creak of the door opening and shutting. Several footsteps, then nothing. The eerie silence disturbed me because why weren't they using the stalls. Or if they came to wash their hands, why wasn't there water running?

When two sets of boots appeared in front of my door, my stomach sank as dread filled me. Those were men's boots. "This is the women's bathroom," I said, standing quickly and pulling up my panties.

Tap, tap, tap.

Ice filled my veins as he knocked on my stall door. When he stopped, it felt just as dangerous.

Shit! My phone was in Kelly's vehicle because I didn't want to carry it around.

As the silence dragged on, my gut screamed danger. Before I lost the ability to do anything, I screamed. "Help! Two men are in the bathroom! Help!"

"You stupid bitch!" I recognized the voice as he yanked at the door. He was the old man from the restaurant. It didn't take him long to rattle the lock loose. As soon as he opened the door, he yanked me out of the stall. I kicked and punched, desperately trying to hit him.

"Why are you doing this?"

The man backhanded me, and my head rammed against the wall. Although dots clouded my vision, I didn't have a chance to recover. He grabbed my throat and pulled me to his face. He squeezed until I coughed. "You think you can move this far away with *our* money, and we wouldn't know?" he asked.

"Jerry. We were only going to scare her enough to talk," the other said. "I never agreed to attack her."

"How much of our money did your boss give you to keep quiet while he ran off?" The pressure on my throat hurt so badly. If he tightened his grip further, I wouldn't be able to breathe.

Fear clung to me as my heart roared in my ears. I tried to speak, but no words came out.

He slammed my head into the wall.

My teeth clanked together, and everything went black for a second.

"Stop!" the other man yelled. "You're going to kill her."

"It's what she deserves," Jerry said. "Look at this place, Phillip? Ain't no way a waitress could doll herself up like this and live in a nice cabin off her wages."

Oh, God. He was delusional, which only made the terror pumping through my veins stronger. Everything good that happened to me was the result of a good man taking care of me. "This company belongs to my boyfriend's family," I tried to make him understand. "The cabin is his—"

He punched me, and pain radiated up my nose. Blood spewed. "Where is Danny?"

The restroom door cracked open a bit.

"Genie...?" Finley called out.

Phillip swore, catching the door as it closed back. "The kid fucking saw us and ran to get someone! I'm out of here, man."

"Where is Danny?" Jerry yelled, shaking me like a doll. "You think I won't kill you? You've taken all of my money. Why would I care what happens next?"

"I don't know where he is," I slurred.

The taste of copper filled my mouth, and my head hurt so bad. I couldn't keep my eyes open.

"Hey!" Jerry smacked me. "Tell me!"

The door burst open, but all I saw was a blur behind Jerry. Then everything went black.

45

EUGENE

A STEADY BEEPING PIERCED MY CONSCIOUSNESS. I GRIMACED AS THE SOUNDS around me became more distinct. Someone talked in hushed whispers. The throbbing in my temples, a pain that slammed into my head like waves, worsened. My neck ached. A flood of anxiety and fear burst through me as I remembered the old man in the bathroom. I sat up quickly, gasping. Awareness trickled through me as I opened my eyes. Immediately, the bright lights made me wince. Too bright. God, my head hurt, and my eyes felt like someone tried to yank them out.

"Easy," Kelly said, standing quickly.

Kelly, Sue, and Finley were in the room with me. I was in a hospital with an IV hooked to my arm. I winced again.

"Dim the lights, Finley," Sue said.

"I'm glad to see you're awake." Kelly squeezed my hand. "Do you remember what happened?"

"Yes," I croaked.

"Go tell them she's awake," Sue ordered the kid. The door clicked shut as Finley left the room. Sue stood and waddled to the bed.

I glanced around the room. "Where's Hudson?"

Kelly glanced at Sue quickly, and something about the nervous way she looked churned my stomach. But Sue ignored her and grabbed my hand. "He went with Finnick to the police station."

"Jerry and Phillip were their names," I whispered. My head still throbbed, and I felt exhausted. "Did the police manage to detain them?"

"Ya misunderstand, dear," Sue said. "Hudson and Finnick are *in* jail. Finnick caught the one running, and Hudson walked in on the one attacking ya." Her grip tightened.

"The one who did this to you is currently in ICU," said Kelly. "He's in stable condition, but let's hope he lives."

My throat burned, and the shame crept in. None of that would have happened if I confided in Hudson before I was attacked. I winced, and my body trembled from the constant pain. "Is Hudson responsible?"

"Landry couldn't get him off the man," Kelly muttered. "The man was screaming that he was going to kill you."

Oh, God. It was all my fault. Instead of telling Hudson that someone was harassing me, I chose to ignore it because I didn't want to be a burden. What a dumb choice. That was me—always making the wrong decisions. Hudson was in jail because of *me*. Because I was afraid when I shouldn't have been.

I was nothing like the family members I feared becoming. Yet, I didn't know how to ask for help without thinking of Gran.

"Hey, it's okay." Kelly patted my shoulder. "Landry's getting them out."

"No, it's not. Hudson—"

"Is going to be fine," Sue finished.

The doctor and nurse stepped in, rattling off a bunch of tests they needed to do. I had a concussion, and with the number of blows to my head, they wanted to observe me overnight to check for brain bleeds.

When the nurse administered more pain meds, I quickly fell asleep.

The pain was the first thing I noticed when I woke again. The second was the darkened room, and the man asleep in the chair beside my bed. The monitor beeped as I stared at Hudson. I was instantly relieved to see him. He still had the suit on, which meant he came straight there after leaving the jail. His normally slicked back hair was in complete disarray. I sniffed as the tears threatened to spill. Crying only made my head hurt worse, so I really didn't want to do that.

Suddenly, he gasped and jumped up. As soon as he locked eyes with me, the tears spilled, and my shoulders jerked from how hard I sobbed. "Baby," he whispered, leaning over me. He was careful with my face and head. The heat of him being so close was soothing. "Baby," he said again, rubbing my arm. "Shh, shh. It's okay."

"No, i-it's not." I hiccupped. "I don't want you in trouble because of me."

"I'm not in trouble," he murmured. "The fucker deserved worse. He would have done worse to you if I hadn't gotten... He's going to live when he doesn't deserve to." Hudson wiped my eyes, and I winced. "Sorry," he croaked. "I can't fucking touch you because of that fucker. I could kill him, and I wouldn't bat an eye."

"Don't talk like that," I said.

"You haven't seen yourself," he said, his breath hitting my cheek. "He mentioned that sleazy lawyer you worked for to the police. Most likely, they'll question him in the morning. Have you encountered anyone else regarding the lawyer's disappearance and the settlement money?"

I stiffened.

Hudson looked down at me. "I won't play around when it comes to your safety. If there's anyone else harassing you, I need to know."

"Just those two," I said. "I'm sorry. When the old man visited the restaurant and said some strange things, I should have known he was up to no good. He also left a note on my car in your driveway."

"In the driveway?" Hudson's voice dropped an octave.

"I figured he was just trying to scare me. He thought I was working with Danny and took some of their money. I didn't, so why did I have to walk around like I was guilty? I didn't want to tell you because I was scared."

"Scared?"

"Things are so good between us. I didn't want to ruin anything."

"Why would that problem ruin anything?"

"I don't know."

He squatted beside the bed, running his thumb over mine. When he kissed my hand and I felt a teardrop fall onto my skin, my heart shattered into a million tiny pieces. I hadn't meant to upset him, but my issues with feeling like a burden were becoming a rift between us.

"What am I doing wrong, baby?" His voice cracked. "To make you think you couldn't tell me."

I had to let the past go. If I didn't, I'd continue to make mistakes, thinking I had no one to confide in. I had Hudson, and I didn't think he saw me as a burden.

I squeezed his hand once. "Maybe it would help you understand me if I told you about my family," I said. "My reasoning for not telling you had nothing to do with you. It's my own problem. I feel like a bad person if I ask people for help. Growing up, I watched my family use the only person to take care of me and my brother. My gran's screen door is so vivid in my memories because I can remember how busy her trailer stayed. How often people were in and out, asking for money and things she didn't have. Now, I'm scared of taking advantage of you the same way I loathed seeing Grand being used."

His jaw tightened. "You're *not* your family, Eugene. No one would ever think you'd use someone. You'd suffer before asking for anything. The worst thing that could have happened, happened because of that. I want you to come to me, for anything, because you're my family."

My heart raced. He called me his family.

"I didn't want to be a pain," I admitted.

"You're not a pain. That's what I'm fucking here for. To take care of you. So let me, Eugene."

"I'm sorry. I didn't want you to find out I'm more trouble than I'm worth."

"I'd never see you that way. Why do you speak about yourself this way? *Who* made you doubt your worth?" His voice sharpened as his brows furrowed. "I never said anything because I didn't want to pry, but I noticed your reaction when Max tracked mud in the house. You flinched when I stepped near you in the shower, like I might hurt you. You haven't done it lately. But I noticed how fearful you were in the beginning if you made the littlest mistake."

Hudson noticed. Feeling lightheaded, my head swayed, and my stomach twisted in knots.

"It's okay, Eugene," Hudson murmured. "I'm sorry, baby. Forget I said anything. You'll tell me when you're ready." He kissed my knuckles suddenly. "You've got me hooked around these tiny fingers. I'm going to do better, so you'll understand my shoulders are yours to rely on."

My chest tightened when I felt his hand shaking.

"His name was Jared," I said. "Just an ex who liked being mean if the house wasn't clean enough for him. I just don't like talking about him because I'm embarrassed that I let someone treat me that way."

Hudson's eyes were glassy as he swallowed, then he shut them. "Oh, God. Is that why you think you need to clean up after us?"

"No," I blurted, then winced as pain sliced through my head. "Well, it might be a habit out of fear, but I truthfully like washing the dishes and things. You cook for us, so I want to do something in return."

"You. Are. Not. A. Burden." He placed a kiss on my hand between each word. "Do you hear me?"

"*Yes.*"

"I love you."

Those three little words from him had my heart soaring.

"I love you, too," I said, and we both cried. "Please don't be mad. I'm going to work on my issues about feeling like a burden."

"Don't apologize. Never apologize to me. I'm not mad, just upset that all these people from your past made you feel like you couldn't come to me. From now on, you're going to tell me when something's wrong."

"I will," I promised.

"Do you need pain meds?"

"Yes, and I got to pee."

After Hudson made sure it was okay for me to get out of bed, he helped me to the bathroom, pushing the IV stand for me and holding most of my weight with the other arm. My vision blurred, and I swayed as I walked, and Hudson had to steady me. I glimpsed my image in a mirror. I had a bruised nose and a black eye. By the time I finished up in the bathroom, I felt physically drained. When Hudson helped me on the bed, I scooted over and patted the spot.

"I don't want to accidentally hurt you," he murmured.

"My IV's on the other side. It's fine. I'd rather us sleep on this twin bed together than you sleep on that chair." When he stood there staring at the little bed, I added, "Please. I'll heal and sleep better beside you."

He took off his shoes, then crawled in beside me, careful not to touch my face.

46

HUDSON

Eugene had been home from the hospital for two days and kept asking if the police had called. She constantly told me how bad she felt that I ended up in jail for a few hours. No matter how often I tried to assure her there was nothing to worry about, she still fidgeted with her hands and peeked out the window, as if the police would show up to arrest me.

My heart ached seeing her so anxious all the time.

The fucker named Jerry was awake and wouldn't dare press charges. Since I wasn't allowed anywhere near him, a family friend who worked at the hospital snuck me into his room. I made sure Jerry knew about Eugene's innocence in her old boss's case. Finnick roughed Phillip, Jerry's accomplice, up. Phillip claimed he hadn't touched Eugene, but he was there to threaten her all the same.

I didn't get it. How could they look at Eugene and think she could steal from anyone? Even after the man nearly killed her, she still looked at me and said it wasn't fair for them either. "*A lot of people were depending on that money Danny stole.*" As if that fucking mattered. That didn't give anyone the right to attack someone, especially Eugene. She was innocent.

I could feel the anger boiling to the surface thinking about it, so I stood and walked to the kitchen while Eugene napped on the couch. She slept a lot because of the head trauma. The doctor said she would make a full recovery, but it terrified me. The thought of something happening to her had me staying home with her. I wouldn't dare go back to work until she was healed.

The fact that someone attacked her still enraged me. When I walked in that bathroom and saw the man pummeling Eugene into that wall, I never knew such fury. I lost it. I would have killed him if they didn't tear me off him. I still wanted to kill him. The bruises on her beautiful face were turning blue and yellow in some spots, but it would be another week or more before the bruises would fade completely. Closing my open hand over my trembling fist, I shut my eyes and took a deep breath.

She was attacked because she lived in my fucking cabin. For whatever reason, Jerry and Phillip thought that because she lived at my place, she must have taken off with some of their money.

I was livid just *thinking* about what the police told me.

And what Eugene confessed about her past at the hospital replayed in my head constantly. To think that she assumed she was bothering me hurt me. I should have been nicer to her in the beginning instead of trying to deny my instant attraction to her. Maybe then, she would have told me about Jerry and the note sooner.

"Just an ex who liked being mean if the house wasn't clean enough for him."

My chest tightened as my pulse throbbed at my temples. Yes, I should have been kinder. My girl had been through enough.

All I wanted to do was wrap Eugene up in my arms and hold her. It would be the only thing to soothe my agitation, but I couldn't. I might hurt her head if I dozed off and hit it with my arm.

I ran my fingers through my hair and took a deep fucking breath.

"Blondie?" Eugene stepped into the kitchen. My heart cracked in two when I spotted the swollen eye and nose, and the bruises. She had a blanket wrapped around her. Max had stayed at her side since we returned, like he could tell she was injured.

"Do you need me to turn off the light?" I hurried over to the switch.

"No, the headache's actually starting to ease today," she said.

"Really? That's good, baby."

I walked over and lightly kissed her forehead. The contact wasn't enough. I was beginning to ache from the loss of touching her the way I wanted. My heart and mind would be at ease once she was better.

"I'm fine. You can go back to work."

"Absolutely not. When you return to work, I'll go back. They're managing fine without me." Since Eugene entered my life, I realized how little I was needed at my restaurant. Of course, I still dealt with all the paperwork and things at the cabin, but I left Randall and Daisy in charge of the truck orders. So far, they hadn't disappointed me.

The doorbell rang. Eugene's eyes widened as she stepped closer, and she asked, "Is it the police?"

I hated that she was seriously scared for my sake. No matter how much I told her everything was fine, she was worried. She walked to the door with me. I opened it, then smiled as Edwin and Francis stepped in.

"Your eye is looking better," Francis said as she leaned into Eugene for a hug.

"Be fucking careful." I pulled Francis away from her.

"It's fine, Blondie." Eugene hugged her while I glared at the two women.

Edwin held up two bags of takeout. "We brought food, but I'm not sure we ordered enough."

A second later, Holly strode through the door. Eugene smiled warmly. "You shouldn't have come. You know you didn't have to."

Holly waved her hands. "Be quiet. Let me see you."

I tensed as another person touched Eugene.

Holly muttered, "I'm going to kill the jerk! What hospital is he in?"

"It's fine. Everything's fine." Eugene's voice cracked.

The room went silent.

Nothing was fine about what happened. Her injuries were proof. Holly hugged Eugene, or else I would have. Eugene looked on the verge of tears. She needed that normalcy with her friend, so I helped Edwin carry the food to the kitchen.

After everyone left, Eugene napped for about an hour. We offered Holly a room to stay the night, but she wanted to head back home. I fussed and cared for Eugene in front of everyone. I didn't give a damn what they thought, but I was still on edge. I wanted her to recover sooner than later. Her sleeping a lot, constant headaches, and blurred vision were eating me alive. How could I be at peace until she felt better?

I made brownies. When she woke, she ate a hot fudge brownie. Her appetite was getting better. She inhaled the dessert for me.

As I took the plate from her, she blinked up at me. "Want to bathe with me?"

I froze. She looked so adorable yet vulnerable, sitting on the couch with a bruised face. My heart ached. Yes, I very much wanted to bathe with her, but I was scared of hurting her. Picturing the old fucker slamming her head into the wall as I opened the bathroom door haunted my thoughts.

"How about I bathe you?" I suggested. "Let me go wash this plate, then I'll run you some water."

But when I finished in the kitchen, Eugene wasn't on the couch. Walking into my bedroom, I heard the faucet running and went to the bathroom. Eugene was naked and sitting in the tub as it filled. Her nipples were hard, likely due to the chill in the cabin.

Besides the bruises on her neck and face, she was fine everywhere else.

I dropped to one knee beside the tub. "You should have let it fill up before getting in," I grumbled as I noticed the goose bumps on her arms. "What am I going to do with you, baby?"

"Get in here with me." Her voice was a seductive whisper as she grabbed my wrist and tugged.

The last thing I wanted to do was get a fucking hard-on while she was still injured. But that was exactly what happened as I looked at her. "I don't want to hurt you, and we both know I'll manhandle you if I get in there."

She giggled, then let her eyes droop, biting her lower lip. "You won't, because I'll be on top." She breathed heavily, causing her breasts to rise and fall.

My cock strained against my pants.

"We can just slip your dick inside me and relax. And maybe you can rub my clit, or you can watch me rub my—"

She stopped talking when I stood and yanked off my shirt. The idea of my cock snug in her pussy while we relaxed sounded like heaven. I could convince myself I wasn't overtaxing her because we wouldn't be moving. My dick throbbed as she watched me undress. When I finished, she stood, so I could get in. I sat down, then she straddled me. I groaned when she gripped my cock, fisting it tightly before guiding it to her pussy. When she lowered herself, I swore I saw the fucking Milky Way as I stretched her open. She was so wet that I eased right in. When I filled her completely, she panted, laid against my chest, and wrapped her arms around my neck. I rubbed her back, dipping my fingers in the water and letting it drip over her skin.

Like she said, we stayed locked together. And it felt really damn good. It felt torturous and heavenly being inside her without attempting to move. I could get off if I wasn't careful. I didn't want that to happen. Not when I wanted to stay there as long as possible. When the tub started to get full, I had to use my foot to twist the knob. The small movement made Eugene whimper, and she wiggled, causing me to groan. Pleasure edged through me, and I inhaled her hair as I went back to rubbing her body. I slid my hand down her ass cheeks, caressing them enough that her pussy pulsed, and the head of my cock felt like it would explode. I slid my thumb over her asshole lightly, and she jerked against me. I almost came right then and there because her pussy pulsated around me. I knew she was close. I needed to get her to that sweet oblivion.

She squeezed my neck. "Hudson."

The word was a plea.

"Don't move unless it's to put your tits in my face," I warned. "Otherwise, be good and sit still like you said we'd do."

"Please," she whined. "*God, Blondie.*"

"Just let it build, baby," I whispered against her ear, causing her to tremble. "It's going to be so good when you come."

I didn't give in completely. Not yet. I kept teasing her with my thumb, breaching her back hole enough that she moved, and it was fucking bliss. Torturing her was torturing me, but what a perfect torment.

"You're going to come for me," I said. "You're going to come without me touching that clit."

To touch her there, she'd have to sit up, and she felt too good pressed against me as I fondled her ass. Besides, by the way her pussy tightened around me, she was close to shattering.

I squeezed her ass, then gripped her hips, lifting her slightly. She moaned at the action. Her walls hugged me. I would come if I took it any further.

"Don't stop, don't stop," she begged. "I'm coming."

"Then take me with you," I rasped as she sank back on me.

My cum filled her as she rolled her hips, riding out her release.

With her arms still around my neck, she lifted her head, smiling. "We did good, see? I kept my head on your chest and only moved my hips occasionally."

I chuckled. "You did good, baby."

"I like having you inside me," she whispered right before she kissed my lips.

"Careful, please," I said. "I don't want to bump your bruises."

"You're good, Hudson. Do you know that?"

"I wouldn't say I'm good." I thought back to any of the fuckers who hurt Genie. I could kill Jerry or her ex and never feel guilty if given the chance.

"You are. You're a good person, a good *guy*. I honestly didn't think I'd trust someone like I do you."

My heart felt like it would jump right out of my chest. "I'm good because of you."

"I love you, Hudson. Truly. I felt so guilty when I found out what you did for me. I didn't tell you what was happening when I should have. You hate what happened, and so do I. I now see my mistakes. I know I'm not someone you pity. I'm not someone you'll grow tired of when things get hard. We're just in this life together. And I am happy since meeting you. So happy, Hudson. I hope you stop worrying because I'm fine."

She wiped my eyes.

I took a moment to compose myself before saying, "I'll stop worrying when you go for the checkup. Or maybe when the bruises are gone. But I'll always fuss over you, Red, because you're my girl. I can't be happy if I don't see you happy. I love you so damn much."

47

EUGENE

Six months later

I'd just come home from work. Hudson's truck was parked in the driveway, but I didn't see him anywhere. It was one of those rare occurrences where Hudson didn't work, and I did. "Hudson?"

No response.

As I stepped into the main room, I spotted Max hunkered down near the recliner. "What are you doing, Bear?" I asked, then noticed something black in his mouth. "What is that?"

He army crawled away when I tried to get closer before darting into the bedroom. Hmm. Clearly, Max knew he wasn't supposed to have whatever was in his mouth.

Following him, I found him sitting beside the bed with a black box in his mouth. Then I heard the shower running in the bathroom. So, that's where Hudson was.

With a smile, I dropped down beside Max. "What do you have?"

As soon as I took the black box, it became apparent what it was. All the blood rushed to my face as my heart hammered.

It's an engagement ring!

My brain had already decided what it was before I opened the box. Then I opened it and saw the sparkly diamond ring. My brain said again, *"It's an engagement ring!"*

I fanned my face because it was so hot. My heart literally felt like it grew wings and took flight. I giggled as my eyes watered. Oh, my God. Was that really what I thought it was? Hudson wanted to marry me. He was going to propose.

Suddenly, the shower cut off. Panicking, I closed the box and shoved it toward the dog. "Where did you take it from?" I whispered.

Oh, fuck. That couldn't be happening. I couldn't let Hudson know I knew and ruin it all. Maybe he wasn't going to propose, I told myself. It might not even be for me. But I knew better. There were too many signs. Hudson kept kissing my ring finger, saying odd things, and asking me to call him *hubby* when he wasn't sick. The overwhelming happiness built up in my chest. He'd been easing me into the next stage of our relationship. My heart knew it.

Not wanting to be caught, I left the box with Max and ran from the room before Hudson got out of the bathroom.

HUDSON

As soon as Eugene's footfalls faded, I opened the bathroom door and grinned at Max. Scooping up the box, he strode over and gave it to me. I petted his head and gave him the treat I had in my pocket for that purpose.

The box was covered in drool, but it didn't matter. "What do you think? It's a good sign if you ask me."

I heard her gasping and sniffling even when I had the shower turned on. When I saw her pull into the driveway, I ran to the bathroom. My ear had been plastered to the door ever since she entered the house. After encouraging Max with enough treats, he led her to the bedroom.

I found her in the kitchen, drinking water. She was flushed head to toe, with a glassy look to her eyes. Since she was so flustered, she didn't notice that my hair wasn't wet, and it didn't make sense for me to shower that time of day anyway. A lot of times we showered or bathed together.

"How was the restaurant?" I walked over and kissed her.

"It was good." She averted her gaze.

It seemed I would have to propose that night. I couldn't let her remain so awkward around me, although I found it cute. August's nights were nice, so I could make a fire outside and roast some marshmallows. She'd like that more than taking her out and making the proposal a public affair. It would be fun, and the quicker I had the ring on her finger, the happier I'd be. I needed that woman to be my wife six months ago.

"What's wrong?" I teased.

"What do you mean?" she said, but we were interrupted by my phone ringing. It was my mom. "Hello?"

"Turn on the news," Mom said quickly.

I frowned. "What's wrong?"

"Just turn it to channel six."

"I don't have cable," I said. Honestly, I streamed programs and watched Netflix.

Mom groaned. "Just go to their page, and you'll see. The money wasn't stolen."

"All right. I'll call you back." I hung up the phone, feeling puzzled.

"Is everything okay?" Eugene asked.

"Mom said for us to look at the news," I replied. "Come on. I'm sure I can find whatever it is on their Facebook page."

Eugene followed me into the main room. I plopped down in the recliner, and she sat on my lap as I went to the news page. When I saw the article about Danny Hopkins, I clicked on it. There was a video.

Eugene gasped as we watched the footage. I couldn't blame her because no one had the story right. Danny Hopkins was dead. The police found him in his vehicle at the bottom of Lake Campbell, a place in Eugene's old town. There was suspicion of foul play. An autopsy would be performed. More interesting was that his missing wife had been found in California under an assumed identity. When the woman had a medical emergency, her information matched the missing person's report.

I assumed she might be involved. The police learned of her whereabouts around the same time they found Danny's body. The police weren't saying anything to confirm or deny her involvement yet.

"Holy shit," Eugene said.

I didn't think much about Eugene's attack those days, but I was livid after reading that article. According to the article, the police confirmed the checks weren't cashed. Although the police leaked that the money had been stolen, the lie led to Eugene's attack.

"You should have never been attacked over this fucking mess," I muttered as I put my phone away.

Closing my eyes, I leaned back and frowned at the ceiling.

"Jerry will likely feel guilty now," she whispered. "You know, for hurting me."

"He didn't just try to hurt you." My eyes slid over her. "He tried to *kill* you."

Jerry got off too easily. Eugene refused to press charges, and I knew it was because she worried that he would retaliate by messing with me. He couldn't have, but she didn't understand how much power my father had.

"I love you." she said, kissing my cheek.

I felt the tension drain and said, "I love you, baby."

"This is good news. At least people will get answers. Maybe they'll get their money, too."

"I don't really give a damn as long as they stay the fuck away from you."

"Do you like this nail polish?" she said as she laid her head on my shoulder. Her hair tickled my cheek. I smiled as she waved her hands toward my face. Her nails were painted red. She dropped her right hand, keeping her left hand up as she brought it closer. She was being so obvious about staring at her fingers that I kissed her hair, watching her fingers flex.

"It looks good," I told her.

"It's missing something, though. Don't you think?"

"Yes, it is."

"Hmm."

"Hmm."

She burst out laughing, burying her face in my neck as she curled up on my lap.

Bliss. That was what that was. Fucking bliss.

EPILOGUE

EUGENE

Three years later

"Is this the bookstore?" the old lady asked right as she peeked into the door that led to and from Homestyle. When Hudson added to the restaurant, he created a hall leading to the bookstore. He oversaw the dessert menu that I offered, so he needed direct access to my building. Plus, I believed he wanted a direct connection to me.

"Hello. Welcome to *Books & Caffeine*. We also have cakes and other desserts for anyone who has a sweet tooth," Georgianna said to the old lady, only for her to greet another customer with the door chimed again.

It was opening day for my bookstore.

My palms were sweaty, and I was jittery with excitement. I couldn't believe how many people were walking around *my* place, looking through the book aisles. The bookstore existed thanks to my husband, his dad, and Finnick, who built it within a couple months.

Hudson constantly told me it was me who made my dreams happen, but I liked to think we did it as a team.

To the left of the bookstore, I had the cash register. There was an entire bar of desserts, including donuts, cakes, and cookies. We also decided to try custom orders to see how it went. Daisy liked the idea of baking sweets when Hudson couldn't. We also decided to offer milkshakes and smoothies for those who didn't like coffee. I would try a little of everything at the beginning to see what the customers liked.

While I felt bad that I stole Georgiana and Loretta from Home-style, it didn't take my husband long to find waitresses. I'd grown close with the women and wanted them working in my store.

When I saw a couple of women walk into the monster and alien romance aisle, I grinned. Right below the aisle name there was a sign that read: *The bookstore is not liable for your newfound obsession with alien men. Read at your own risk!*

I put the children's books on the opposite side of the store, so there would be no mix up with the romance books. Besides, I thought there were too many signs for all the categories of books. While the majority of my books were dedicated to the romance genre, I included aisles for non-fiction, science fiction, mystery, and young adult.

When I glanced away from the alien romance aisle, the little old woman stood in front of me. "Are you the wife?"

"Huh?"

She smiled, and an older gentleman stood behind her, grinning too. "Are you the owner of this place and the wife of that man who keeps giving out these vouchers in the restaurant?" She held up the voucher Hudson printed to hand out to his customers.

My chest warmed. "Yes, that would be me."

"Your husband is stopping everyone at the door before they walk out of Homestyle and asking them to walk over."

Oh, Hudson.

I laughed as my cheeks heated. "It's opening day. I think he wants to see the store do well."

She patted my shoulder. "No. I believe he wants to see his wife happy."

"Yes, you're probably right."

The old woman looked up at the man and said, "How about we grab us a cake, dear?"

A few minutes later, I had their cake boxed up and waved them goodbye as they left. By then, I had a long in front of the register. Only two people had books, but I had high hopes more readers would come.

I didn't know how much time had passed when Loretta nudged my shoulder. "Randall texted me. He needs Hudson in the back helping with orders, but he's out front, telling everyone to visit his wife's bookstore."

I laughed. "So, I'm guessing Randall wants me to go send my husband to the kitchen?"

"I reckon you should," Loretta said. "I'll take care of the register."

I entered the restaurant and immediately shook my head when I saw Hudson handing a young couple one of the vouchers near the front entrance.

"The bookstore belongs to my wife. Make sure to check it out," he said as they hurried out the door.

Behind him, one of the new hires had his arms folded over his chest. "You said wife five times in the last sixty seconds."

Hudson turned around. "Only five. I'm slackin'."

Once I was closer, I cleared my throat. As soon as Hudson saw me, he wrapped me in his arms and kissed my forehead.

"What are you doing out here?" I asked.

"Making sure people grab the voucher on the way out."

"What a good hubby you are," I whispered into his ear. "But Randall needs help. The bookstore has plenty of traffic."

"Has anyone said anything about the alien romance section?" Hudson asked, waggling his brows.

I snorted. "A few people have browsed the section, but no one has had questions yet."

"Don't worry, there will be people interested in it like you." He waggled his brows again.

I rolled my eyes, smiling. "Would you stop?"

"The alien shit is actually good. I understand the hype."

My husband was yanked away from me by Randall.

"Go work." I blew Hudson a kiss.

"You got this, baby. You're going to do great."

"I am going to do great."

"That's my girl."

My heart felt like it could burst from the love I had for Hudson.

I stood there for a minute, just smiling, when someone tapped my shoulder. It was a young woman. "Are you okay, ma'am? You've been standing there a while..."

"You know what. I'm more than fine," I told her. "Everything's perfect."

THE END

NOTE FROM THE AUTHOR

Thank you so much for reading my book! I hope you enjoyed Eugene and Hudson's story. If you want to leave a review on Amazon, that would be amazing. Reviews are helpful for authors and readers.

Hudson and Eugene's story started when my sister sent me a video from TikTok about a man cooking. Of course, I loved the idea of a man being the one to take care of his special someone. As for Eugene, I'm someone who also has negative thoughts, wondering if I'm a bother to people. Those kinds of thoughts are exhausting. I loved writing Eugene slowly, understanding she could rely on Hudson. I feel like unlearning a negative thought process is hard, but I think it's so important we take care of ourselves mentally. And that requires us to work on our inner turmoil. Here's to hoping I conveyed a little of that in Eugene! Like my character, I'm working on myself every year.

MICHELLE'S ROMANCE COLLECTION:

You can find all the books on Amazon.

One Percent of You:
*Standalone
*Small town
*Slow burn
*Single mom/grumpy tattooed neighbor
*Rough first encounter
*He falls first and harder

All Our Secrets:
*Heavy on the emotions
*Standalone
*Small town
*widow/late husband's best friend
*Late husband is a ghost haunting her home (literally)
*Secrets/miscommunication
In the book you'll find...
The consequences of anger, regret, and guilt. Each character

represents one of those emotions. This is not an easy book, but I loved writing it. Main couple has a happy ending, but still sadness within these pages.

Fall From Grace:
*Childhood friends to lovers (book starts with them as kids)
*He has a rough childhood (parents with drug addiction)
*next-door neighbors
*He's always loved her
*Timeline spans through their childhood and teenage years (not a teen read! This is meant for adults.)

Just Enough:
*Friends to lovers
*Next-door neighbors
*They're with different people during part of the book.
*He's always loved her but pushes it to the side all the time.

MICHELLE'S PARANORMAL ROMANCE COLLECTION:

Seven Deadly Series:

The devil curses the children of Grim, each with the seven deadly sins. Lots of actions, romance, and ongoing fight against an entity known as Harvest. Each book focuses on a different couple and romance. You'll find each character and their romance is slightly different.

Soul Food:

A standalone romance between a demon known as a soul reaper and a human rapper named Ruth.
He's cold hearted, but cracks under her seduction. Too bad she doesn't know she's seducing the demon!

Heartbeat Girl:

A standalone romance between a vampire and human. He's one of three vampires in a rock band and she's their manager. He's been obsessed for a while, but she doesn't know that...yet.

The Grim Awakening Series:

A story about a girl who sees ghosts and finds love with the Grim
Reaper. This is my baby series. I wrote this when I had no clue what I
was doing.

ABOUT THE AUTHOR

Michelle is from a small town in Eastern Kentucky where possums try to blend in with the cats on the porch and bears are likely to chase your pets—this is very true. It happened to her sister's dog. Despite the extra needed protection for your pets, she loves the mountains she calls home. She has a man and twin girls who are the light of her life and the reason she's slightly crazy.

As a kid, she was that cousin, that friend, that sister and daughter, the talker who could spin a tale and make-believe into any little thing so it was no surprise when she found love in reading, and figured all these characters inside her head needed an outlet. They wanted to be heard, so she wrote.

The voices keep growing faster than she gets the time to write.

The stories are never going to end. That's perfectly okay, though. We never want to stop an adventure.

She writes and loves many different genres so sign up to her mailing list to keep updated on her releases!

Join Mailing List here:
http://eepurl.com/cRXrUX

f facebook.com/michellegrossauthor
X x.com/AuthorMichelleG
⃝ instagram.com/michellegrossmg
♪ tiktok.com/@authormichellegross